Bridging the Gap...

"Believe me, Hrrula, our people saw no trace of yours. You have no idea what a shock you gave us."

"If we do not object to your presence here, why do your elders?"

"Because of the nature and history of my race," the human replied. "Look at that bridge. We have all we need on the other side. But soon, because we are inherently greedy, we will want something that can be found only on your side . . . and we will cross the bridge."

"But it was we," Hrrula replied, "who wanted the bridge, Terran."

Hrrula was a cat. A six-foot-tall cat. One of the natives of Doona.

Or was he?

decision at doona

anne mccaffrey

A Del Rey Book

BALLANTINE BOOKS • NEW YORK

A Del Rey Book
Published by Ballantine Books

Copyright © 1969 by Anne McCaffrey

All rights reserved under International and Pan-American Copyright Conventions. Published in the United States by Ballantine Books, a division of Random House, Inc., New York, and simultaneously in Canada by Ballantine Books of Canada, Ltd., Toronto, Canada.

ISBN 0-345-27864-X

Manufactured in the United States of America

First Edition: April 1969
Seventh Printing: October 1978

To Todd Johnson—of course!

Contents

	Characters	viii
I	Conference	1
II	Escape	7
III	Surprise	13
IV	Contact	25
V	Return	31
VI	Reaction	41
VII	Bridge	45
VIII	Interference	52
IX	Arrival	57
X	Problem Child	62
XI	The Feast	76
XII	Rescue	82
XIII	Red Letter Day	89
XIV	Third Message	102
XV	Interlude	109
XVI	Barn Raising	118
XVII	Search	132
XVIII	Hereagin, Goneagin, Finnegin	142
XIX	The Wrong Side	148
XX	Turnabout	163
XXI	Returnabout	171
XXII	Delaying Tactics	184
XXIII	Intervention	195
XXIV	Proof Positive	200
XXV	Vigil	220
XXVI	Tumult and Shouting	227
	L'Envoi	243
	About the Author	246

CHARACTERS

Hrruban:

First Speaker Hrruna
Second Speaker for External Affairs Hrrto
Third Speaker for Internal Affairs
Fourth Speaker for Education
Fifth Speaker for Health and Medicine
Sixth Speaker for Production
Seventh Speaker for Management
Eighth Speaker for Computers
Senior Scout Chief Hrral

Hrrestan—elder of village
Mrrva—his mate
Hrriss—their son
Hrrula—young man of the village
Hrran—Duty Officer on Hrruba
Mrrim—Technician

Terran:

Kenneth Reeve, jack of all trades
Patricia Reeve, his wife
   Ilsa, 10, Todd, 6
Hu Shih and Phyllis Hu *leader (+ metropologist?)*
Sam and Aurie Gaynor
Victor and Anne Solinari
Lee and Sally Lawrence *sociologist*
Macy and Dot McKee
Ezra and Kate Moody *doctor*
Bill Moody—their son
Martin and Fawzia Ramasan
Alfred Ramasan—their son
Ben and Akosua Adjei
Abe and Becky Dautrish
Buzz and Anneck Eckerd

Captain Ali Kiachif of the ship *Astrid*
Commander Al Landreau, Spacedep
Mr. E. K. Chaminade, Codep (Colonial Department)
Admiral Afroza Sumitral, Alreldep (Alien Relations
   Department)

Chapter I

CONFERENCE

▼▼▼▼▼▼▼▼▼▼▼▼▼▼▼▼▼▼▼▼▼▼▼▼▼

THE PLANET RECEDED to a small, blue-green sphere, the lesser of its two satellites beginning to pass across the retreating face of its primary, a pearly tear in the northeast hemisphere. The film ended with such abruptness that there was a pause before the viewers reacted with the customary throat-clearing and chair-shuffling.

The First Speaker motioned for silence and bowed courteously toward the Senior Scout whose inner apprehension defied his attempts to suppress it.

"Thank you, Senior Scout, for such an effective visual presentation," the First Speaker began blandly. "The planet is, as you have reported, a pastoral jewel."

"Exactly!" And the Third Speaker rose to his feet, turning slightly to First but not waiting for permission to address the group. "Exactly. A pastoral jewel and utterly useless since its mineral and metal deposits are too negligible to warrant the high cost of extraction. We'd do much better working on that turbulent volcanic planet in Sector—" he glanced at his notes, "9A-23. It's far more important for us to increase our stores of the rare elements so abundant there than to mess around with pastoral jewels."

The Senior Scout and the Chief of Extraterritorial Ex-

1

plorations exchanged quick, concerned glances, but when the Chief leaned forward to their sponsor, the Second Speaker, he received a barely perceptible nod of reassurance.

"I believe Fourth has information relevant to 9A-23 and its exploitation," First suggested.

The Fourth Speaker rose, shrugging his robe into place over his shoulder.

"There is, unfortunately, no possibility of opening 9A-23 to an exploitation venture." He gave a wry grimace. "There have been no applicants for the courses required to train personnel for the complicated mining procedures necessary to such a closed unit project."

"I find that hard to believe," Third muttered indignantly.

Fourth swiveled slightly toward Third, his attitude mildly rebuking him for his aside.

"In fact, there have been very few applications for any training courses in recent years except . . ."

"We'll go into your report in detail in a few minutes, Fourth," the First Speaker broke in smoothly. "However, Fourth merely underscores one of the many reasons why we are here to consider the opening of that lovely pastoral planet to colonization."

"Colonization?" Third exploded.

"Exactly. And immediately."

"I fail to see how opening that useless planet to colonization can help us get trained personnel to man a mining operation on 9A-23."

"With your kind permission?" said First, his irony so uncharacteristic that Third subsided instantly, looking chagrined. "This lovely place, graciously endowed with clean, fresh air, land, water, lakes, streams, fields, mountains, deserts, abounding with all manner of wild life, yet none sentient enough to violate our Prime Rule, vast stretches of uninhabited space—" and he caught the involuntary shudder that seized the Third Speaker. "A planet so close to what our home world *once* was as to be its twin is perfect as a retraining ground."

Undaunted, the Third Speaker rose to his feet, his eyes round, his visage reflecting distaste and concern.

"Good sir, a hundred years ago the Ruar System proposal was overwhelmingly rejected by 87% of the voting adults. You cannot be proposing to revive that old wheeze about a return to the simple, pure, primitive life. Why, who'd put up with such deprivations?"

The Senior Scout wondered if he could control himself.

"A hundred years ago," the First Speaker answered gently, "our suicide rate among young adults was not what it is today, nor had the last major continental mass of our fourth planet been dormitized, destroying the remaining natural land; the sea harvests were still adequate for our population's basic subsistence diet. Today we are faced with so grave a crisis that I fear for the future of the race itself. In our search for freedom from want and to remedy the inequalities of opportunity by the suppression of physical competition on all levels, we have literally destroyed initiative, ambition and vitality. The once vigorous hunter has become the enervated observer.

"Fourth Speaker will shortly give us his report but let me repeat the most distressing statistic: in the generation now approaching maturity, only one half of one per cent have indicated interest—oh, nothing as decisive or binding as actually applying; just an interest—in training for technical or administrative careers. I need not tell you that this falls disastrously below even the minimum requirements for the replacement of essential personnel.

"We have become a people so passive, so pacifist, so detached and unemotionally involved that *even the effort to propagate our species has become too great.*"

The Fifth Speaker for Public Health and Medicine nodded gravely, his fingernails unconsciously tapping on his own distressing report.

"The Computers predict that, unless we immediately—" and First paused to impress on each of the Seven Speakers the gravity of his pronouncement, "immediately begin to reverse this effect, our civilization will collapse of its own dead weight within three generations. Therefore," and the First Speaker rose to his feet, "I, as First Speaker, have already chosen family units to settle on this lovely new world, to begin an intensive re-education, stressing those racial characteristics which allowed our ancestors to conquer space and . . ."

"To hunt and kill?" breathed the Third Speaker in a horrified whisper.

"To hunt, yes. And to kill, yes, for food," the First Speaker agreed in a gentle, reasonable tone, "with as primitive a weapon as is effective. There are no sentients on this planet, Third Speaker, no creatures of any great intelligence or sensitivity. It is, as you saw from the films, ecologically balanced on the kill-or-be-killed natural order. Yet, even if we were forced now—on some other planet—to consider the destiny of another rising species, I trust that we have come far enough along evolution's scale by now to remember the terrible lessons of past errors and to profit by them. Indeed," and his smile was grim, "we have almost come too far along that scale for the perpetuation of our own race. Therefore, as the truly rational intelligent beings we profess to be, let us discuss this necessity from all angles. I cannot, of course, presume to override anyone's honest beliefs and principles. Fifth Speaker, you have comments relevant to this crisis, do you not?"

With a haste inconsonant with the dignity of his office and his years, the Fifth Speaker rose and, in a voice hoarse with distress, gave his devastating report. He did not try to gloss over the frightening rise of suicide deaths, including the irrational waves of mass, masochistic self-destruction; a crushing apathy in some strata balanced by insensate violence in others; the decreasing birth rate in the higher intelligence percentiles; a disproportionate increase of mental retardation in the lower brackets; an overall picture of racial decay and indifference.

The Fourth Speaker was asked to report more fully on Education. The good gentleman glanced down at his thick report for a moment, then let it fall from his hands to the table.

"The statistics are here. First Speaker has already acquainted you with the essential one: one half of one per cent of the maturing generation indicates—not applied for, has indicated only—interest in further training. When there is no incentive to learn anything, why bother? With the performance records presently in hand in elementary levels, there is really no point in my speaking at all. Soon there will be no teachers left to teach those who do not wish to learn anyhow."

He shrugged and sat down, his chin sinking to his chest in an attitude of disconsolate defeat.

The Sixth Speaker stood, clearing his throat, trying to dispel the gloom cast by the Fourth.

Halfway through his own report on production and manufacturing he, too, stopped and his report slapped quietly back to the table.

"There's no point in my going on either. Perhaps I'm fortunate in that most of my department's operations are automatic, so personnel training is not presently a problem. It will be. And soon."

The Third Speaker glared around at his peers, unable to catch anyone's eye, until he reached the Second Speaker.

"And I suppose that you, too, are going to hang your head with still more disgraceful mouthings of inefficiency and indifference."

"On the contrary," Second replied, looking first to his left for the Prime Speaker's permission. "My Department attracts trainees constantly. Of course, we have to reject many of them due to physical unfitness. Others are disappointed because, unfortunately, the appropriation for Exploration and Defense falls woefully behind its needs. Consequently, we get the best of our vital young men and women. If Sixth is agreeable, I believe I can put it to the Corps to volunteer to man the mining colony proposed for 9A-23, until such time as other personnel can be found and trained."

There was something about the way Second made his helpful proposal that irritated Third far more than First's rejection of the 9A-23 priority over the pastoral planet. The reports, so devastatingly pessimistic, must be exaggerations of actual fact. Moreover, the whole thing smacked of collusion. He intended to check the printouts in the Computer. However, before he had a chance to gather his arguments, the First Speaker was taking a vote on colonizing *his* pet project. The Third Speaker naturally felt obliged to abstain from voting and was then forced to suppress his horrified indignation when the other six Speakers voted in its favor.

The First Speaker wasted no further time but turned the meeting over to the Chief of Extraterritorial Explorations.

The Chief rose, feeling a respect bordering on admiration for the Prime Speaker's masterly handling of a tricky meeting. The Chief bowed to him, catching no hint in the benign eyes that the re-education program which the Chief was about to outline had, in actual fact, been initiated twenty years ago.

Chapter II

ESCAPE

▼▼▼▼▼▼▼▼▼▼▼▼▼▼▼▼▼▼▼▼▼▼▼▼▼

IT REQUIRED EVERY ounce of self-control Ken Reeve had developed over the frustrating years of his adulthood to keep from shouting, singing, jumping or committing a number of other social solecisms.

As it was, he received stern, remanding looks from the other passengers in the express lift for the wide smile he couldn't repress.

He did make an effort to compose his face, to moderate his breathing to the proper shallowness, but the mere knowledge that in the very near future he would have a whole new world to breathe in made it difficult for him to conform.

Nevertheless, because he couldn't risk an official summons which might delay his triumphant return to Patricia, he did hunch his shoulders forward, tucked his elbows tight to his straining rib cage, sucked in his guts and pressed his knees together in the proscribed stance socially acceptable in an elevator.

It was still impossible to limit his exultation, which he was evidently broadcasting, judging by the constant surreptitious looks he received as the cage plummeted down to the dormitory levels.

Never before had Ken been so aware of the weight, warmth and aroma of humanity, or of the crowded life

7

that had seemed inescapable; from which he was actually going to escape. As never before, he was conscious of the odor of a confined crowd: a composite of inefficient multiscented perspirant inhibitors, breath cleansers, digestive neutralizers, the acrid overtones of body-warmed inorganic fabrics, the hot-metals-old-paint stink, and, over all, the air-conditioner's deodorizer, which had never been successful.

Stale air breathed by stale people into stale lungs to prolong stale lives in a stagnant society!

The hydraulics were faulty again, Ken noticed, for the elevator stopped with a sickening jolt. There had been a newscast recently, urging young adults to apply for a career in maintenance. Not even the failure of two high-speed freight elevators had stimulated any response to the call, though there had been wide muttering about the lack of public spirit in the upcoming generation. No one in his packed cage appeared to notice the jerking stop, but then, Ken thought as he felt the pressure of soft flesh against him, we're so tightly jammed in, no one could get hurt in a free-fall.

The wide doors slid reluctantly open. Ken mastered the incredible urge to stride recklessly through the socially acceptable shuffle of the disembarking. Heads, shoulders bobbed forward around him. The hair on his shins stood out in radar-like sensitivity to the constant proximity of other legs. He gritted his teeth, wanting to race down the walk-belt of the 235th Hall, but he doggedly matched his step with the other hundreds in that rippling sea of bodies. The creeping pace was endurable if he thought of the fields and hills he would soon be able to stride over. Did anyone—any one of his presently close fellow travelers—know what a 'field' was? A 'hill'? He'd wager they'd never even applied for a day at their local Square Mile.

But the wager he'd made after *he* had seen a Square Mile had paid off. He, his wife, Pat, the two kids, Ilsa and Todd, were going to leave the land warrens of Earth for the naked soil and sky of Doona. Doona! The name had a talismanic ring: a fresh air ring, a real food ring, a landscape ring—a freedom ring!

The 235th Hall had never seemed so long to him, nor the walk-belt so slow. It crawled past block after block until Ken felt every muscle twitching at the restraints he had to impose on himself. But Proctors were everywhere in the Hall, just waiting for a misdemeanor to break the monotony of their four-hour watch. Ken had heard it rumored that Proctors received extra calories for every conviction.

Well, if that were so, he snorted to himself, innocently returning the shocked glances cast in his direction as he turned guilt from himself with practiced ease, their Aisle Proctor ought to be one helluva lot fatter than he was.

Up ahead, he heard a murmuring. He glanced over the barely bobbing heads, lucky enough to be taller than most of the run of his generation. He could hear a snuffling, the outraged mumble, the slight flurry of moving bodies.

A case of flatulence, no doubt, he decided with an inward chuckle. That offense'd reduce a lot of calories for someone if the criminal could be identified.

Fortunately, before he reached the scene of the crime, he got to his Corridor turn.

"Turn, please," he murmured in the properly distressed tone required of a citizen imposing on his fellows.

With mechanical promptitude, the bodies directly to his right squeezed either backward or forward and permitted him space enough to slip sideways to the edge of the moving walk-belt and onto the stationary plastic floor.

"Corridor, please," he repeated endlessly as he sidled, a step at a time, toward the 84th Corridor.

Christ, but it would be great to walk out without having to consult the schedule for Pedestrian Traffic in Hall and Corridor Routes. He could have been home from the Codep Block four hours ago. Of course, it had been great meeting the rest of the Phase III group. Their leader and the metropologist of the group, Dr. Hu Shih, was quite a guy; soft-spoken but firm, he seemed to know every frame of the Spacedep survey and the Alreldep reports. Hu Shih must have just got in under the age wire, too.

Ken spared a moment of wonder for the courage and tenacity of the many, many Codep assignees who never had made it off-planet, or who had turned overage before Spacedep released even a resources planet to Codep. God, to live a whole lifetime with nothing—nothing but a dream that would never be realized! To put up with the inferior quarters all inactive Codepers were given, the subsistence allowance, the disrespect, the sneers and condescension—and then never get off-planet? Well, that had been one of the arguments of his friends and family when he'd applied: Codep men died young—suicides!

But not Ken Reeve. He and his were going. And the dream that had taken fire the day he'd stood on the amazing soil of his Regional Square Mile, felt grass, seen sky above him, blue and limitless, was going to be fulfilled.

Inadvertently Ken had lengthened his stride in the Corridor and trodden on the heels of a citizen in front of him.

"Your number?" the man rasped out indignantly.

"I'll be off-world before you can bring it to Court," Ken replied in a loud, carefree voice. Suddenly he no longer cared about earth-bound conventions—not when he would soon have a whole planet to conquer. "I'm going to Doona!"

Indignation turned to shocked outrage.

"Off-world? He's mad!" "Idiot!" "Social deviant!" "Anarchist!" were some of the clearly projected whispers around him.

"Your number!" the offended citizen demanded again.

"Sweat it, man," Ken advised him crudely and hopped off the Corridor, ducking down the Aisle three up from his own. Let that proper citizen search for him there! And Ken didn't care that it would take him another fifteen minutes—even at the acceleration permitted in an Aisle—to double back to Aisle 45.

At a heel-thumping walk, he passed two shuffling women, arm-locked, faces nose-to-nose as they carried on a private mutter.

They squealed thinly as he thudded past them, but he had put too many other pedestrians between himself and them before they could form a protest.

Fortuitously his own Aisle was sparsely occupied— Todd had driven away any resident who could wangle a transfer. He lengthened his stride, passing others without the customary obsequiousness, ignoring the exclamations of those who did recognize him. Their complaints, too, would not come up on the docket before he left. And thank God, Pat and the kids would be transferred to Codep's Cubed Block now that the whole family was on active assignment.

Active assignment! He chanted the alliteration like a prayer. Maybe now they rated additional acoustical shielding so that Pat wouldn't suffer so much ostracism because of Todd's asocial traits. Active assignment aids additional acoustics, he expanded the litany, grinning foolishly.

As he threw open the door to their two rooms, he heard Pat's startled warning. He managed to prevent the door handle from jamming into the thin back threatened by his precipitate entrance.

"Mr. Reeve, it is easy to see where your son received his unsocial tendencies," a whining whisper informed him.

Quickly closing the door behind him, Ken stared down at the socially correct, emaciated skeleton that housed the petty spirited Proctor of their Aisle Section.

"A pleasant day to you," Ken replied with such jaunty good humor that Pat, who had obviously been taking a terrible tongue-lashing, stared at him with dawning hope.

"How can it be pleasant when a steady stream of tenants report insupportable noise emanating from these rooms?" Proctor Edgar demanded.

"Oh, but it is the pleasantest of days. Now take your nosy intolerant bitching elsewhere!"

"Ken!" Pat screamed in a well-trained sotto voce. Then the strain and pallor of her face were replaced by incredulous joy. "Active assignment?"

"You bet!"

"Mr. Reeve. Moderate your voice this instant. Your family has already been reported nine times this week for social misdemeanors. I am reluctant to reduce your calorie allowance any further but I must demand . . ."

"Demand away," Ken encouraged him, beaming at Pat. "You have no jurisdiction over us any more. We're out of it. We're going to Doona!"

"Doona!" Pat stifled her elation but she could not suppress the relief she felt, even in the presence of non-family observers. "Oh, Ken, is it really true?"

"True-true-true, Pat," and Ken, deliberately aggravating the outraged Proctor, picked up his wife and kissed her lustily.

"Reeve!" the Proctor's protest was barely audible over the smack of the embrace.

"Get out if you can't stand it," Ken advised. "Go invade someone else's privacy on the excuse of official business." He kept his hold on his wife with one arm as he opened the door and shoved the Proctor back into the Aisle.

At the door's resounding slam, Pat came to her senses.

"Ken, you're mad. He'll, he'll—" she floundered helplessly.

"He can't do a damned thing to us, not ever again," Ken assured her, burying his face in Pat's silky hair and hugging her for the joy bursting inside him. "We're going. We're going to be free to run and yell and stride and—*feel!*"

Chapter III

SURPRISE

▼▼▼▼▼▼▼▼▼▼▼▼▼▼▼▼▼▼▼▼▼▼▼

"WELL, GENTLEMEN," Hu Shih announced as they finished breakfast that morning, "the town is in good order, all winter damage is cleared away, fences mended, fields plowed and sown, and our houses await our families. I believe it is therefore safe to inaugurate those secondary projects we planned during the long months of our winter."

When the cheering died, Ken Reeve pointed across the table at Sam Gaynor. "C'mon, pal. Our project is the other side of the river."

"Damn walk-about nut," Gaynor growled with an anticipatory grin spreading across his face. "Remember, you guys, every man jack heard Ken bet he could walk me, *me!* off my feet."

"Anyone who *wants* to walk after the winter we put in," Lee Lawrence exclaimed, throwing up his hands in disgust, "is queer."

"It's spring, man, you don't need snowshoes," Ken countered, grabbing up a handful of lunch rations.

"Spring! When a man's fancies should turn to more than long tiring walks," Lee Lawrence remarked sourly.

"Speaks the sociologist?" Macy McKee taunted, for Lee was famed for his ingenuity in avoiding exercise.

"Walking won't be so bad now it's spring," Vic Soli-

13

nari put in. "And next winter won't be so bad either, now we know what it's like during winter on Doona," he added, thinking of the exigencies which he, as storemaster, had had to practice over the incredible ten-month winter season.

"Long and cold," Sam quipped.

"But next winter," and Lee leered significantly, "we'll have our wives with us."

Ezra Moody, the doctor, groaned. "God, I'll be busy next spring!"

"Who's going to let you wait till next *spring?*" Lee demanded, bringing his chair down with a crash.

"They'll be here any day now," Ken sighed with a sudden harsh yearning. "C'mon, Sam, shake a leg!" he urged and started for the door.

Their exit signalized an exodus from the mess hall in which they had spent so much of their time. In fact, by the time Ken and Sam were depositing their gear in the small powered skiff at the river's edge, only Solinari was left in the Common.

An hour later, when Ken and Sam returned at a dead run and in a kind of incredulous wrath, they had to hang on the air whistle for five minutes before anyone returned.

"What'n'hell's the matter with you, Reeve?" demanded Lee Lawrence, the first to arrive.

"We're not alone on Doona, Lee," Ken cried, waving the quick-prints at the startled sociologist. "We're not alone!"

"You're round the bend, man!"

"No, he's not," growled Sam Gaynor, his face set in hard, bitter lines. "There's a village across the river in that grove of porous wood trees, where the river widens below the falls. A big village, full of furred, tailed cats that walk on their hind legs and carry knives."

Lee sat down slowly on the top step of the mess hall porch, staring at the photographs Sam thrust in front of his face.

"If I didn't have these, I'd've sworn it was a mirage or

something," Sam went on. "Because, Almighty God, I couldn't believe my eyes."

"And there was no village in that clearing when we were there last fall or last winter," Ken added, white beneath his tan.

"It stinks!" Lawrence grated out. "Oh God, you didn't talk to 'em? You weren't seen?" he added, reverting to his professional self.

"Hell, no. I shot the camera and we sloped out of there," Ken assured him.

"Oh God, what do we do now? Phase IV is already started," Lawrence groaned.

"One thing's sure," Ken reminded him sourly, "they can't reach the ship in warp drive to turn it back, and it's not scheduled to stop this side of Doona."

At that moment, Hu Shih, Ramasan and Ben Adjei came running across the Common and by the time the others had reported in, Sam, Ken and Lee had somewhat adjusted to the unsettling discovery. Hu Shih was already running through the tapes and films of Phase I and II for any references to the porous wood forest in which the village so blatantly existed.

"There is absolutely no evidence of any habitation in that area on any of these reports," he said in a decisive tone, his face inscrutable. "Not a house, not a roof, not a shingle in sight." Hu Shih picked up one of Ken's quickprints, regarded it thoughtfully a moment before placing it carefully beside the inaccurate films.

"Well, the place is now crawling with cats," Sam Gaynor said into the silence.

"I thought cats lived in caves," Eckerd, the other jack-of-all-trades, remarked inanely, looking up from his elaborate doodle in spilled sugar.

"That is not as odd," Dautrish, the botanist, added, "as the fact that there is no other even faintly felinoid species on this planet. Strange that only one would evolve and to such a dominant position."

"Hmmm, a very interesting observation, Abe," Lee

drawled. "Nevertheless, it does not bear on the fact that our noble Spacedep has committed a grave error."

"Error?" cried Victor Solinari in mock horror. The storemaster's voice was edged with bitter sarcasm. "Our noble spacemen fallible?"

"But how could the Phase II scouts have missed a village as big, as well established as this one?" Gaynor demanded, jutting his chin out with ursine aggressiveness.

"Tell you what," Lawrence suggested, waggling a finger at Sam, "I'll bet those Phase II-ers experimented with that local red berry and they thought the pussycat people were just hallucinations! Last night I went upon a bat, and saw a tawny six-foot . . ."

"This is no joke!" Gaynor snapped.

"Son," drawled Lawrence, his mockery gone, his voice rough, "iffen Ah doan laff, Ah sure as hell stinks am gwanta cry!"

Silence gripped the eleven men as each fought to control his emotions at this crushing blow; this unexpected denouement to years of training and hope.

The grotesque injustice of it all threatened to overwhelm Ken Reeve. He thrust back the childish desire to deny what his eyes had seen, to disregard the evidence of the pictures he himself had taken. He thought of the incredible effort required of them throughout the past ten months; physical, mental and emotional. Not merely the hard work of building the colony's headquarters and family homes, of enduring the unfamiliar discomforts of a long hard cold winter, but the psychological upheavals of adjusting to something as fundamental as open sky, broad fields—everyone had experienced some agoraphobia—organic foods which, no sweat, had had to be *killed* by men who had never before ended the life of an ant. However, once they'd run out of their pre-packaged protein supplies, any reluctance had quickly disappeared with the onslaught of hunger pangs. But such minor things as learning to shout to bridge distance, to run, even to be able to hike for miles at a time—all these new skills had had to be learned in painful adjustments. The idea of having to return to Earth and its stale, antiseptic sham life was grossly repellent.

"There must be a mistake," Reeve heard himself say.

"No, we're the mistake," Lawrence replied bitterly. "If the cats are here, we shouldn't be. Simple as that. And at that, we have already broken the guiding principle of the Colonial Department."

"Sweat the goddamned stinking principle," Gaynor said obscenely. He lurched to his feet and faced Hu Shih. "We're here. We've worked, we've bled, we've—sweated . . ."

"Gentlemen," the colony leader cut in sharply, rising to his feet. He turned to Gaynor, waiting until the engineer had subsided to his seat. "It would be nice to believe that the evidence of these pictures is a mistake—a mirage, as Sam suggested. But such houses are all too solid and cameras do not lie, despite the Phase I and II inaccuracies. Such houses do not grow overnight. Although I could wish that they did. We might then establish a prior claim to our lovely Doona." He surveyed his fingertips contemplatively before he continued. "How such evidence of habitation can have escaped not only the robot cameras of the orbiting probe in Phase I but also the trained eyes of the scouts is beyond my comprehension. But," and he paused to sigh deeply, "they *are* there. And we are here! And we have broken the Principle of Non-Cohabitation, by existing here with another and obviously sentient species."

"And when our families land, what do we tell *them?*" Ken demanded softly. "Do we say, 'Hello, honey, how are you? Have a good trip? Well, that's nice because we're going to turn around and go right back home.' Home!" And into that last word Ken crammed all the bitterness, frustration, disappointment and black anger that boiled inside him.

Home! A planet so overpopulated you married at sixteen to get on the list to have one of the two children allowed you before you were thirty—that is, if you could prove that you had no hereditary genetic faults or handicapping recessive traits. A planet so crowded for space there were only twelve Square Miles of international backyard remaining. He'd been eighteen before he had touched dirt, seen grass or smelled a pine tree. A trip to the local Square Mile had been his cherished award for being top man in Section Academy. The poignant memory of the experience had motivated and sustained him during the frustrating years of intensive study necessary to qualify for immigration under Colonial Department jurisdiction.

Once a man met the basic requirements of Codep, he was put on another list which permitted him to study specialties, one of which might get him a place on a Colony list. That is, if he had been lucky enough to choose a specialty needed on the very few planets turned over by the Spacedep and the Alien Relations Department to the Colonial Department.

In order for a planet to be relinquished to Codep control, it must meet two simple requirements: 1) Humans must be able to support themselves on it without atmospheric or gravitic adjustment. 2) It must be devoid of any dominant intelligent species.

In a hundred years, only nineteen of the two-thousand-odd worlds examined had been cleared by both Spacedep and Alreldep to Codep. Small wonder that this pastoral planet, with its earthlike atmosphere, its slightly-less-than-Earth gravity, presented such a desirable Eden. Even the fact that its sidereal year was twice that of Earth, with winters and summers lasting ten months, did not form an unsurmountable obstacle to its settlement. True, Doona was light on metals, but it was larger than Earth by some two thousand miles in diameter. Doona's two satellites might possibly have some mineral or light metal deposits that could be developed later on. The first job of the initial colony was to farm the land, experimenting with both Terran and indigenous grains, adapting Terran livestock to Doona and, if possible, domesticating the herd animals which roamed Doona's pasturelands. When the colony had proved itself

self-supporting, it would be augmented from Earth's teeming millions. Considering the relatively few transport ships in Codep service, this would take decades.

A constant source of bitterness between the three departments were the miserly appropriations allowed them by the Amalgamation Congress. With government funds constantly drained for new ways to ease housing and food shortages, to provide entertainment for the restriction-ridden masses, Spacedep, Alreldep and Codep got short shrift despite their logical pleas that, if more money were allocated for shipbuilding, for explorations, for immigration, the strain on Terran resources would naturally be eased.

True, not a large percentage of the population desired to move from the tri-D tube and the work-saving mechanisms which provided the bread, beer and tranquilizers that made their convention-rimmed life supportable.

There were still enough Ken Reeves, Sam Gaynors, Hu Shihs to fill Codep rosters; men and woman eager and willing to accept hazard and struggle rather than a life of restriction and boredom. However, pastoral planets were not high on the preferred list. Worlds with quantities of ore or rare minerals had preference. Man could always live on hydroponics and synthetics while he mined rocky planets like NC-A-43 or water worlds like SE-B-95. Fortunately, the zoological lobby had helped put Doona on the preference list. Livestock such as horses, cows, buffalo, deer, chickens, dogs, cats and other once common animals and fowls were dwindling to extinction, despite Preservation's techniques, so that a pastoral planet would have to be opened to perpetuate the useful animal species once common on Earth.

A subtle campaign had been waged on Earth through Tri-D, brain-washing a generation of children with ancient movies of animal heroes, by blackmail, by subliminal posters. When the bill to colonize pastoral Doona came up before the voters, it was passed by a landslide.

As Ken Reeve's bitter words echoed through the mess hall, Hu Shih thought rapidly.

The arrival of their families would only underscore the enormity of this catastrophe. There is always a solution to any problem, the colony leader told himself, firmly turning his mind from a static round of recriminations, but it may be difficult to accept the necessary solution.

This incident was the first infringement of Codep's guiding rule, the Principle of Non-Cohabitation. He forced himself to review the terrible Siwannah tragedy which had resulted in that very same Principle. And never, since the mass suicide of the gentle Siwannese, had a colony been set up where another intelligent species had been discovered by Spacedep. He shuddered, strengthening his flagging resolve that another such infamous incident must not be recorded about Doona. But any moment the transport ship, and their families, would arrive, compounding the original error. He took what comfort there was in the knowledge that his Phyllis would have a few days on Doona, walking in its lovely forests, smelling the cinnamony bark of the—Hu Shih's thoughts halted. He rose.

"Home? Yes, Ken, home. We will have to go home. Because, gentlemen, we can argue until the cows land," and he smiled, surprised at his inadvertent humor, "and still not change the fact that we are bound by the rules of our home planet. We cannot—*cannot*—remain on a planet already inhabited by an intelligent species.

"Not only have we unwittingly fractured that rule, but our very proximity to the natives places us in a still more delicate situation. We cannot simply ignore them as we might have been able to do if they were on the other side of the planet. Then we could simply pack up our equipment and leave when the Phase IV ship comes.

"At any moment, one of *them* may discover *us*.

"So, we must first apprise Codep of the existence of these natives by homing capsule. Even at faster-than-light speeds, it will take four and a half days to reach Earth . . ."

"And probably four and a half weeks while Codep fumbles to any decision," Lee interjected.

"And another four to five days before we receive an answer. In the meantime, the Phase IV ship will have arrived with our families." Hu Shih paused, exhaled deeply. "It is impossible to leave this site until they do arrive; otherwise we could simply pack up right now and eliminate the danger of contaminating this species with a premature contact with us. No, we are constrained to stay. We must also prevail upon the captain of the Phase IV ship to remain, pending subsequent removal orders."

"Shih," Gaynor interrupted, "those transport ships are so tightly scheduled, they can't lay over any longer than it takes to unload."

"In an emergency of this nature, I'm certain discretion will override commercial interest," the colony leader replied. "The captain will certainly understand the delicate situation at a glance and adjust to necessity."

"What about the livestock?" Ben asked. "There would be only fodder enough for the outgoing trip."

"That is why we must wait for instructions. I think you must agree with me, then, that we will have at least a nine day interlude, during which time the natives are certain to discover us."

"How in hell did they manage to camouflage that village, Shih?" Ken demanded. "Where have they been all winter?"

"Nomads?" Lawrence suggested. "There's an easy route from the southern part of the continent, come to think of it, beyond the range."

"Where they came from is not as important as what to do now they are here," Hu Shih reminded Lee gently. "Consider the relevant problem, please.

"Undoubtedly, if someone from Alien Relations Department had been included in our number, he would know exactly what course of action should be, must be taken. But unfortunately, Codep did not see fit to include someone with any xeno training in our number," and he smiled less tentatively now. "Besides, we have natives, not aliens, to deal with and there is nothing in our copious instructions to cover this contingency."

Lee Lawrence choked on a burst of derisive laughter while Gaynor glared at him savagely. It had become axiomatic that whatever manual of procedure was consulted, the guidebook failed to cover the major emergencies encountered on this non-mining world. There were also large areas in which theory fell far short of practical need. The 'experts' who had compiled the guides had no actual colonial experience and were far too conditioned to stocked storerooms, planetwide resources or frequent supply ship runs.

"It does seem reasonable to me," Hu Shih continued, "to try to communicate with our—landlords—in an effort to cushion their cultural shock . . ."

"*Their* cultural shock?" Lee cried out.

"They may well be nomads."

"With houses like that?" Gaynor protested.

Hu Shih held up his hand for order. "As I mentioned, we cannot ignore them; they are just across the river. *We* are the trespassers, against the law of our own home world." 'Home' had been delicately stressed. "In all conscience we must do what we can not to compromise their cultural evolution, or worse—precipitate another Siwannah. Once we have established in our own minds their level of civilization, we can continue intelligently. Therefore, since Ken is the only one among us with any semantic training, he will make the initial contact."

"Now wait a minute," Sam protested. "They carried knives. And big cats on Terra used to be carnivores, didn't they, Dautrish?"

"Well, yes," the botanist agreed.

Ezra Moody raised his hand. "Judging from the lack of protruding eyeteeth—or fangs, I'd hazard that they have evolved beyond the chase-hunt level. Here, Ben," and Ezra indicated one particular photograph to the veterinarian, "look at this jaw. Don't you agree?"

Ben nodded cautiously.

"Fangs don't indicate temperament," Lawrence said.

"True," Moody agreed seriously, "but you'll notice the absence of anything more lethal than a knife in their belts. No clubs or . . ."

"A knife is lethal enough," Ken said. "And I plan to carry one too," he asserted, turning to Hu Shih.

"Oh, that's definitely in order," Lawrence agreed. "Lack of a knife might mean emasculation. Ritual, of course," he added hastily with a laugh as he caught Ken's startled glance.

"Exactly what do you want me to do, Shih?" Ken asked.

"Mainly, tape as much of their language as possible. Alreldep is sure to want it as a basis for their own investigations. We ought to sleep-learn as much as we can synthesize in order to deal with the natives." He sighed. "Of course, it's not the best way to learn a language, for no adult ever learns another's tongue properly, but we must somehow get across to them that our stay will be brief; that we did not know we had trespassed . . ."

"And you want Ken to walk in there armed with a lousy knife and a tape recorder?" Sam exclaimed. "Those cats are six feet, Hu Shih . . ."

"Christ's sake, Sam, take it easy," Ken said, though he appreciated Sam's solicitude. "You're spoiling for a fight."

"Fight? No! But common sense tells me those babies can be dangerous. And for you to walk in among fifteen-twenty of those males?"

"One unarmed man constitutes no threat," Hu Shih replied firmly.

"And leaves ten to defend our position here," Sam interjected.

Hu Shih regarded him with mild reproof for a moment before continuing. "And one man can tape sufficient language and shoot enough additional film for the departments interested to have some foundation on which to base their assessments of the damage we have inadvertently done to a less advanced species."

"If they are not advanced, is there a chance we could cohabit? With their permission?" Lee suggested softly.

Hu Shih held up his hand to dispel such false hope.

"We are bound by the Principle of Non-Cohabitation, gentlemen. This is our first consideration."

"It wasn't our fault!" Ramasan said, his dark eyes sparking.

"What were those Phase II buggers using for eyes?" Vic Solinari demanded, slapping the table with the flat of his hand.

"All true," Hu Shih agreed. "However, it is useless to waste time in idle recrimination. We will go back to Earth but we do not need to return empty-handed." The remark gained instant attention and Shih was inwardly relieved. Obviously none of them had thought beyond the immediate problem. "Doona is full of treasure long since lost on Earth: the fragrant bark of the porous wood tree, the wood itself which polishes to brilliance; the translucent river pebbles, the . . ."

"He's right!" "No sweat, man, we could buy our way anywhere with a handful of that quartzite." "Ben, where'd you find those silver traces?" "Those berries . . ."

The sudden possibilities turned the men from despair to constructive planning, each vying with the other as to what would command the highest credits back on Earth.

When Hu Shih reluctantly left them, to compose the formal message he must speed to Earth by homing capsule, he knew that they would be able to salvage something from this disaster. And they would have at least eight or nine days, even with the faster-than-light speed of the capsule, before Codep could instruct him on procedures. Yes, there would be time to gather enough of Doona's treasure to ease some of the problems of their return.

Chapter IV

CONTACT

▼▼▼▼▼▼▼▼▼▼▼▼▼▼▼▼▼▼▼▼▼▼▼▼▼▼

KEN REEVE reached the top of the rocky saddle above the valley where he and Gaynor had seen the catmen's settlement. He paused for a moment to hitch the recorder to a more comfortable position on his shoulder. Like most burdens, it had seemed to gain weight with every mile. With a shrug he swung it off and, striding to a reddish boulder, sat down in the shade of the stately ribbed porous wood trees.

I'll need a break before the show starts, he told himself, removing his wide-brimmed hat and wiping his moist forehead. After nearly a year, he was still as unused to the pressure of the headband as he was to the smell of sweat. He squinted up at the warm spring sun, orange against the green-blue sky.

Gazing back the way he had come, Reeve grunted when he realized that their own settlement, nestled in an outcropping of trees, was no more visible to him than that of the natives. Far below in the river valley, beyond the second loop, the rising heat haze hid the slim metal spire of the homing beacon, despite the fact that it occupied dead center of the landing site.

The foothill of red-grained rock formed an additional barrier to mutual discovery. No smoke came from the Terran encampment because they still had converted heat. His eyes swung to the natives' valley and only because he looked carefully and long was he able to detect the faint gray plume of smoke, like a vague tentacle against the deep olive of the porous-tree needles.

He grunted again, confounded that the preceding two phases of allegedly meticulous survey could have missed such evidence. Now, if this were a hibernating race, he conceded grudgingly, perhaps they had been in their burrows or caves by late fall. But it hadn't been late fall when the orbiting robot had photographically mapped the planet. He sniffed and the aroma of burning wood touched his senses faintly. Faintly but unmistakably, burning wood. The two human scouts shouldn't have missed that in thirty days, Reeve argued. They were in our valley and, unless they goofed off in their reports, in this one too, because a description of this stand of wood was mentioned.

Late fall, though, Reeve mused, that's cold here. But, if they use fire in the spring, they surely use it in late fall. So how come? How come? Reeve swore softly to himself and sighed deeply.

He could barely accept the unalterable facts intellectually, let alone emotionally. Whatever the diplomatic repercussions, he was rebellious. And grateful that Pat and the kids would at least be able to touch down. God, it had been such a long time since he had had Pat. And a year made such differences in a child. Would his Ilsa be the same grave-faced, girl-woman he had left, so determined not to upset her daddy with tears? And Todd —well, it was odds to even that he'd probably shriek; from five to six was a long time for a kid to remember his father. Reeve smiled as he pictured the reunion.

Then the injustice of his situation closed in on him again. He still couldn't see how Spacedep and Codep could have slipped so badly. *And we're left holding the bag!* He picked up a piece of the red shale, examined it closely in sudden interest. *A bag of rocks!* He skipped the shale across the ground, watching the puff of dust it kicked up as it ricocheted off the rock wall.

You wait and you wait and you hope, and bribe, and cajole, and suck up; all for a chance to get out of the man-run on Earth. You get the chance, by taking the long-shot gamble of specializing in nothing and everything, and by the grace of adroit maneuvering and the proper slots on the IBM card. Then some nearsighted, stinking, half-assed Scouts—they probably never moved from their damned ship for fear of a purple fungus—report unoccupied a world very obviously too well occupied.

Savagely Ken launched another rock after the first.

He was examining another stone, a white one with lavender flecks, when a distant sound caught his ear. He paused but heard nothing more than the sound of the winged life in the trees, cackling and chirruping with complete freedom. Slowly he rose, slinging the recorder to his back. As the searching tongue prods again and again at the aching tooth, Reeve looked back over the valley where he had hoped to live his life and raise his children. He sighed and settled his hat on his head, well back so his face was fully visible. Then he turned back to the forest.

I cannot give this up, Ken vowed as he started resolutely down from the ridge. A memory of the greenless, treeless, granite and aluminum jungle of his home Sector superimposed itself on the forested slope. I want *this* for my children. And, God damn it, I want it for myself.

The forest enveloped him coolly. He kept his eyes open for any other sign of life. The porous wood trees grew to sixty or seventy feet, branching out twenty feet above the ground with widespread limbs, twig ends tufted by green, three-sided needles. Survey pictures showed that in fall the needles turned a deep red-purple. The ground was covered by the yearly droppings, now a rich reddish-brown, making a springy mulch. Grass and seedlings would find it hard to push their way up through the dense cover, so the forest had an uncluttered, parklike look to it.

The houses of the village (Gaynor had counted fifteen

while Reeve was busy snapping shots), were not yet visible. They were closer to the river in one of the natural clearings where an outcropping of the red rock had made rooting difficult. Aerial maps of that area, again showing not a single habitation, indicated that the river, dropping a sudden five feet, created a natural fall thirty feet across, flanked by great slabs of rock, flat, gently sloping up to the forest edge.

If the cats wore clothing, Reeve smiled, an excellent place for women to wash and spread things to dry or for fishermen to spread their catch to cure. If, he added to himself, their culture was advanced enough.

The fish—and Reeve ran his tongue around his teeth at the thought of the succulent red flesh—edible without a hint of the aftertaste of artificial origins. On his father's salary, real food had been an impossibility. Pat had tasted honest beef meat once, but she had found it tough to chew. She wouldn't find the well hung game here tough, Reeve vowed to himself smugly. He'd become quite adept as a butcher and was trying his hand at smoking and quick freezing meats.

A flurry of birds drew his eyes upward and he stopped, looking to see if any feathers dropped. You could bring back hundreds of feathers. Wait a minute. Had his passage set them in flight or something else? Were the catlike natives aware of his presence, and watching him secretively?

It makes little difference when we meet, Reeve told himself, so long as I have a chance to get enough of their language on tape so we can communicate. If I can only talk to them and tell them how much it means to be able to . . .

He had rounded a cluster of trees when a sphere, in an all too homey shape, bounced off a tree trunk and rolled to a halt at his feet. Instinctively he bent to pick it up as two small bodies came bounding toward him and skidded to a stop. The two species froze and regarded each other with surprise.

Reeve picked up the ball and the other two, eyes

wide, moved closer together as if for support in confronting the unknown quantity before them.

Close up, the resemblance to cats was uncanny, Reeve thought, returning the solemn stares solemnly.

The great green eyes regarded him from under straight wide brows, dark pupils narrowed against the orange sun. Flattish noses were broad at the nostril over the lipless wide mouths. The chins were short bridges in the middle of the wide hinged jaw. The lobeless ears had tufted tips. Each child—for their very appearance and attitude cried youth to Reeve—wore a belt around his middle. A short sheathed knife hung from it without covering their obvious maleness. Their skins were a light fawn, like a soft velour, but their heads were covered with a darker tan mop of hair that hung to their ear tips. Visible between their spraddled legs were short, tufted tails, stuck straight out behind them in surprise.

Careful not to smile for fear a smile might mean hostility to them, Reeve made several one-handed catches. He pointed slowly to the taller of the two cubs, then indicated that he wished to return the ball to him. With an easy, underhand throw, he returned the ball. Solemnly the cub, ears twitching briefly, caught the ball, holding it in both hands without looking at it. Reeve saw the retractable claws unsheath just long enough to secure the catch.

"That was a good catch, fellow," Reeve said quietly, putting all the approval he could into his tone.

Both sets of ears twitched rapidly. The two looked at each other a moment, then turned their attention quickly back to Reeve. He held up his hands suggestively and crouched like a catcher. Two pairs of round green eyes widened further. The taller cub, keeping careful hold on his ball, blinked and nodded hesitantly. Reeve sensed it was gratitude for the return of the ball. Neither cub appeared afraid of him but clearly they had never seen his like. Reeve had the impression of two well-brought-up young men waiting for the adult to speak.

He straightened up and pointed toward the village. "Could you boys take me to your father?"

The taller cub turned to his companion and Reeve hastily thumbed on the recorder. He caught the last part of a growled collection of sounds. The smaller cub shrugged and made a grimace that suggested, "How should I know what to do next?"

The tall cub growled out another phrase, his wide mouth in profile open almost to his ear.

The other shrugged again and turned around, starting off toward the forest. The tall one regarded Reeve seriously for one more moment. Then, inclining his head toward Reeve, turned, leaving Ken to follow him.

Chapter V

RETURN

▼▼▼▼▼▼▼▼▼▼▼▼▼▼▼▼▼▼▼▼▼▼▼▼

REEVE WONDERED if the homeward trek seemed shorter because the agile native led him to a lower saddle of the ridge or because he was so elated by the initial contact. God knows the stinking recorder felt no lighter and, in the hot midday sun, both he and Hrrula were becoming fragrant. The native smelled—different: a not unpleasant difference, Reeve decided, though the odor brought no comparison to mind.

Hrrula's narrow feet with their vestigial webbings and claws gave him a springy step and more purchase in the slippery shale and the thick ground cover than Reeve's boots. A tail would be a handy thing in mountain climbing, Reeve thought inconsistently as he panted up the slope behind Hrrula. You could do without body ropes, maybe. How much pull would a tail take, he wondered, resisting an all but uncontrollable urge to grab the appendage as an assist to the top of the ridge.

Hrrula fortunately stopped at the summit, looking questioningly at Reeve. Ken wondered if the Hrrubans might possibly be telepaths and that Hrrula had caught his thought.

"Our colony is down there, across the river," Reeve began briskly to cover his momentary embarrassment. He pointed, watching with fascination as the Hrruban's eyes narrowed to slits. The houses in their grove, similar to the Hrrubans' village, were invisible through the trees.

What was obvious from this angle was the plowed field in which various forms of Terran grains were already planted. Beyond that were the fenced pastures awaiting the arrival of the precious farm livestock on the colony ship.

The Hrruban gazed out over the valley, his sensitive ears twitching. He turned his head, its dark mane cropped close to the skull in the manner in which most of the natives Reeve assumed to be young wore their mane hair. Hrrula's yellow-green eyes glowed with the first trace of excitement or interest Reeve had detected. All the Hrrubans seemed possessed of superb dignity and poise. Reeve hoped he had been able to mask his own nervousness. A guy's sweat got sour with nervousness. The Hrrubans' noses twitched so frequently, they must be sensitive to odor.

Hrrula now nodded at Ken and the two resumed their trek.

Reeve was not sure whether he was pleased or annoyed at Hrrula's walking language exercise. The native stopped to name each new bush or tree they passed. He would frequently point to one he had already identified, look questioningly at Reeve to see if he remembered. It kept Reeve alert, not alone trying to retain the mass of new information but looking ahead in order to see which specimen might be indicated next. But he remembered to get all of it down on tape.

That Hrrula insisted Reeve learn the native name for everything caused a complex reaction in the Terran. Dautrish, the colony's botanist, had already lovingly catalogued each new species. Well, maybe Dautrish could sell that catalogue for its esoteric value. Reeve's respect for the Hrrubans, however, increased with this insistence on the use of their own words. Of course, there wouldn't be time to learn much Hrruban but the practice might just help Reeve wangle a transfer to Alreldep. Ken shook his head, those rolled 'r's were hell to get and he was sure this was a pitched language as well, like the old oriental dialects. One misplaced inflection and you had delivered a gross insult back to the first generation.

There, again, was incongruity. A pitched language is the mark of a very old civilization, with plenty of time for shadings and nuances in expression of ideas.

Hrrula had stopped by one of the ironwood trees on which grew an immense parasitic vine. Reeve recognized it immediately as the one that had given Dautrish violent cramps from a simple smear-sampling.

"*Rroamal. Rroamal,*" Hrrula said, very soberly shaking his head from side to side. He made as if to touch it and drew his hand back quickly, shaking it as if it hurt.

"Bad? *Rooamall,*" Reeve tried, then grabbed his belly as if he had a case of Dautrish's cramps. He added a realistic groan.

Hrrula's mouth widened and he nodded appreciatively.

Another item of information to add to my list, Ken thought. Our body chemistries react similarly to at least one common irritant.

Hrrula held up one digit and repeated the word for the vine carefully. Inwardly Ken groaned again and motioned Hrrula to repeat the word once more. The native did and Ken made another attempt to get what he thought he heard as a rising inflection on the second vowel sound. Hrrula, listening attentively, approved the result and they moved on. In his mind, Ken kept practicing the sound, trying to impress on himself the correct inflection.

By the time they reached the river and the plastic skiff moored there, he had a variety of useful words, three with similar sounds but different inflections. With what he had on the recorder, this was a good start. Hu Shih ought to enjoy it, Reeve thought.

Hrrula knelt by the boat, oblivious both to Reeve and the sudden appearance of Gaynor and McKee on the opposite shore. Hrrula carefully got into the skiff, looked at the far side, felt on the coamings and then spread his hands wide, questioningly.

He is used to a paddle, Reeve decided, smiling to think how surprised Hrrula would be when he started the tiny motor. The river current was too swift for a paddle-propelled vehicle.

Instead of a surprised or fearful reaction, Hrrula nodded approvingly as the engine took hold and the skiff cut the current efficiently. Hrrula hunkered down quietly, curling his tail around his toes, folding his arms around his knees, facing the Common.

Reeve threw the mooring line to Gaynor and stepped off quickly.

"By God, they are cats," Gaynor said. "And he stinks!"

"Watch it," Reeve said, keeping his face and voice pleasant. He turned a bit so that he could dig Gaynor warningly in the ribs. "This is Hrrula who seems to have some position in the village and was sent with me by the chief, Hrrestan."

Hrrula debarked and stood, completely at ease, his eyes on the trio. Although Hrrula now had a clear view of the buildings, the experimental greenhouses, the park-like Common, he displayed no overt interest.

The guy's got innate manners, Reeve found himself thinking.

"Hrrula, this is Gaynor," Reeve said slowly, pointing to Sam. "Sam, this is Hrrula. They greet by touching palms, extend yours palm down."

"That character's got claws," Gaynor said, returning the greeting. "I could get used to that—but not the stench."

"If he likes you, I gather he keeps his claws sheathed," Reeve remarked drily.

"Yeah, but when does he turn off that stink?" And Sam turned his head away to sneeze lustily.

McKee hastily stepped forward and touched palms with Hrrula.

"I've got a recorder full of their sounds for us to parse," Reeve told his colleagues, "plus a walking language lesson on the dangerous flora of the planet."

"Is that why this Ha-rula came?" demanded Gaynor,

stumbling over the rolled 'r'. Before Reeve could answer, Sam convulsed again into multiple sneezes.

"I couldn't prevent him from coming if we're keeping the friendly image intact," Ken replied.

"How long's he staying?"

"Beats me."

McKee grinned at Hrrula. "Well, let's get conjugating or declining or whatever is necessary to purr."

"Sounds more like growls to me," Gaynor remarked. "I'm no linguist. I'll go feather my bed," and he jerked his forefinger under his nose to prevent another of his body-jolting sneezes. "You'd be smarter to come along, Macy. We haven't got that much time here, you know."

McKee waved him to go on and turned to accompany Reeve and Hrrula to the mess hall.

Late that night, when Ken Reeve decided to take a break from his language dissection and endless playback of the recorder, he found Lawrence holding the floor in the mess hall.

"These Hrrubans are civilized," Lee was insisting vehemently, his argument directed at a glowering Sam Gaynor. "And I don't mean stand-erect, thumb-opposed civilized. I mean, a mannered sophistication. You saw him at dinner; he knew the purpose of utensils and used his own knife to cut meat."

"He ought to. It was sharper," Gaynor retorted.

"Speaking of knives," McKee put in, "notice the workmanship on the handle of his knife? I wonder where he got the stones; that pink-purple one is a beauty. And I've seen nothing like it around here."

"Must come from another section of the planet. They are nomads," Abe Dautrish said thoughtfully.

"I wouldn't ask to see that private knife, not just yet," Lawrence cautioned McKee.

"And let's be cautious in the gemstone field," Reeve suggested as he poured himself coffee. "Some early tribes attach special significance to stones and metals belonging to their gods."

"I just finished pointing out that their cultural level is

considerably above rank superstition," Lawrence said with some asperity.

"Ken, you didn't see a worship center in the village, did you?" asked Ramasan.

"Not a place obviously set aside as sacred," and Reeve scoured his memory of the quiet village. "All the buildings looked residential, but then, how'd I recognize an Hrruban church from a proverbial hole in the ground?"

"Of them we got plenty," laughed Lawrence who had so recently been a fence-post hole digger.

"Do they suckle their young?" Ezra Moody asked.

Ken closed his eyes again to focus on the scene in the village but he had too many details doing a reel in his mind's eye.

"I'm sorry, Doc. I did see young ones, the kids with their balls and some older cubs—I guess you'd call 'em cubs—were playing some involved throwing game. I didn't pay it much attention, you understand, but it looked at a glance like a team game. I didn't see a small baby cub. Some of the women, though, wore garments draped from their shoulders—patterned materials. Some didn't. Difficult to notice mammary development through the fur. A couple of females had a sleeveless top, then the ornamental girdle and a skirt similar to the one Hrrula wears, only they didn't carry knives. So it's obvious that clothing is adornment rather than cover-up. And the women didn't take any part in the conference at the central fire. They came and went. They cook indoors; I did notice that.

"Oh, and I saw a woman milking one of the deer-types in a pen by her house."

"They can domesticate those deer, huh?" Ben rumbled. "I'd thought of trying it, once I could catch one," and then he shrugged. "Deerhorns were once ground up as an aphrodisiac."

"Good Lord!" Ezra Moody exclaimed, staring at Ben Adjei in astonishment.

Everyone was used to Ben's dry teasing humor but occasionally he would succeed with the pragmatic medic.

Now he shrugged again, but there was a certain gleam in his dark eyes as he replied. "The wise merchant stimulates demand for his products and impotence is on the rise in our automated society."

"Why, you wouldn't—you don't mean—" Moody stammered until someone's chuckle tipped him off.

"A moment, though," Dautrish interjected. "Ben has a point. No, of course I don't mean ground deerhorn, Ezra, but I mean, let us be sensible in what we plan to bring back to mother Earth. Let us not duplicate or undercut each other's treasure. I am very tempted to bring back some of those nicotine-rich leaves, Ezra, for I happen to know that there isn't enough available on Earth to treat those circulatory diseases for which nicotine is a specific."

"You can't prepare enough to make its importation valid," Ezra replied. "And can we protect it and Earth from a possible cross-infection? We have to be sure what we bring in can be adequately sterilized, you know, or it will be jettisoned."

"True, true," Dautrish agreed, his enthusiasm waning abruptly.

"Can you sterilize feathers?" Sam Gaynor asked in alarm.

"Yes, indeed. Ultra-violet'll do it. We can put them through an insecticide to remove the quill parasites."

"Parasites?" Sam Gaynor regarded the plastic bagsful of vivid feathers with obvious suspicion.

"Hey, which weighs more? A pound of feathers or a pound of rocks?" Lawrence asked with an all too sober face.

"Huh?" Gaynor was startled afresh. "Oh, knock it off, Lawrence," he said when the sociologist began to laugh. He picked up his colorful treasure and left the mess hall, muttering under his breath.

"Take it easy, Lawrence," Ken suggested. "You know he's got a low boiling point and we don't need to fight among ourselves."

"He may just find there isn't *room* for fine feathers on

the Codep ship," Lee Lawrence replied, no trace of his recent amusement on his face. "Mart's rings, Vic's plasticized flowers, even Macy's stones make more sense than feathers!"

"Yes, but feathers don't have much mass and it's mass that a ship moves," Vic Solinari pointed out.

"Yes but! Yes but!" Lee cut in, his eyes restlessly darting from one face to another, his mouth distorted suddenly with his inner conflict. "Yes, but *why?*"

The anguished question hung unanswered in the tense silence that followed the sociologist's outburst. Each man must have been wrestling with conscience and conditioning, Reeve realized. Wrestling against the inexorable departure from Doona. They had accepted it; at least to the point of collecting items now unobtainable on Earth and therefore valuable; extraterrestrial products with which to buy a decent status. But the emotional shock was seeping past rationalization, past obedience, past all civilized compromise, and every man in the room was fighting to maintain mental balance in the face of this embittering disappointment.

"Why?" Ken heard himself saying. "Because history has shown that two civilizations cannot coexist on the same planet without competing to the point of aggression—and destruction. God knows I don't want to leave Doona either, but I goddam well couldn't live with myself if I stayed—and the Hrrubans got wiped out like the Siwannese."

"One can suddenly understand why our ancestors found genocide to be the easiest solution to their own problems in dealing with minority groups," Ben remarked in his imperturbable fashion. "It was Columbus, wasn't it, who eliminated the Carib tribes completely? Of course, they had only spears, and swords, not rifles and—" his voice dropped to a velvety whisper.

"Are you mad, Adjei?" Lawrence shouted, his eyes wide with horror at the big vet's soft intimation.

"Not from you, Ben?" Moody was stunned.

"You're sick, Adjei!"

"What's the matter with you?"

Ben smiled as he leaned back in his chair. "I just thought I'd say it and it would be said and could be forgotten."

There was no doubt, judging by the expressions in the room, that the thought had occurred to everyone; nasty, niggling, treacherous thought that it was. Ben was right. It was a relief to hear it spoken, to be able to discard it with honest revulsion.

"But it rather forcefully points up why we have a Principle of Non-Cohabitation, doesn't it?" he went on quietly. "However, we have progressed. Your reaction proved that. So we will have the dubious pleasure of being recorded as the heroes of the Decision at Doona."

Ken put down his empty cup. He hadn't had enough coffee but he couldn't stay in the charged uneasy atmosphere of the mess hall.

"Doc, spring me out some stay-awake, will you?" he asked.

"Why beat your wits out over that crazy purr, Ken? What good'll it do you now?" Lawrence asked.

"I don't know," Reeve answered honestly as he waited for Ezra to locate the stimulant, "but it occupies my mind and gets me from today to tomorrow."

"Knowledge is never useless," Dautrish said, riffling the pages of his careful botanical drawings. "I think I'd like to have a list of those Hrruban equivalents of all these. For my records, you know, and," he favored Ken with a wry smile, "my own personal satisfaction."

"Say, is Hrrula going back to his village tomorrow?" asked Solinari. "I mean, I'd kinda like to look around it."

Ken scrubbed wearily at his face, waiting for the pep pill to take effect. "Hrrula didn't indicate any length of stay. I'd like to get one more good session with him on the tape before he goes."

"You know," Lee mused, all trace of his previous disgruntlement gone, "I rather like that—*we* learn *his* language."

"I, too, approve," Ben concurred. "For once, the native

gets the linguistic upperhand. Unusual too, probably unique in contact history. Hmmm. When you've got the glossary, Ken, I'll learn it with you."

The giant veterinary rose languidly, stretched until his joints cracked and, with a step unusually noiseless for one of his physical bulk, walked out of the hall.

"Well!" Dautrish exclaimed, looked around until he saw Reeve grinning at him. "An astonishing man. One never knows what to make of him. Anyone else want to grasp the golden opportunity of learning a real live alien language?"

"Fleeting opportunity, you mean," Lawrence said, then added, "I'd give my sociological left arm to know what's been happening tonight at Hrrula's village."

Chapter VI

REACTION

▼▼▼▼▼▼▼▼▼▼▼▼▼▼▼▼▼▼▼▼▼▼▼▼▼

WHEN THE FILMS and tapes reached Exploration, the Chief, trusting no one else, personally brought them to the First Speaker in the Executive Cube. To his intense gratification, he was asked to remain as the First Speaker ran through the records of that initial contact with another intelligent species.

After the last scene faded, the Chief watched the First Speaker meditate until the silence was unbearable.

"Sir," he all but stuttered in guilty uncertainty, "the Prime Rule is in jeopardy. We will withdraw our people."

The First Speaker regarded him with a deceptively blank expression.

"On the contrary, Chief, we must remain and observe."

"Observe?" The Chief was surprised—and relieved. One of the few pleasures he had in his position was the opportunity to visit that planet.

"Of course we must observe. Surely, Chief, you of all our people have realized that a contact of this sort was only a matter of time. You know how often your Scouts have discovered traces of other space explorations."

"Indeed I do, sir. But considering our wretched history—" he hesitated, arrested by a minute change in the calm face.

"Chief, it is time we stopped making that 'wretched history' an excuse for racial cowardice." The gentle voice in no way lessened the shock of the statement.

"Sssssir?"

"That planet is ideal for a confrontation. It is also obvious that this species intends ours no harm. Indeed, the film is witness to their very earnest attempt to meet us with friendship. Notice, also, the willingness to learn our language—surely no easy task for them. No, Chief, I regard this incident as extremely providential. Extremely."

The First Speaker rose and walked to the windowed wall, turned off the opacity in order to look out at the endless panorama of structures.

"All those people and so few interested in more than the fare on the view and food panels. Something must snap them out of this crushing lethargy. What they need is a good fright! Yes, a blood-stirring fright!"

Gone was the gentle-voiced Speaker. The Chief sucked in his breath at the vibrant ring as he felt his heartbeat accelerate.

"Nothing gets a man more than a threat to his very existence!"

"Sir," the Chief began tentatively, "it will provoke another wave of suicides and our young adults . . ."

A growl deep in the First Speaker's chest paralyzed the Chief completely.

"A suitable end for those unable to face any sort of challenge. No, Chief," and the First Speaker paced energetically, his eyes gleaming with excitement, "this crisis will be the making of us—or the end. And if it's the end, then good riddance to a species that has outlived its purpose. Now, here are my orders for . . ."

A discreet tap on the door was instantly followed by a muffled oath as the door swung open abruptly, framing an apologetic aide trying to restrain the Third Speaker from forcibly obtaining entrance.

"First Speaker, I demand—" the Third Speaker began over the aide's protestations.

The First Speaker raised a reassuring hand to his aide before beckoning the Third in. The moment the door closed behind the aide, the angry intruder erupted into accusations, barely able to enunciate in his rage. The Chief wondered who was the spy in his office. Or had the Third, in his zeal to end the whole project, managed to place an adherent in the colony?

"Aliens on that pet planet of yours. I told you that worthless place would be more bother than use. Pastoral, indeed! With who knows what else running around loose. Call 'em back. Call 'em back before another moment's loss of time. Before irrevocable damage is done. Never should have permitted this ridiculous experiment, First. Never. Doomed from the beginning."

"On the contrary, Third," the older man replied calmly, indicating a chair for his unexpected visitor.

"What do you mean? On the contrary, First? Clear case of Prime Rule. Clear case. No discussion necessary. Call 'em back."

"It is not that simple, Third, nor can we call them back."

"Why not?"

"I believe that you have scarcely had the chance to see the film tapes that were taken of the first encounter," the First Speaker remarked suavely and firmly pressed the Third Speaker into a chair. "If you would be kind enough to start the film, Chief . . ."

A flash of repulsion mixed with curiosity crossed the Third's face and he subsided with a show of reluctance.

During the replay, the Chief kept surreptitious watch on the Third's reactions and tried not to be pessimistic as he realized that the film clearly did not reassure the conservative.

"If you think, First, that I will let any member of our species stand in danger from those—those . . ."

"We stand in considerably more danger from our own

species," the First Speaker interrupted with such fervor that Third stared at him in stunned silence. "Another race, as intelligent as we ourselves, co-inhabits this galaxy. Prime Rule notwithstanding, contact has been made on a *neutral* world. It is my intention to make the most of this fortuitous confrontation to pave the way to a peaceful alliance."

"Peaceful alliance? With creatures like that?" Third was apoplectic with indignation. "You overstep your authority, First Speaker. I am calling an emergency meeting of all Speakers. We shall determine if you have not also overstepped the borders of sanity."

Before the First Speaker could reply to the insult, the other man had swept from the room.

"Sir, what will happen now?" The Chief was aware of the cold slowing of his heart.

"Why, the Third Speaker will convene a meeting, just as he declared. And then we shall indeed see—what we shall see. However," and First's smile was characteristically benign, "since it will take a few days to drag the Speakers back from their various retreats, let us make a few plans of our own. Let us determine what sort of people our new acquaintances are, and what *they* have in mind for that lovely world."

Chapter VII

BRIDGE

▼▼▼▼▼▼▼▼▼▼▼▼▼▼▼▼▼▼▼▼▼▼▼▼▼▼▼▼▼▼

FOR THE HUNDREDTH time, Ken wondered just how it had come about that they were learning the Hrruban language instead of the other way round.

"It must have been my fault," he said out loud. "I made the initial contact. How did I goof? Or did I? Hell, all I did was learn some plant and tree names," he defended himself. "And I did get a language tape. Somehow we've lost the first round. Or maybe—maybe we've won it."

It was now four days since he had trod into the Hrruban village. No homing capsule had arrived from Amalgamated Worlds with instructions. Nor had the colony ship arrived with their families. This caused a good deal of unrest among the men. Ken forced his mind away from that insidious thought.

He wondered what kind of a flap their report of natives on Doona had created in the ultra-conservative Executive Block. It would be like them to reply that indeed there had been a mistake; there *couldn't* be natives on Doona. None had been reported by Spacedep, Alreldep or Codep. He thought of the films and tapes which closely followed the first message: films made by concealed camera of every step of the second day, starting from the instant Hrrula rose, and indicated that he

wished to return to his village, and that he wanted Ken
and Hu Shih to accompany him. Ken had pointed to Vic
Solinari and Hrrula had not hesitated a moment to include the storemaster.

There had been a little pantomime on Hrrula's part
when they were preparing to embark in the little raft.
Ken, thinking Hrrula was concerned over the capacity of
the skiff, tried to reassure him. Hrrula watched the pantomime, lowered his jaw in what was evidently his ap-
proximation of a smile, and got in.

No sooner had Hu Shih and Vic been presented to the
village chief, Hrrestan, and four of the other older natives, than Hrrula began to speak in quick syllables. He
hunkered down on the ground and with one claw delicately drew the outline of a bridge, spanning water.
Grinning widely, Hrrula looked up at Reeve.

"God, he wasn't scared of the river or the skiff sinking," Vic cried in astonishment. "He was planning a
bridge!"

Ken and Hu Shih immediately protested but their
arguments, embellished with violent gestures and cha-
rades, had run into the language barrier. The vocabulary which Ken had struggled to learn was all too
insufficient to express such intangibles as aggression or
isolation, much less the fact that the colonists must leave
as soon as they could obtain transport.

The Hrrubans met every attempt to dissuade them
with bland insistence on the bridge.

"Do you realize what this means, Ken?" the slight colony leader had finally whispered to him. "They do not
resent us."

"Now, wait a minute, sir. Don't you realize what a
bridge . . ."

"No hostility at all. Really I am most heartened. And
their grasp of architectural concepts is quite sophisticated. Have you noticed the dovetailed joints on the
window frame of that house?"

"Shih," Ken gripped the man's shoulder and gave him
a little shake. "We mustn't build that bridge!"

"Why ever not?"

"In the first place, that bridge is the first step toward possible aggression of our race against theirs."

"You refine too much . . ."

"For another," Ken went right on, "why waste time building a bridge we'll never get to use?"

The animation left Hu Shih's face; his dark eyes were thoughtful.

"You're right, of course, but it is difficult not to take a hand offered in such open friendship. They do seem to want to get to know us."

"And how often has our race turned the hand of friendship into a martial fist?"

Hu Shih nodded solemnly and they turned to renew their opposition to the bridge, trying to get the Hrrubans to understand that the colony would not remain long enough for the effort required.

Hrrula, his eyes half-lidded, tapped the diagram of the bridge. He held up two fingers and spoke the Hrruban word for day.

"Impossible," Ken protested and stretched out his hand to erase the dusty sketch in conclusive denial.

A furred hand, talons politely sheathed, slipped adroitly under his, preventing the erasure.

"Yesssss," and the Hrruban hissed the Terran word softly.

Ken regarded Hrrula solemnly, determined to his course. Two other fur-backed hands joined Hrrula's to keep Ken from reaching the drawing. Ken looked at Hrrestan who nodded slowly, to the other Hrruban who dropped his jaw and smiled.

"If you knew how silly you looked, Ken," Vic remarked ironically. "They want a bridge. Okay. We've tried to explain it's a waste of effort. But what harm will a bridge do, Reeve? As you pointed out, we know we're not going to be here long enough to finish it. And if it means that much to them, let's be polite. They obviously know how to build one, so we're not giving them a premature cultural shock."

"Vic, don't you see the principle that's involved? Every single instance of territorial aggression began . . ."

"Don't sweat history now, Ken," the storemaster suggested rudely. "I don't want to think about it. I just want to take each day on Doona as it comes, enjoy the planet as much as I can . . ."

"And find out where the Hrrubans mine those stones?" Ken asked cynically.

"That, too," Vic admitted. "Besides, I'd like to see what they intend to use to span that river. Can you find out?"

"Victor's argument is valid," Hu Shih said.

Thus dies noble principle, Ken thought as he glared from colony leader to storemaster. And yet—we won't be here long; it does not use a cultural concept they don't already grasp—and what the hell!

"Hrrula," Ken said aloud, pausing in fascination at the way the native's ears twitched. He pointed to the suspension beams which Hrrula had scratched in the dust. "*Rla?*" and he enunciated carefully, wondering if he'd swallow his tongue one day getting out that rolled 'r'.

Hrrula nodded gravely, gesturing toward the *rla*-wood tree behind him.

"They use that porous wood?" asked Vic eagerly.

"*Rla,*" Ken corrected him.

"*Errla,*" Vic growled out. Hrrula shook his head patiently and repeated the sound which Victor dutifully tried to mimic. "I can't get that 'r' sound, Ken," he groaned under his breath. "But that wood wouldn't bear enough weight. It's too damned porous."

Ken rubbed his temples, trying to drag appropriate words from his small Hrruban vocabulary. Shaking his head at his limitations, he knelt down again at the drawing. Carefully he drew a wide band to indicate the river. He then sketched the footings on both sides of the river, well back from the verge. He tapped the vertical elevation, showing the suspension, pantomiming the height of the trees with the length required to span the gap. Hrrula nodded solemn understanding.

"Hrrubans," Hrrula said softly, indicating the adults present, "hayumans," he said carefully, tapping Ken and Vic, jerking his head over his shoulder in the direction of the colony, "*rla i zamat rrigam.*"

"*Rrigam* means build?" asked Vic.

"Guess so," Ken answered. "Verb falls at the end of the sentence near as I can figure. I still don't think we should agree," he muttered under his breath and looked around to see Hrrestan pointing vigorously to the bridge sketch, nodding his head emphatically.

"*Um zamat rrigam. La!*"

After one last attempt to explain that the Terrans would not be staying, Ken gave in.

The bridge was planned. And planned, according to Sam Gaynor's truculent opinion, with a sound knowledge of engineering principles, until he found out that *rla* wood was to be used.

"That damned porous wood . . ."

"*Rla*," Ken corrected automatically.

"*Erla*, then," snapped Gaynor, "are too pulpy to hold any weight at all, not to mention a span. Damn fool notion."

"They treat the wood, Sam," Vic Solinari explained. "Don't know with what, although Harrula tried to explain. But he showed me the coating on the house timber and I couldn't crack it with a ball-peen hammer."

"And the house's owner politely requested him not to chisel it," Ken added with a grin at Vic's embarrassment.

"I hope they know what we're doing," Gaynor said, for he could not remain long in Hrruban company without titanic sneezing. Moody had treated Gaynor empirically with massive antihistamines but could not isolate the specific factor without examining an Hrruban. Such an occasion had not yet presented itself.

It worked out by the end of that day that the Terrans would cut timber for the footings on their side of the river, the Hrrubans on theirs; the Hrrubans indicated they already had sufficient timber cut for the span. The foundations had been dug on both sides when two Hrrubans arrived with a large wooden tub full of a hot gray viscose liquid.

Taking paddle-like brushes, Hrrula and Hrrestan began to coat the footing logs, working quickly and taking care not to splash the hot liquid on their bodies. The logs for the footings were lifted into position by Hrrubans wearing protective hide gloves. More liquid was sloshed on the now upright pilings. After an arbitrary pause, the Hrrubans filled in the dirt around the footings and turned to the first of the span logs. Again they worked swiftly, coating the log and then easing it out across the rapid flow of the river until it was in its assigned place. It was rapidly anchored with tough vines which were also painted. The Terrans watched as, after a second pause, Hrrula tested the log with a judicious claw. Apparently satisfied with the hardening of the paint, Hrrula astonished everyone by leaping up and racing down the length of the log to prove its firmness. He then indicated that the Terrans should examine the Hrruban workmanship and duplicate it on their side of the river.

"It's the same transparent stuff," Vic assured Gaynor after he had poked and scraped, and made no mark. "Tough as a plastic."

"Seals the wood and strengthens it, huh?" Gaynor murmured, sniffling constantly as he examined the span and the coated footings. "By God, we could use that wood for pretty nearly all our building needs and not have to wait for a plastics extruder. Find out how they make that, will you, Ken? And the rest of you guys, c'mon. Let's build our end just the way they did."

"Good? Hmmm?" asked Hrrula, grinning at Reeve as the skiff took the first load of men back to their side.

"Very good," Ken agreed. "What is it by you called?" he asked carefully in Hrruban.

"*Rlba*," Hrrula replied and Reeve groaned.

The 'l' became liquid but the 'r' took a savage roll and the upward accent fell on the final vowel.

Hrrunka, another of the Hrrubans whom Ken could

now recognize on sight, was stirring the *rlba*, which had been placed over a small fire to keep it at boiling point. The smell was pungent, reminiscent of the scent exuded by *rla* bark when sun-warmed. Hrrunka gestured Ken over, pointed to the *rlabans* behind him, pantomimed boring a hole, the sap running out, heating the sap to boiling point, brushing it on, waiting an arbitrary time; then, Hrrunka indicated, the sap hardened completely.

By the end of that day, the bridge was completed, twenty-six feet long, seven feet wide, sturdy enough for the colonists' power sled, constructed of native materials and with native ingenuity.

Chapter VIII

INTERFERENCE

▼▼▼▼▼▼▼▼▼▼▼▼▼▼▼▼▼▼▼▼▼▼▼▼

"IF—" AND THE First Speaker's voice projected sharply through the startled hubbub caused by Third's empassioned peroration, "we abandon the planet now, with no logical explanation for the disappearance—and I see no logical explanation short of killing our people outright and leaving their bodies to be found . . ."

"Really, sir," and Third was on his feet with indignation, "that solution—your solution—is the most . . ."

"Then let me continue!"

The stern disapproval in First's voice effectively quelled Third's brashness.

"By leaving the planet without logical explanation for such a *retreat*," and he delicately emphasized that word, stirring long forgotten pride in many chests, "we invite trouble to come to us—here! At the moment, we can contain it there—" he pointed to the star map and the red-flagged planet under discussion; it was obviously at a safe distance from the home system. "And we can probe, observe and, above all, think deeply on which course to pursue."

"The Prime Rule already states every single contingency . . ."

The Third Speaker's reliance on that Rule struck the Chief as totally inconsistent. For a person who constantly quoted platitudes and proverbs, he showed a remarkably different stripe in a crisis which he couldn't explain with a trite phrase.

"The Prime Rule states every contingency—except this one," the Fourth Speaker in charge of Education interrupted. "As any fool could see," and Fourth's nostrils twitched with disapproval, "the planet had no evidence of sentient life when we established our communities. The project prints out most creditable results in the short time it has been in effect. I do wish, now, that we had not specified that these units be withdrawn during the long cold season. The youngsters could just as easily have taken instruction there as here and we might not have lost the colony."

"We haven't lost it yet," the First Speaker reminded him gently. "I believe the Eighth Speaker has a computer analysis of the situation?"

Eighth rose and bowed with composure to the assembled before he unfolded the tapes in his hand. He scanned them quickly and, with the slightest smile on his features, placed them carefully down on the table.

"The data is insufficient for a prognosis," he said and sat down.

"Insufficient?" Third protested above the polite murmurs of the others. "How can that be?"

Eight rose slightly from his chair and passed the tapes across to Third. He looked at them nonplussed, his jaw dropping with astonishment.

"Yes, the data is indeed insufficient," First remarked.

Privately the Chief was twitching with delight. He would never have guessed that the Eighth Speaker might be on their side, willingly or unwillingly guided by the infallible tapes of his computer banks.

"Common sense," First was saying, "deep meditation and—and these tapes—point out the inadvisability of rash moves. Therefore, let us hear from Eight what additional data must be collected before probability curves can be plotted."

"And you'll abide by that?" Third leaped on the compromise.

"Of course," the First Speaker agreed easily and indicated that the floor was now Eighth's.

"We shall need to know, first of all, the language. I understand strides are being made in that direction already. It would be helpful to know their cultural level, scientific abilities, some indication of their moral values as regards family life, goals, customs . . ."

"Nonsense," sputtered Third, looking directly at Second who had been remarkably quiet throughout this meeting. "What we *need* to know is the strength of their weapons, their space fleet, the position of their home worlds, the . . ."

"That is quite enough, Third! You are interrupting Eighth."

"But you aren't dealing with the core of the matter at all, First. You know you aren't." Third's voice rang with an angry note in which the Chief detected a ring of fear. "We've got to be able to destroy them before they can . . ."

"And who has prated most of the Prime Rule, Third Speaker?" The anger in First's tone was not fear-based; it was the indignation of a patient, overtried man. "Destruction has not been our operational aim in thousands of years. Let us not retrogress to it in this crisis. Let us, instead, learn as much as we can of our new friends— yes, friends, Third, not enemies! For it would be race suicide for us in our present decadence to consider them anything else until we have good cause to do so. And I, for one, do not believe we shall have cause."

"We must protect our people," Third insisted, pounding the table with his fist. "We cannot permit them to be slaughtered as our team on . . ."

"Withdrawal can be effected instantly," Second remarked calmly.

The Chief longed to speak but could not even catch First's eye.

"Can you imagine the effect on our new friends," First

continued, "if our people just—disappeared? They are not unintelligent, for they already have *space* travel, and our disappearance can only precipitate more speculation than we wish. Indeed, I believe it will be only a matter of time before one of them adds up the anomalies we have already presented them. It is far better for us to preserve the facade of low-culture post-nomadic . . ."

"A ridiculous notion; degrading, a spurious protection . . ." Third muttered audibly.

"Are any of your *stripe* there?" First asked with mild concern.

"Of course not. More sense than to participate in such an outlandish idea."

"Considering the volume of space separating us from this planet, how high is the probability of their race finding our home world?" Fifth asked Eighth.

Fifth was another unknown quantity, the Chief knew, for it was only in the past year that Fifth had shown an interest in the botanical, pharmaceutical and mineral resources of the world. Specimens had been quickly procured for his research laboratories but Fifth had issued no reports on his findings.

"I have run that probability through the computer," Eighth replied slowly, "but again, the data is insufficient. We know nothing of the tenacity and aggressiveness of this race."

"Which brings us right back to the point under discussion," First remarked smoothly. "We must know more about our new friends. We must learn to communicate with them so that we can assess their basic psychological reactions . . ."

"Such as their ability to build bridges?" Third snapped. "I insist, by virtue of my prerogative as Third Speaker for Internal Affairs, that our people be protected from those—those bareskinned beasts. By forceful means if necessary. Place a defensive screen around that planet . . ."

"A moment, Third," First intervened in a steely voice. "Let us examine the matter calmly."

Third spluttered a moment longer until it finally bore through to him that his vehemence was jeopardizing his cause.

"I have been hasty," he apologized, "but my concern is all for those valiant pioneers, defenseless against the unimaginable machinations of these unknown bipeds."

"Your concern does you credit," First murmured and then beckoned to Eighth who had been patiently waiting to continue.

"I propose a compromise until we have amassed sufficient data to plot a probability curve. Am I correct in understanding from the translation of the tapes that the families of these—bareskins are due to arrive shortly?" Eighth received a confirmation. "I assume that they also must have informed their home world of our presence?" The Chief nodded. "Then let us permit the family transport to land, for to prevent that would be heartless and would also hamper one facet of our investigations. However, since we do not yet know the psychology of the bareskins, let us agree that our people be instantly transported back to their base as soon as any other vehicle is detected approaching the planet."

The instant approval of this concession was so overwhelming that First, who foresaw the problems inherent in the compromise, felt it wiser not to protest.

Chapter IX

ARRIVAL

▼▼▼▼▼▼▼▼▼▼▼▼▼▼▼▼▼▼▼▼▼▼▼▼▼

SINCE ITS COMPLETION three days ago, the bridge had had heavy traffic. The morning's visiting Hrrubans were already crossing it. Solinari and McKee passed them midway, pausing to say hello, then hurrying on to meet their own guides. They were off to the groves the Hrrubans cultivated for a rich nut which they ground for meal. Solinari and McKee had an idea about importing seed pods, speculating that the trees might be grown hydroponically. They hoped to get a Food Resources Grant and thus avoid a reduced status when they returned to Earth.

Reeve pulled on his coverall, aware that his private ruminations would make him late for his own appointment.

Hrrestan and two unfamiliar Hrrubans were expecting him at the mess hall. He had got used to distinguishing the natives by the variations and shadings of their velvety fur and eye markings. Gaynor might grumble that he couldn't tell one cat from another, but there were differences in the color of the backbone stripe and eye markings almost as distinct as the onetime differences in Terran skin shades. Lawrence suggested that this might be due to dietary differences rather than tribal or ethnic variations.

Ken hurried out of his cabin, down the trail to the mess hall, where the Hrrubans were awaiting him on the porch. He managed to growl out a respectable Hrruban apology to which Hrrestan replied with courteous denials. Reeve was delighted to be able to understand every word Hrrestan spoke. Progress in one direction, at least.

Hrrestan introduced the older of the two men as Hrral and the other Hrrto. Hrral was older than Hrrestan, his body fur so deep a brown it blended with the backbone stripe. His face fur was flecked with white, yet there was no other indication of approaching debility in the straight, strong body.

Hrral returned Reeve's carefully enunciated greeting with grave courtesy.

"Hrral is the elder of our largest settlement," Hrrestan explained. "I sent messages requesting him to visit us at his earliest convenience. Hrrto lives not far from Hrral and accompanied him."

Reeve felt his expression of welcome must be frozen on his face from the shock of Hrrestan's words. Why had it not occurred to anyone before that there would be more such settlements on Doona? It should have been obvious that Hrrestan's village could not be an isolated instance of humanoid life. A trained alienist would have undoubtedly checked that out immediately. Hell, his training had been in planetary exploitation, not diplomatic relations. Codep was damned lucky he'd taken up linguistics at all. At least some attempt had been made at establishing communication. He was a settler, damn it, up against a situation nowhere mentioned in fifteen years of extensive training.

"It is our way," Hrrestan continued smoothly, "to live in small groups so that our numbers are not a burden on game and other resources."

The horror of his home Sector's warren-like levels was superimposed for an instant over the Hrruban village and sent an additional internal shock through Reeve. He mumbled something about their wisdom.

"There has been mention made within my hearing of your sky-traveling ships," Hrrestan continued. "The young Hrrula says your mates and young will soon be joined with you. Hrral," and here Hrrestan made a curious bow to the elder, "great as is his learning and long as is his life has never seen such a wonder as a ship that travels in the sky."

Hrral seemed afflicted with a cough and his tail tip twitched.

"This is truly said to you by Hrrestan, Hrral," Reeve replied earnestly but slowly. "For how else could men travel from one world to another? This is how we have come here."

Reeve caught a glimpse of Hrrula's jaw dropped in silent amusement and wondered frantically what word he had mispronounced.

"It would be our great pleasure," Reeve began to see what Hrrestan was leading up to, "if the noble Hrral would remain as our guest until the sky ship comes?"

Hrral and Hrrestan exchanged glances and Reeve wondered if he had exceeded his authority in making the invitation. He looked around for Hu Shih. The courtesy and self-effacing manners of the Hrrubans were considerably more in the metropologist's manner than Reeve's. Sometimes Ken felt that he compared unfavorably with an untrained Hrruban cub with his habit of blurting out what he thought instead of couching it in the properly elegant phrases.

How the hell did anyone find out anything from Hrrubans, he'd like to know, when you had to lead up to what you wanted to say from the opposite direction? Sure, they should be finding out all kinds of facts about burial techniques ,child education, status symbols, tribal government, so that Alreldep would have what it needed. But the formal Hrruban language did not adapt itself to blunt inquiries. The inquirer—and Reeve was not alone in this frustration—was likely to find himself involved in a pronunciation lesson. So often in his dealings with Hrrula, Reeve would arrive at the opening he

needed to insert a leading question, only to find himself
involved in a grammar lesson. By the time he had been
lectured on the exceptions to that particular rule, he had
forgotten his question. It never seemed intentional at
that time but, in retrospect, Reeve wasn't so sure that
the Hrrubans hadn't discovered an exceptionally deft
evasive trick.

Expressing surprised pleasure at the invitation, Hrral
argued amiably with Hrrestan about the great inconve-
nience to which he would put his host. By the time he
had reassured Hrral, Reeve found that he was also committed to conducting Hrral around the colonists' installation.

They were about to step into the mess hall when both
Hrrubans stopped suddenly, throwing their heads up to
the sky, their ears twitching rapidly. Confused, Reeve
scanned the sky to see what could have attracted their
attention. Hrrula was also standing stock-still, head skyward.

"The eyes of the Hrruban are farseeing," Ken remarked politely. "May I know what they see in the sky?"

Hrrestan, his ears still working, his pupils adjusting
his vision to normal range, widened his mouth in the
Hrruban version of a smile.

"The sky ship is descending. Observe the sparkling."

Ken peered over the velvety shoulder, glanced along
the angle indicated and, sure enough, a metallic flash appeared in the sky at the tip of the pointing claw. Faintly
now, Ken could hear the boom of retroblasts as the ship
braked.

It took all Reeve's self-control to keep from reacting in
the idiot way of the others. Someone had sense enough
to set the air whistle blowing in report-in sequence. Hu
Shih emerged excitedly from the mess hall, nearly tread-
ing on Hrral's tail in his haste. Reeve managed to make
the proper introductions as the metropologist bowed his
apologies. By the time Hu Shih realized that Hrral came
from a distant village, the glint of sun on metal was con-

stant. The speck that was the ship enlarged noticeably with each passing second.

"We will not intrude on the reunion of families so long separated," Hrral demurred, politely, edging away.

He seemed in an all-fired hurry to get away suddenly, Reeve thought, when a moment ago he was so anxious to stay. Maybe Hrruban ears couldn't take the noise of descent. Every Hrruban ear was flat against the skull.

"It is a joyous occasion we would share with our new friends," Hu Shih replied graciously.

"Stay. There is no need to leave," Hrrestan remarked quickly to Hrral. "A great feast has been planned by our women to welcome their women."

"Such thoughtfulness will be treasured memory," Hu Shih answered.

Ramasan came tearing around the corner of the building.

"Shih, there are—oh pardon," he added in stumbling Hrruban. He plucked at the metropologist's sleeve to draw him to one side. "Those females are digging a pit and there are I don't know how many deer carcasses in my kitchen—and I can't understand . . ."

"Evidently their women wish to help prepare the welcoming feast," Reeve told him.

"Oh—oh," Ramasan murmured, "there'll be so much to be done—and I simply don't know enough Hrruban—" but he dashed off before Hu Shih or Ken could reassure him.

Omigod, thought Ken with a sudden panic. All these cats and no one on board that ship knows about it!

Chapter X

PROBLEM CHILD

▼▼▼▼▼▼▼▼▼▼▼▼▼▼▼▼▼▼▼▼▼▼▼▼▼

THE GIANT squatty transport ship had made planetfall,
the event punctuated by the steam rising from the
burn-off. The men, moving with clumsy haste, sprayed
down the chemical neutralizer, then pumped water on
the flat burned ground to hasten cooling. The sooner
that was accomplished, the sooner their women would
disembark. Each man had known that there was no way
the ship could be contacted by Codep and diverted once
the existence of the natives was known. Yet everyone
had been haunted by the fear that somehow they might
be denied even a brief reunion with their families.

The ship was a silver exclamation point to their relief
and welcome. As the water stopped boiling away, the
steam cleared and the upper lock slid open, a black eye
on the silver skin. Two men emerged, scrambling agilely
down the passenger steplift. With great leaps they
cleared the burn-off area, looking around. Hu Shih hastily plowed through the men who crowded the burn-off
edge, trying to wave to the women who now filled the
open lock.

The captain, swarthy-faced and possessing a bizarre
sprouting of facial hair, frowned at the Hrrubans before
he saluted Hu Shih.

He started to speak but could not make himself heard

above the babble caused by the men shouting to their wives aloft.

"Belay it," the captain bellowed with lungs developed communicating across blast-off bedlam. "Y'can yell yer-selves sick, but until I turn my papers over to your chief here, no one steps off the ship or on it." He glared imper-sonally at everyone before continuing in a milder tone, "and I'll not flip a frame forward in the midst of riot."

The men, not without a little grumbling, quieted down. With a two-fingered touch to his cap brim, the captain handed over a tube of film to the metropologist.

"Ali Kiachif, commanding officer of Codep Ship *Astrid,* passenger and cargo manifests. I'm to request all aid and assistance in unloading to facilitate my depar-ture in good order at sunrise," he rumbled off in a bored voice. "Anyone we know?" he added in an undertone, jerking a long stained thumb at the Hrrubans.

"Captain Kiachif, an emergency has arisen," Hu Shih began with much throat-clearing, "which may necessi-tate your remaining . . ."

"Oh no, nooo," Kiachif countered, palms up in dis-agreement, his brows half-moons over his very wide eyes. "None shall detain this courier from the course of his carefully plotted and closely allotted tour. I'm due at Codep Provisionary Planet number oh-who the-hell-cares. And I'm leaving tomorrow," he rolled his eyes heaven-ward, "with an empty ship because that's the way my orders're cut. In the meantime, if you had a little—a little —" his voice trailed off expressively.

"This way, Captain Kiachif," Hu Shih hastily indi-cated, gesturing toward the mess hall.

"We can't unload the livestock, Shih," Ben protested, blocking their path.

"Whaddya mean—you can't unload the livestock?" Kiachif demanded, scowling fiercely. "You gotta. I'm to pick up rare metal ingots on that godforsaken provision-ary hell."

"That's the emergency," Hu Shih repeated urgently. "It is only a matter of hours, I'm sure, before we will receive orders from Codep. They will undoubtedly include our instant removal from this planet."

The captain shot a stunned glance back at his ship, frowned blackly at the Hrrubans and then brandished his order tapes.

"What shall it be? Leave your families and all here—or dump 'em off in the mining dome of a chlorine world? You know how big domes are and what sort of man is sentenced there. You've got the choice, because I have none. That rare ore has to be taken to Elerell 4."

There was no doubt that the feisty Kiachif would do exactly as he threatened, though it seemed an irrational and inflexible stand to take, considering the emergency.

The upshot was that the unloading began. Questions from the women, who were startled at seeing the Hrrubans, had to be given short shrift. Everyone, with the exception of the three smallest children, was pressed into service in the unloading.

Ken found himself leading a groggy mare down the gangway and realized that he had never touched a live horse in his life. The mare's velvet hide was warm to his touch and it exuded a pungent odor not at all unpleasant, though intangibly different from that of the herd beasts he had slaughtered here. She had been blindfolded and was trembling, her hooves daintily seeking footing on the ramp with a nervous grace that fascinated Ken. She snorted, tossing her head and, not knowing what else to do, Ken spoke to her reassuringly, patting her neck with tentative strokes, uncertain whether she would resent being touched.

"Lead her forward, man, she won't break," McKee yelled behind him. He and Ben were the only two who had had any direct experience with the Terran animals. "Hiyup, girl," McKee added, swatting the mare with the end of the halter rope he held.

With an indignant squeal, the mare leapt forward and Reeve, hanging on instinctively, ran with her down the ramp.

"I'll make a horseman of you, Ken, if there's time," McKee said as he trotted his mare beside Ken.

"If I may assist, Rrev," hissed Hrrula softly at Ken's elbow.

The Hrruban, although he addressed Reeve with his innate courtesy, had eyes only for the mares. With a sure instinct the Hrruban let the nervous horse smell his hand while he soothed her with a soft purr. Before Reeve realized it, he had relinquished the rope to Hrrula and the mare, calmer now, was being led away toward the plastic shed that would serve as a temporary barn.

"Hey, Reeve, here's someone for you," he heard Lawrence yell and, turning, he saw Pat flying toward him.

Between kisses and incoherent monosyllables, Ken got the impression the voyage here had been horrible for a reason he was unable to fathom. The feel of Pat's body against him and the touch of her lips, the spicy smell of her was too much for him to pay close attention to anything she was saying.

"You've got to *listen* to me," she insisted, pulling out of his grasp, just as a shrill shriek sounded right behind him.

Startled, he wheeled to see the stallion, groggy as he was from deceleration, lunge out of the ship. Throwing Pat to one side out of the horse's way, Ken made a frantic grab for the trailing halter rope. He missed, thrown heavily down in the dust by the force of the stallion's passing. As he jumped up, he saw someone flash past him. Hrrula, with speed and an agility he had not previously exhibited, raced after the animal. He snagged the trailing rope and, stopping with incredible abruptness, yanked downward on the lead, jerking the stallion's head down and back. The horse reared in protest, bucked and backed as Hrrula, going hand over hand up the rope, reached the horse's head to calm him.

Ben met Hrrula as he led the stallion to the stable and talked earnestly to him, with the result that Hrrula assisted with the rest of the livestock.

Pat, dusting Ken off, blurted out what all the women must be asking.

"Who are *they?* They're not mentioned in the reports. What happened?"

"The question is what happens now?" Ken answered bitterly. "What are *we* doing here, if they are here?"

"Oh, Ken," Pat cried with a rush of horrified comprehension. "We can't go back to Terra. I couldn't stand it." She clung frantically to him.

"Honey, get a hold of yourself, you're here—today, at least," Ken tried to reassure her; anything to wipe the stricken look from her face.

"Ken!" Victor called urgently. "Translation, please!"

"Ken, don't go. Not yet," Pat cried, desperately hanging onto his arm.

"Honey, later. Later we can talk," and he pulled away to join Solinari who was trying to explain to three Hrrubans where he wanted them to put specially marked crates.

Ken had no time that morning for more than a quick welcome hug for Ilsa, who was then taken off to check crate numbers at the storehouse.

On the whole, Ken was proud of all the women and children. With no time for more than the briefest explanations, and no reassurances for their future, the women worked right beside the Hrrubans, smiling and gesticulating where words were not available. The children were trying very hard not to stare at tails that flicked out of the way of bouncing crates or stumbling feet, but gave no sign of fear. The last bundles, personal luggage, were being handled out of the cargo holds when Reeve, standing near the steplift, saw Kate Moody, the colony pediatrician, descending. She was having a time, holding onto the rail of the lift and the struggling child in her arms. Reeve wondered why the hell she just didn't put the kid on his feet. Then he noticed Ilsa waiting for Kate, a strained look on her little face.

When Kate reached the ground, she still did not release her charge but asked Ilsa a question. The girl pointed toward Ken, and Kate, grim-faced, plowed forward to him.

Her face was a study of professional neutrality as she approached, but her strong hands were very busy defending the softer parts of her body from the thrashing arms and legs of her burden. With a heave, she deposited the fierce little boy in Ken's arms.

"This, Ken Reeve, is yours," she said with a great sigh of relief. "We've all had our turns with him and he is now yours, all yours. You'll have to take my word for it that it is absolutely unfair for you to turn him over to his mother now. Which is probably what *you* may feel you should do. The one thing Pat needs is a rest from him."

"I don't understand," Reeve exclaimed as he held the rigid little body.

"It won't take you long, believe me," Kate retorted, her brown eyes flashing.

In wonder, Reeve looked down at his son's face. Solemn blue eyes regarded him from a narrow triangular face. The strong jaw was set obstinately, lips firmly pressed together in a thin line. The direct challenge in the child's expression was curiously adult and definitely wary.

"You probably don't remember me," Ken began tentatively, disconcerted by the apprehensive rigidity of the young body. Kate had walked quickly away with Ilsa.

"You're supposed to be my father. They said they were turning me over to you as soon as they landed," said a defiant voice.

The dead silence that followed was pregnant with childish challenge. There was no doubt in Ken's mind that he had been held as a threat to subdue the child and he resented this tremendously.

"And what am I supposed to do with you?" asked Reeve, trying vainly for the proper reassuring attitude. It was incomprehensible to him why supposedly well-trained personnel had descended to such tactics, poisoning his reunion with his son.

"Make me behave," Todd replied flatly, jerking his chin belligerently forward.

"Well," Reeve began, hoping to redeem the situation, "I can imagine it was tough on a small space like a ship but for a while anyhow, you've got a whole planet to play in and—" he trailed off because the small body, which had begun to loosen, stiffened again. Todd looked fixedly over Reeve's shoulder. He held that position for a moment and then began to squirm.

Obligingly, Reeve let him down, turning to see what had attracted such absorbed attention. Todd made a beeline toward Hrral, who was talking to Hrrula by the corral. Reeve ambled after him when Pat, wild-eyed, rushed past him to intercept the child's line of march. For a march it was. There was definite purpose in the boy's attitude.

"Stop him, Ken," Pat screamed. "There's no telling *what* he'll do."

Puzzled but spurred by Pat's frantic concern, Ken started to jog. Todd had a good headstart and, before either parent reached him, he had gone straight up to Hrral, taken that worthy's inviting tail in both hands and pulled as hard as he could.

Pat stopped, shocked, covering her eyes with her hands. Appalled by his son's action, Ken swooped the child up in his arm, administering a sharp swat on the buttocks. Todd became an unmanageable tangle of arms and legs, flailing in all directions, determinedly trying to free himself from his parent's grasp.

Pat raced up to Hrral, her whole body portraying her apology and horror.

"Tell him, Ken, tell him. They say you speak his language, tell him," Pat wailed.

"My mate begs earnestly that you forgive the inexcusable attack on your person by our child," Ken said as he struggled to control Todd's contortions.

A threshing foot caught him painfully in the groin and Ken reacted by slapping the child's face with a little more force than he intended. The boy went rigid, solemn, defiant blue eyes regarded him with stunned hurt.

"It is the nature of the very young to be curious about all manner of things," replied Hrral graciously, flicking his tail around his toes. Out of the corner of his eye, Reeve saw Hrrula do the same. "Since your race has no caudal appendage, it is natural for him to wish to inspect mine."

"What's he saying, Ken? Has Toddy done it again?" cried Pat nervously.

"Fortunately he's understanding about the very young," Reeve reassured her. To Hrral he expressed deep gratitude for the elder's attitude. Then he excused himself and he and Pat marched without a word toward their plastic cabin.

"He certainly couldn't know he was doing wrong, Pat," Ken temporized as they walked.

"Oh, don't be too sure about that," Pat contradicted bitterly. "If he wasn't the image of your father, I could swear I had given birth to a changeling."

"Pat!" exclaimed Ken, astonished at her vehemence.

Pat stopped and turned to her husband, her fists on her hips.

"I kept hoping that he'd improve once he understood we were leaving Earth. And for a while at the Codep Block, he was almost human. But the minute we got on board—" she paused, her eyes round with distressed tears. "That child has been the bane of the whole journey. There isn't a person who hasn't had trouble with him. They had to double the watch on the drive room, control room, and hydroponics section. The engineer finally put a special time lock on our cabin. We couldn't leave it from seven at night til eight the next morning. During the day, either an adult or one of the older children was assigned to watch him every single blessed minute—in four-hour shifts. There isn't one of us that isn't bruised by his kicking and pinching. Kate has tried tranquilizers, sleep training, everything. He is—he's—he's incorrigible!" and Pat whirled to lean against the nearest tree trunk in tears.

"Kate's a psychologist, why didn't she . . ."

"Kate had to give up!" Pat gulped. "We all have, from the captain to the swabber, from the eldest child on down. He simply doesn't think like any normal child."

In the process of trying to comfort his wife, Ken put Toddy down. The moment she felt Ken's arms around her, she whirled in terror.

"Don't let him go," she screamed in panic, pointing over his shoulder. Ken looked; the sturdy boy was making tracks right back to Hrral and Hrrula.

"Gotcha," cried a passing crewman as he snagged Todd. "Not like the morning you got into the communications spares, huh?" and he grinned sardonically as he handed Todd back to his father.

After much debate with Pat and still not quite sure why such precautions were necessary, Ken carefully locked Todd in his room and went back to work.

"Are you sure he can't break that window?" she asked anxiously.

"Hon, it's the toughest plastic extruded. Besides, I smacked him hard enough so I doubt he'll risk more of the same."

Pat, only partially reassured, was then pressed into service by Kate Moody to check medical supplies. Ken watched her slim body for a few moments before he resumed his own task.

He would play a very active father role, he told himself, for the boy had obviously missed the masculine father figure. Ilsa had always been socially well oriented and conformable. Then Ken had to attend to checking the bills of lading.

Damn Kiachif for putting them to this wasted effort. He could have had all these hours with Pat.

When he had finally located the elusive crates on his manifests, he took the papers up to the mess hall where the captain and his supercargo had set up a temporary office. Kiachif, the super, Ben Adjei, Gaynor and McKee were grouped around the table. Only the super appeared concerned with the problems of unloading.

"Don't know why I bother. Ridiculous waste," the supercargo mumbled as he scrawled his initials on the sheets, "It'll all have to be burned when you leave but I'd never hear the last of it if I didn't get 'em all checked. Though how they'd know if it hadn't been checked is utterly beyond me."

Ken stared at him in annoyance and dislike.

"Yes, I agree," Captain Kiachif was saying, "that it might be more sensible for me to wait for the homing capsule. But, my friends, I have a schedule. Nasty things, schedules. Particularly a closely figured one like mine. It's so close there's not so much as a sneeze computed in between hops. So *I've* got no choice. I've got to keep it, discovery of natives—which I agree is no sneeze —notwithstanding. And frankly," Kiachif jerked his chin down onto his chest and peered around at the listening circle, "if you get what I mean, it's to *your* advantage to let me depart on the sneezeless schedule."

"You mean, it'd take you that much longer to figure on touching down here again," McKee said hopefully.

"Ah, you get what I mean," grinned the captain.

"But, Captain, certainly you see the unusual circumstances . . ." Hu Shih began persuasively.

"Shih," McKee interrupted, clearing his throat, "what the good captain means is, if he waits and we get a clear-out, we have to clear out. If he's already gone, they have to send us another ship and that'll give us more time here," and Macy smiled brightly at everyone.

"Exactly what worries me, gentlemen," Hu Shih said with uncharacteristic sternness. "We may do untold prejudicial harm to a delicate situation. None of us is trained in establishing the proper contact with an indigenous population."

"I'd say you'd done all right, if you get what I mean," Kiachif commented, waving at the scene outside where Hrrubans and Terrans worked easily together, covering stacked crates with plastic cocoons.

"We have, it is true, established an outwardly harmonious relationship," Hu Shih agreed cautiously, "but we are also forced by circumstance to expose a less advanced race prematurely to certain aspects of our culture which may well jeopardize their proper evolution."

"They've exposed us to a few aspects of their culture that make ours look sicker than it is," McKee reminded the colony chief drily.

"Look, Hu Shih," Kiachif said, rubbing his chin thoughtfully, "you guys work like trolls for three hundred days, with nothing worse to deal with than the local carnivores, because Codep has said this planet's uninhabited. Okay, Codep goofed. You didn't. You're here, you've got your families—if you see what I mean." He cocked his head, his eyes glinting as a knowing smile parted his thin lips. It faded abruptly as the captain sighed in patient exasperation. "I see you don't see what I mean," and he pointed significantly at the distant hills.

"Oh, no. Absolutely no," Hu Shih declared as he suddenly grasped the Captain's meaning. "We must leave when Codep's orders arrive, for that is the honorable thing to do."

The captain's hooded eyes narrowed slightly and one stained index finger speculatively scratched a hairy cheek.

"Why?" Kiachif drawled.

"Why, because of the Principle of Non-Cohabitation."

"Why?" Kiachif repeated stubbornly.

"Because of the Siwannese, man," McKee snapped impatiently. The captain was pointing out an alternative that was all too tempting.

"Why, because of the Siwannese?" Kiachif pursued ruthlessly. "That Siwannah affair happened over two hundred years ago. And they were dolts, those Siwannese, anyway."

A shocked silence filled the room at such irreverence.

"Aaah, by the walloping widow, you've all been taken in," the captain scoffed. Hitching his jacket up on his shoulders, he planted both forearms on the table and leaned earnestly forward.

"So one paranoic race commits mass suicide and the

tender conscience of our planet backs away forever from the challenge of contact with *any* intelligent species." His scathing look called them all cowards. "Have ye never wondered what'll happen when we meet our equals? Oh, none such as those domesticated cat creatures. But our real equals. What'll the tender-minded do then? Humph. I suppose it'll be our turn to commit ritual suicide. Not that that's not what all the land-siders are doing right now, crowding everyone into lifetime coffin-sized rooms," he snorted contemptuously. "If you get what I mean."

"You forget, Captain," Hu Shih said gently, pressing his fingertips together, "that the Tragedy at Siwannah must be the last outrage our race perpetrates against a helpless minority. It must be the last one. We have so many to regret. Starting with the Egyptian treatment of the wandering Semitic tribes, the decimation of the Caribs, the annihilation of the Amerinds, the German massacre of the Jews, the Chinese Attempt in 1974, the Black Riots of 1980. One goes on indefinitely until the Amalgamation of 2010 which was probably bloodier than any previous pogrom. We are all products of that decision from which we retain only ethnic surnames," and Hu Shih's graceful wave included everyone. "It isn't reassuring to wonder what further terrible incidents man would have on his conscience with such a background were he not restrained by the Principle."

"Yechk!" Kiachif said derisively. "Pure luck. Wouldn't have happened on any other planet!" His stained finger pointed accusingly at the metropologist, who regarded it with hypnotic fascination. "And it wouldn't have resulted in such stupidity as that fool Principle if Terra hadn't just recovered from that nasty Amalgamation." The stabbing finger swung 180 degrees and shook out the window at the busy scene on the Common. "D'ye think those cats would have curried their fur and placidly lain down to die? No! Far better for our poor overpacked planet if we'd met *them* first." Kiachif's eyes widened to incredible circles of white, emphasized by the regular half-circle of black eyebrows. "Have any of you," he asked softly in a sudden switch of mood, his eyes narrowed again, "ever read the transcript of the Siwannach? What? Ssshuuu," Kiachif whistled in disgust. Up went his hands in a gesture of exasperation, one descending with a loud clap to his knee, the other to resuming its remorseless probing.

"So! You must know you were being drugged into automatons on Earth. You certainly risked the indignities that they always heap on Inactives, in order to get away. But," the finger jabbed toward Reeve, then McKee and finally to the metropologist, "you don't rouse yourselves enough to question what you've been taught. You hate a cramped, machine-made existence but don't question why you have to endure it. You question the emptiness of life but not *why* you have to wait so long for an opportunity to leave it. And you never question why this doesn't change. There have to be changes in a world if it's to grow—and I don't mean spread out—I mean grow up—you see what I mean?" The captain's voice was cajoling. "Haven't you ever really looked at the beginnings of those idiotic restrictions?"

"I have read the original Siwannach transcripts, Captain," Hu Shih said, gently firm. "And I know to what you refer; that one little phrase that some believe was innocently mispronounced. That one little phrase that caused a whole race of profoundly gentle, devout people to commit suicide. It is a case in point of what I have always said: no adult ever really learns the nuance and rhythm of another language perfectly." He sighed deeply. "At least the Amalgamation provided one common language in which all express themselves, even as the ancient Chinese philosopher Lao Tze suggested 6500 years ago. However," and Hu Shih held up one slender hand, a contrast to the large blunt-fingered fist of Kiachif, "it was not only regret at such an occurrence and a desire to avoid a repetition which prompted the Non-Cohabitation Principle. It was the feeling that the greedy acquisition of more planets on which to spread the products of our then uncontrolled breeding was not the real answer to our problem. It was the knowledge that we have no right to take away from another species their own peculiar road toward self-fulfillment. What role might the Amerinds have played in history if the white man had not weakened them with measles and small-pox and whisky? What tragedies might have been avoided if the black man had not been wrenched from his own continent by gold-hungry exploiters? Oh, the list of intentional atrocities is so long. No," and the gentle voice was as inexorable as Kiachif's histrionics, "the Non-Cohabitation Principle is a sound one, a just one and, to my great shame, we have broken it. That is why we must perpetrate no lasting harm on these pleasant friendly people."

"The captain is also right, Shih," McKee put in quietly. "He has to follow his schedule. That means we stay until Codep recalls us, if you get what *we* mean."

Hu Shih drew himself up and looked so disapproving that McKee blanched and dropped his eyes.

"I get what *you* mean, Macy. And I repeat—we leave when we are ordered to. And if that homing capsule arrives before tomorrow's blast-off, we leave tomorrow."

The metropologist did not see the not-if-I-can-avoid-it expression of Kiachif's face.

"Super," the Captain boomed out to break the awkward pause, "all your papers in order? I'm getting mighty hungry for what smells like honest-injun food. By the Great Horned Toad, that aroma's killing me," and he drew in a massive breath from the open window. "If you get what I mean!"

Chapter XI

THE FEAST

THE HUGE BONFIRE burned with a bluish-purple, orange-tipped flame, lighting the Common spectacularly. Trestle tables had been set up and hastily improvised benches had been extruded from plastic scrounged from the ship's supplies. To men long celibate there was the wonderful presence of women, coming and going between the mess hall and the barbecue pit. There Ramasan presided over the spit with the huge prong-horned *urf* buck, slain by the joint efforts of Hrruban and Terran hunters for the occasion. Torches moved down the long slope from Saddle Ridge, across the river, as still more Hrrubans came to the feast. As the firelight threw shadows of grotesque parodies, Ken wondered that there were so many Hrrubans in the one village.

The women had pitched into the preparations with a determination that proved they were avoiding all thought of the future and its problems. Ken was not the only man grateful for feminine reticence, and thankful to whatever instinct prompted them to make this night one to remember.

Aurie Gaynor, as if to make up for her husband's allergy, stood at the bridge to welcome the Hrruban guests.

"Julie O'Grady and the Colonel's Lady, whoever they were," she had flung at Lee Lawrence when she volunteered herself. "And if I can't purr, I can radiate charm, wit and personality."

Phyllis Hu, a delicate-appearing woman with luminous beauty, had taken a rapturous inventory of the available supplies of local produce. She told Ramasan he had been chef long enough and to please go turn that buck so it wouldn't char. She'd handle the rest. Imagine, letting a man fool with *real* food.

Akosua Adjei and Ann Eckerd (known as Anneck to distinguish her from Anne Solinari) took charge of setting up dining facilities. Sally Lawrence unpacked her treasured guitar and Ezra Moody proved how successfully he had been able to use local animal gut to restring his violin. Dot McKee and her twin teen-age daughters volunteered as scullery crew.

Aurie Gaynor sent a message to Ken Reeve that the Hrruban women were coming laden with food and what did one do?

"Just show them where to set the stuff down," Reeve told young Bill Moody. "With the exception of two tubers and some local fungi, we tolerate the same foods. And, Bill, those round purplish nuts are the best eating on this world or the next."

Reeve had settled himself with Dautrish and Hu Shih and they were shortly joined by the captain and the supercargo.

"Like the old-timey pioneer days in the nineteenth century, if you get what I mean," the captain was saying as the men watched the well-organized chaos around them. "How much of this local smokable you got on hand, Mr. Botanist?" he asked Dautrish, relishing the taste in his pipe.

"Well, not a great deal. The Hrrubans don't smoke," Dautrish began. "I gather it has medicinal properties for them rather than—whatever you call smoking."

"I feel," Hu Shih remarked, "the evening supplies its

own pleasant intoxicants of good food taken in the presence of loved ones long missed, and of new-found friends."

"I get what you mean," Kiachif agreed with patient resignation.

Out of a pool of darkness cast by a small shrub, Hrrestan and Hrral stepped toward them. Reeve rose immediately and introduced the two Hrrubans to Kiachif and the supercargo. As he stepped aside to allow the two elders to seat themselves, Reeve caught sight of Hrral's tail carefully curling under the bench, and remembered his son.

"Good Lord, that child's still locked in his room," he exclaimed with guilty remorse.

Hrral's wide mouth dropped in the Hrruban grin.

"But no, he has found that the tails of our cubs also do not come off. He was at the bridge and himself made a personal inspection. Or so I am informed."

Reeve felt suddenly sick.

"How can I—" he began apologetically.

Hrrestan grinned and Hrral held up his hand politely to interrupt Reeve.

"He does not trouble, and our own young are curious that he has no tail. I believe the young of both races will be friendly together in the way of the young."

"Young Master Todd in trouble again?" boomed the captain, his eyes sparkling with amusement, for he couldn't have understood the interchange.

Heartily embarrassed, Ken related Todd's breach of etiquette and his own remedy.

"What I don't understand is how he could get out of that locked room," Ken finished, puzzled.

"Perhaps Pat let him out," Dautrish suggested.

The captain's chuckle started deep in his belly. The super regarded his captain with disgust. "That young man won't be kept within any bounds. It's a jolly good thing, mister," and the pipe was waggled at Reeve, "that he has a whole planet in which to range. He'll need it, and you will too, if you get what I mean."

"Todd'll get what I mean," replied Ken grimly, determined not to allow a six-year-old's precocity to stride roughshod over an entire colony.

The supercargo's snort of derision spoke volumes for Ken's good intentions.

"Is it permitted to ask whether they speak of your young one?" asked Hrrestan politely.

"To my embarrassment, yes," Reeve replied.

"Speak of the devil," the supercargo growled and two small figures stalked out of the shadows. One was an Hrruban cub, a full head taller than his Terran companion. Reeve recognized him instantly as the taller of the two ball players he had met in the woods. The cub's tail was wrapped around the waist of young Todd Reeve.

Ken sat down weakly as the two marched directly up to Hrrestan.

"This one is sad, father," the Hrruban cub said, "because he has no tail and wishes mine. I have told him I cannot give him mine. He asked where I got it and I told him. So he asked me to take him to my father so you could give him a tail, too."

The humor of the request evidently did not escape the cub but he made his recital solemnly.

"Hrriss, my son, you have great kindness," Hrrestan replied with equal solemnity. He put his arm around Hrriss. "But tell me, since you do not speak his language nor he yours, how did you understand his desire?"

The cub looked surprised. "He is understandable," he said finally with a shrug of his narrow shoulders.

"I want a tail," said Todd, suddenly vocal and, after a longing look at Hrrestan's appendage, he leaned trustingly against the elder's thigh.

"Little one, we cannot always have what we want," Hrrestan said, circling Todd's shoulders with his other arm.

"Hrrestan said—" Ken started to translate.

"I heard him," Todd interrupted bluntly.

"How can you? You don't know his language," Ken demanded, his words tinged with anger.

Todd turned his head to look at his father, his lips pursing with disgusted exasperation for adult obtuseness. "All you have to do is *listen* to him," he explained reasonably.

The captain guffawed so hard he choked on the smoke he had just inhaled. The supercargo pounded him on the shoulder blades until the captain was reduced to a weak, weeping rasp of a laugh.

"All—you—have to—do is listen, the child says," the captain finally managed to get out.

"Hrriss," Hrrestan said, releasing both boys and turning them toward the Common, "take Zodd (he could not quite master the labial stop of the 'T') and play together, listening carefully to each other. That is the way to make friends—to listen."

The two moved off without a comment, Hrriss's tail tucked around Todd's waist.

"Your youngest will gather much credit for you," Hrrestan remarked, turning around to the adults.

Reeve set his jaw against a swift flash of jealousy that Todd would so easily accept the native and disregard his own father.

"Hrriss shows the wisdom of an adult," he managed to say, politely turning the compliment.

"If I were you, mister," Kiachif said, having cleared his lungs and stopped wheezing, "I'd let the catmen raise that young man of yours. He's a throwback in more'n those blue eyes of his. He needs room.

"Are you suggesting I can't control my son?"

The captain guffawed wheezingly and the supercargo gave a short bark of derisive laughter. At this moment, Pat, wild-eyed, came rushing up to Ken.

"Oh, Ken, I've looked everywhere. Todd's broken out of his room. I mean, really broken out. That window— the whole frame was unscrewed."

Grabbing her hands to calm her, Ken reassured her.

"He was just here, and he's in good—hands, Pat," Ken

said, feeling more and more antagonistic toward the subject of son Todd with each passing second.

"You mean, we've got a tail on him," the captain exploded, roaring at his own witticism. "If you get what I mean," and he dissolved into another paroxysm of laughter.

Ken half-turned, about to pounce on the captain, when the air whistle cut across the babel in the Common, and Phyllis Hu announced over the loudspeaker that the feast was now ready to be served.

Under cover of the cheer of approval, Pat pulled Ken back to her, giving him a moment to get his anger and resentment under control.

Chapter XII

RESCUE

▼▼▼▼▼▼▼▼▼▼▼▼▼▼▼▼▼▼▼▼▼▼▼▼▼

"Daddy, daddy," said a soft voice in his ear. Ken roused himself from the lovely depths of sleep to the urgent tug at his shoulder. "Daddy, please wake up," cried Ilsa, an almost hysterical note of pleading in her voice.

"Whassa matter, Ilsa?" he asked, blinking his eyes into focus.

"Todd's got loose," she said, her little face contorted with her concern. She was wringing her hands in an unconscious imitation of her mother.

Ken groaned and struggled to a sitting position. Reaching out, he dragged the coverall from the foot of the bed and started to struggle into it.

" 'S not your fault, Ilsa, 's not your fault," he reassured his daughter. "Get in with your mother."

He slipped into his boots and, snatching up a jacket against the cool dawn air and a rifle against any carnivores who might not yet have made their kill, he lurched out of the cabin.

The brisk morning air was pungent with many smells: the lingering aroma of last night's barbecue, the wood fire still glowing in the pit; the scent of fresh water mists rising from the river, the cinnamony flavor of the forest behind him warmed by Doona's orange sun. Reeve blinked the last of sleep from his eyes and surveyed the Common.

Trestle tables dotted the green but the debris of the feast had been cleared away. The area had a forlorn look compared with his memory of the crowded jollity of last night. A few oddments of tableware could be seen in out-of-the-way places, shadow-hidden from the cleaning squad. For a non-alcoholic evening, it had been a very high-spirited one.

Todd was nowhere in sight, in any direction. Reeve sneezed sharply as he trotted across the Common to the mess hall. Equipping himself with several rounds of ammunition and a pair of binoculars, he set out toward the bridge.

Takes no mental strain to guess where that little bugger is headed, Reeve thought. And the Hrrubans got to bed a lot later than we did. No one will be glad to see that snot-nosed idiot at *this* hour.

During the evening, Todd had found a length of rope somewhere. He had hacked at the end until it resembled the tuft of an Hrruban tail, and then atached it to his pants. It had dragged, a pathetic imitation, in the dirt behind him. When Reeve had looked for the child at midnight, he had found him, 'tail' in hand, and Hrriss's tail curled around his waist, the two fast asleep in each other's arms. It had been an unsettling sight for Reeve. For the first time, he saw his son's face unguarded, his brow relaxed from its habitual frown, his mouth in a gentle, unstubborn line, the long dark lashes outlined on the fair cheek. Todd looked the six-year-old he was, sweet, young and thoroughly lovable. A responding chord of paternal affection was touched in Reeve's heart and he felt the desire to love and protect this exasperating child. Cradling the limp warm body in his arms, tail and all, Reeve had carried Todd to his bed, kissing him as he laid the blankets snugly around him. Toddy, stirring in his sleep, had smiled with contentment.

It wasn't paternalism that stirred Reeve now, nor any affection for the child who would pull such a stunt.

Plain resentment boiled in Reeve for having to get up before he had to.

Sure enough, in the dust on the other side of the Bridge, Reeve found the wiggling line of the rope tail, a wispy giveaway, aiming spang toward the ridge and the village.

He sure keeps his eyes open, Reeve grunted, but would the child, in his single-minded march on the village, have the sense to look out for other dangers? A pang of fear stabbed at Reeve as he thought of what marks the bearlike *mda* claw would make in that tender body. Todd would have no defense against the *mda's* lightning attacks, nor any warning of its silent-footed approach. Reeve consoled himself with the thought that the *mdas* had not been seen in the lower valley since the bridge had been built. The constant traffic had driven the *urfa*, the *mda's* usual prey, away from this end of the valley. Maybe all the *mdas* had followed.

But Doona had other traps, like the *rroamal* vine or the poisonous red *sser* which smelled deceptively sweet. Reptiles, too, had been catalogued, venomous spiders the size of dinner plates, and invertebrates, exuding oily substances which stung agonizingly.

Anxiously, Reeve plunged up the slope, purposefully noisy in the hope that he might startle any stalking carnivore. He had to check his forward rush at the first dusty clearing, half a mile up the slope, for he no longer followed the straggly mark of the dragging tail. Cursing, Reeve retraced his steps through the grasses, fearful of seeing the signs of a struggle. He cried out with relief when he saw the indentation in the grass where a small creature had passed. For some reason, Todd had struck out in a westerly direction, paralleling the river. His trail led away from the high saddle of the ridge, to the woods that bordered the river.

It made sense, Reeve admitted. The child would see the slope to the ridge as a real obstacle. He couldn't know that the ridge was a more direct route to the village. And he wouldn't know that those woods were far more dangerous. Reeve moved forward at a jog. Maybe he should have roused someone else to help him search, but how could he know the child would have such a headstart. What on earth drew the boy so powerfully to the Hrrubans? Surely not just a tail? Such an instant affinity!

Last night it had been amusing to see Todd's intent little face, absorbing Hrriss's voluble explanations of this and that. Todd, one hand always on Hrriss's tail, would nod seriously. Then the two would indulge in mild wrestling or another of the games all children seem born knowing. But, Christ, did the brat have to get up two hours before dawn to pick up where sleep had overtaken him the night before?

Reeve forced himself to slow down as he approached the underbrush at the edge of the woods. It would never do for him to fall into one of the very obstacles he worried Todd might find. The child had walked up and down here, trying to get through. The opening Todd had found was not wide enough for Reeve. Carefully he examined both sides and saw no vines or thorny bushes. He pressed back the foliage with the rifle butt and stepped through. Then stopped. The ground, covered by the porous-tree needle mulch, retained no marks as did the dirt or grasses. Todd had come through at this point, but where had he gone from here?

Think like a six-year-old, Reeve told himself. Yeah, but Todd doesn't. Well, there's the line of least resistance, Reeve decided, and made off in as straight a line toward the village as the intervening trees permitted.

The terrain sloped down to the river, always visible through the trees. Now, would Todd try the bank? Reeve shook his head, anger for his son's truancy gaining ascendance over his fear for his safety. Well, I can see the river bank from this angle, he thought, and paced forward purposefully, eyes and ears alert.

When I get my hands on that child! Reeve promised himself retribution. The river wound northward now and Ken had to change direction to follow it. Soon it would bend back and flow past the village. The forest animals and birds were waking as the sun penetrated the gloom of the forest. It made visibility better and the noises were comforting. If carnivores had been abroad, there would have been an ominous silence. A sudden clatter of outraged birds attracted Ken's attention. The loud squawking was on his right, nearer the river. He detoured and located the disturbance high in a tree. A silent shadow on the trunk moved with dappled grace. Reeve decided a tree snake had attacked a nest. The chirping subsided and the noise of the river, fast over the rapids above the falls, came to his ears. Also a faint coughing sound, faint but unmistakable.

Gripping his rifle in both hands, Reeve wove rapidly through the trees at a lope. He broke through the forest, onto the rocky edge of the river which foamed and tumbled over the boulders in its bed. Where the river started to turn back again toward the village, a moving speck caught his eye. Hastily adjusting the binoculars, Reeve saw the shaggy brown body of a huge *mda*, pacing up and down the verge, snarling and coughing. The animal paused, started to step out onto an upthrust boulder, but the distance was too great and the current too swift. Snarling with frustration, the *mda* resumed its nervous pacing. The object of its interest was a small figure, crouched on a boulder some ten feet out in the stream. It was Todd, hugging his knees up under his chin, evidently hoping that if he made himself small enough he would be rendered invisible.

Frantic, Reeve checked the range. It was too great for an accurate shot and he couldn't risk a wounded *mda* loose in the forest so close to the Hrruban village. Todd seemed safe enough, although how he had made it to the rock was beyond Ken.

Ducking and dodging, stumbling over decayed limbs and rocks, Reeve closed the distance between himself and his son. The snarling cough of the hungry *mda* became louder. Reeve was grateful that he was downwind from the beast and that the rushing river covered the sound of his hell-bent advance. He paused to catch his breath, because he realized he was panting with fear and exertion. The sinking feeling, cold and heavy in his guts, constantly overrode discretion, urging him to greater speed.

He could see the *mda* clearly now. Again the animal put out a tentative paw, settling his hindquarters as if to spring. With a coughing snarl, he ducked his head, swaying back and forth from side to side, still undecided. Ken could now see the fallen tree trunk, half-caught between the first stone and the one on which Todd crouched. God, the child had had sense enough to dislodge the log after he'd crossed it.

Suddenly the *mda* froze, turned his wide skull upriver. The snarling stopped. Something else was approaching from the village side and the bear had caught the smell. The predator crouched and began to slink from the edge of the river. Reeve trained his glasses on the forest but he could see nothing. Disregarding the necessity for quiet, Reeve plunged on, taking the safety off his rifle as he ran. The village could not be far away and the Hrrubans had only rudimentary weapons. Hrrula had told him they always hunted in small groups, leaving the *mdas* and another carnivore they called *ssorasos* alone. They did not, apparently, hunt for sport. A single person, a woman perhaps, coming to the river edge for water unsuspecting, would be easy, quick prey for the hungry, angry *mda*. Reeve, struggling for a second wind, broke out of the forest onto the ledge opposite Todd. The boy sprang to his feet with a sobbing cry of relief. Reeve waved reassurance and plunged on just as he heard the *mda's* charging roar. A terrible scream broke the stillness of the morning. Reeve, bursting into a small glade, took the scene in at a glance. The *mda* lay, writhing on the forest floor, trying to dislodge the spear in its shoulder. Just beyond it, Hrrula stood, a second spear raised and ready.

Reeve, shooting as he moved forward, emptied the rifle into the *mda* in a wild fit of relief, anger and fear.

Hrrula and he stood looking down at the twitching corpse, the one with spear poised, the other with a smoking rifle.

"I heard the beast coughing and knew he had something trapped," Hrrula said. "It filled me with concern to see it was Zodd."

Reeve, trembling with reaction, nodded weakly.

"It was a deed of great bravery," he managed to say, a tremor in his voice he couldn't control, "for certainly your life is worth more than that of a child."

Reeve was amazed at the savagery in his tone when he spoke of Todd. Hrrula looked at him with an expression akin to dismay.

"Is it not true in your world that a leader is known early by even his childish actions?"

"Leader? Todd? No! Troublemaker, yes!"

Hrrula smiled, leaning against the spear he had grounded.

"The father of my mother's mate, Hrral, and Hrrestan, spoke most highly of your youngest."

Reeve snorted, annoyed that these natives could see something in his child that he did not.

A thin cry of "Daddy," uncertain and frightened, came from the direction of the river. As one, the two moved off to rescue the child of whom the Hrrubans thought so highly.

Chapter XIII

RED LETTER DAY

▼▼▼▼▼▼▼▼▼▼▼▼▼▼▼▼▼▼▼▼▼▼▼

By THE TIME Ken and Hrrula had found a log and thrust it out across the supporting boulders to Todd, Hrrestan and other catmen had joined them, roused by the cries of the *mda* and the shots.

White-faced, Todd scrambled across the log, his rope tail dangling into the river. Reeve gripped the small shoulders tightly and gave the child a fierce shake, the urge to beat him soundly postponed by the presence of an audience.

"You're lucky you weren't killed, you little fool," Reeve said between clenched teeth.

"I was all right out there," Todd replied stoutly. "But I got scareded that Hrrula'd get killed. He only had a spear."

"If he had been killed, young man," and Reeve broke off significantly, shaking Todd. "Can you understand what would happen? Can you?"

"We'd have to leave Doona?" Todd cried, tears unexpectedly starting down his cheeks.

"We'd have to leave," Reeve reaffirmed, expressionlessly. How could he explain to a six-year-old the colonists' dilemma.

"I only wanted to see Hrriss," Todd cried with plaintive snuffling.

God give me patience, thought Reeve, he *is* only a child!

Todd sneezed, looking cold and small with the tall men of both races towering over him. Reeve's mood switched from frustrated resentment to concern.

"The child is cold and must be warmed. Come now to our fire and eat with us," Hrrestan offered them graciously.

Todd planted himself squarely in front of Hrrula, looking up at the young Hrruban, tugging at his hand for attention.

"Hrrula, please forgive me for nearly getting you killed. Don't make us leave Doona," he said earnestly although his teeth were chattering.

Hrrula hunkered down to Todd's eye level, one hand under the boy's chin. "First, promise never to walk in the woods alone again," he demanded.

"I promise, oh, I promise," Todd agreed fervently, his eyes wide and solemn.

"Good," purred Hrrula, releasing the square little chin and standing up.

When they had started off toward the village, Todd wrapped in his jacket and cradled in his arms, Reeve realized that the Hrruban had made his demand to the child in good Terran. Before he could pursue this, the women had rushed out with much purring and hissing over Todd.

Reeve was glad enough to sit in front of a warm fire and let its warmth ease the tension in his body. He didn't protest the delay when the women insisted that Todd be given a warm bath and be dressed in a furry robe. He enjoyed the thick soupy beverage that was served him, delighting in its aromatic vapor and the feeling of well-being it spread through his system.

Then there was the matter of skinning and gutting the *mda*. Ken tried to mask the revulsion he felt during the process, particularly since the business was done under Todd's fascinated eyes. At first pleased that the boy did not disgrace them by becoming ill, Reeve turned mildly surprised at Todd's detachment as the carcass of his former hunter was butchered and hung.

Todd grinned at Hrriss with pleasure when Hrrula told him, in Hrruban now, that the skin would be cured for Todd's use.

At least, Ken thought grimly, the skin would provide enough credit to soundproof a room for Todd back on Earth.

Hrrula then cut thick steaks from the flank, rolling them up in the wide leaves of a river plant for Reeve to bring home.

Reluctant to leave this pleasant scene, Reeve was finally roused by the unmistakable roar of a blast-off. He grinned to himself in sudden relief and self-awareness; by God, he'd been procrastinating in an unconscious desire not to be jerked away from Doona a moment sooner than necessary. And now that Hu Shih hadn't been able to persuade Kiachif to remain until the Codep reply arrived, they had another reprieve.

"Todd, we've got to get home. That was Kiachif's ship leaving."

Todd nodded solemnly but clung to Hrriss's tail. As if looking for a cue, Hrriss turned to Hrrestan. The Hrruban growled a brief spate of sound at the cub, who hung his head sadly. Gently but firmly he uncurled Todd's fingers from his tail and put the hand down at Todd's side. He flipped his tail straight out behind him.

"Tomorrow?" asked Todd with plaintive resignation.

Hrriss's eyes flicked back to his father, saw the assent and his jaw dropped in a smile. Todd's face lit up beatifically and he moved to his father's side.

"I have promised the big one (the Hrruban description of Ben) to help with the hrrsses," Hrrula said to Reeve as he accompanied them out of the village after the farewells required by Hrruban etiquette.

Reeve grinned back at the Hrruban, amused by the catman's obsession with horses. Since they'd probably have to leave the beasts here, they'd be well cared-for. Maybe, even—Ken cut off that half-formed thought. He set a pace easy enough for Todd to follow and the three moved along in a companionable silence.

The moment they reached Saddle Ridge, Reeve sensed something else must have happened down at the colony. There was no activity in the clearing by the river or among the houses. He held up his binoculars and, training them on the Common, brought into focus the colonists sitting in small groups at the tables, obviously waiting.

He tried to tell himself that perhaps Hu Shih had ordered a day of rest for everyone to recuperate from yesterday's feverish unloading and last night's festivities. But these people weren't laughing or enjoying themselves. They were waiting anxiously.

"The sky ship has left," Hrrula said at Ken's shoulder.

"Yes, thank God," Reeve sighed, lowering his glasses. But, he told himself, it is only a reprieve by any stretch of the imagination, won by a conniving captain. But Ken was grateful.

If the message capsule had arrived before the ship had left . . .

Reeve swung around to look back at the hills. Christ, he and his could live comfortably in those hills. Caves had been found. It'd be hard, dangerous, but anything was better than a return to the constrictions of overcrowded earth. Let those who liked that sort of semi-existence, regimented, regulated, restricted, have it. His eyes had had to learn to see distances. He could no longer entertain the thought of shortening his vision to the confines of the standard 10 x 12 room in an apartment warren or the straight, short horizon of a Corridor or Hall. He lengthened his stride, an unconscious revolt against a return to a planet where a free-swinging stride was a social insult.

Christ, social insult? The whole structure on Earth was one social indignity after another heaped on its members. And to what end?

Maybe that nardy captain was right! And the whole Siwannese mess was a travesty, perpetrated by cowards, moral and physical, on an apathetic, indolent majority.

Spacedep had made a mistake. Maybe Codep could force them to—no, Alreldep was also involved. Was there any chance that Alreldep could be made to bargain? There was that other continent. We could go there and let the Hrrubans keep this one.

His eyes, sweeping desperately across the valley he coveted, stopped at the Bridge. The Bridge—his shoulders sagged in resignation, aware of the futility of his hopes and his position.

History had taught too many lessons in which man-imposed boundaries were broken; solemnly sworn treaties were abrogated and the honest intentions of one generation put aside by the exigencies of the next.

A groan, the inadvertent protest welling from the bottom of his soul, escaped him. He felt the velvety touch of Hrrula's hand on his arm and turned, puzzled.

"Oh, here, I'll take Todd. He must be heavy," he said quickly, only just aware that Todd was riding Hrrula pickaback.

Hrrula backed off, shaking his head.

"The child is not heavy. Not as heavy as your spirit, Rrev," the Hrruban said. "Is it because the ship is gone and you will see no more of your fellows?"

"We will see our fellows again when we leave Doona."

"Leave Doona? Oh, Rrala, you mean. But why must you leave?"

"You are here," Reeve repeated wearily. He eased himself to the ground, propping his rifle against a convenient boulder.

Hrrula, curling his tail around Todd's leg, hunkered down and waited. Todd watched his father solemnly over the furry shoulder.

"Believe me, Hrrula, our people saw no trace of yours. You have no idea what a shock you gave us."

Delicately extending one arching claw, Hrrula scratched behind his ear thoughtfully. When Hrrula looked around again, Ken was sure he was chuckling, the wheeze of his mirth barely audible.

"You have no idea, Rrev, the shock *you* gave *us* when you entered our village," and Hrrula shook with his amusement. "After all," he added with curious haste, "we've been here long enough to know the world has no bareskins."

"I don't wish to offend you but there are many things that puzzle me," Ken went on, hoping to catch Hrrula in a non-evasive mood. "We have wondered if your people sleep through the long winter in some protected place. That would explain why we saw no sign of you. But how did you take your homes with you?"

"If we do not object to your presence here, why do your elders?" Hrrula countered.

Evasion again, Reeve sighed to himself. "Because of the nature and history of my race," he said aloud and waved toward the colony across the river. "Look at that bridge. We have all we need on the other side—right now." Reeve paused, trying to explain abstract philosophy in his still limited Hrruban vocabulary. "But soon, because we are inherently greedy, we will want something that can be found only on your side and we will cross that bridge."

"The bridge was built by Hrruban and Hayuman," Hrrula remarked, looking at Reeve through half-closed eyes. "At Hrruban insistence. Yes, even then I understood that you did not want the bridge. *We*," and his furry thumb jabbed at his sleek chest, "wanted the bridge. Far better than the little boat, particularly when the river runs fast and full."

Reeve shook his head vehemently. "How can you understand why I am against the bridge? I don't have the words to tell you."

Hrrula's jaw dropped into a grin and this time he pointed to the oddly silent boy draped on his back. "I will listen very carefully, as Zodd does, if you will explain."

"All right," and Reeve sat determinedly forward. "Our people are very old. We have kept records of what has happened between our tribes. When one tribe has something another one wishes, and the first tribe has many strong young men with long knives, they attack the other village and take the things they want."

"That's silly," Todd remarked. "Everyone gets the same as anybody else; even in Codep Block."

"That wasn't always the case, Todd, and don't interrupt," Ken ordered. He tempered his reproof with the knowledge that these Hrrubans found Todd unusual and it might be politic not to reprimand the boy too forcefully in front of Hrrula. "We've made an effort on Earth to be sure everyone gets the necessities of life: food, shelter, clothes—" he ignored Todd's contemptuous monosyllable. "Once we found a lovely world, with a gentle people on it who welcomed us. But we did not understand their language completely—we didn't *listen*," and in spite of himself Ken grinned at Todd. "We had much they lacked and tried to impose our wealth on them. We didn't understand that they felt they had all they needed for a good life. And then, through no conscious design of ours, the people all—died. All of them. Every one of them. So, with terrible guilt and shame, our elders made it a first rule that this must not happen again on any other world among the stars.

"So—we do not stay on a world which already has its own people." Ken found that he could not continue. It was a pain in his chest, this wanting to stay on Doona, all the time *knowing* that he had to go.

"But you do not want anything in our village," Hrrula was saying, as he absently stroked Todd's arm. "Every day we learn to understand each other better. We have eaten bread together, worked shoulder to shoulder on a bridge. Our women have met and liked your women. We both raise our young to respect traditions. Why then should you have to leave? It is not *our* wish that you go."

"No! We must go!" and Ken forced the words out. "Today I killed a *mda* with this," and he brandished the rifle. "Tomorrow, or a hundred tomorrows from now, something might happen to make me kill—you. I prefer to leave before such an occasion arises."

Hrrula's jaw dropped. "Forgive me, Rrev, but the *mda* was already struck to the heart by my spear."

There was a certain cockiness in the Hrruban's humorous assertion that drew a chuckle from Ken. Well, these Hrrubans had more than once demonstrated a ready humor.

"You have said to me what is in your heart, Rrev," Hrrula went on, his voice little more than a purr. He didn't look at the colonist, apparently more interested in the pattern he was drawing with one claw in the dust, a series of lines and circles. "I will keep your words in my heart for it is honorable not to covet what belongs to another. Rules are made to protect, not restrict." Hrrula looked up from his pattern, saw that Ken was watching him. He let the design stay for another long moment and then erased it with a decisive sweep. "There are many things to be considered."

He rose abruptly, hitching Todd to a more comfortable position. He struck out down the hill, leaving Reeve no option but to follow.

Pat had obviously been watching, for as they came down the last rise to the bridge, she raced across to meet them. Dutifully she tried to relieve Hrrula of Todd but the Hrruban backed away from her, and Todd clung tightly to his neck. She stepped back, blinking, uncertain what to do.

"What has he done now?" she asked in a sad, soft voice.

"He wanted to see Hrriss," Ken replied laconically. "What's all that about?" and he indicated the waiting groups.

Pat caught at her lip and leaned into Ken for comfort. He readily embraced her, taking delight in the feel of her body against his. Hrrula passed them, striding across the bridge.

"The message capsule came in and Hu Shih and Lee are closeted with it. They want you to join them."

"When did the ship leave? Did the message . . ."

Pat flushed and grinned. "No, the ship left *just* before the approach alarm went off."

"What's funny?"

"Well, the captain was trying to pry more of the local leaf out of Abe Dautrish's stores when a crewman rushed in and garbled off a series of numbers. Kiachif got the crew rounded up and into that ship before you could say 'acceleration.'" Pat stifled a giggle. "The ship's radar has a longer reach than the alarm." She giggled again. "I believe the captain's last words to Abe Dautrish were to the effect that cold sober he couldn't take another ninety days of that child."

"You mean—Todd?" Reeve spluttered, caught between indignation and amusement.

Pat nodded as solemnly as she could, trying to conquer the desire to laugh aloud at the look on her husband's face.

"The capsule came five minutes after their exhaust trail dissipated." Pat gave up the effort and grinned broadly as she added, "Macy said the captain cut it awful fine."

Pat's laugh had a contagious quality and Ken found himself unable to resist joining in.

"I never thought I'd be grateful to Todd for anything," Pat sighed, her face abruptly twisted with perplexity. "You'd better get along to the office."

They had crossed the bridge by then and she gave him a loving kiss and a gentle shove toward the building.

Hu Shih and Lee Lawrence were sitting at the metropologist's desk when Ken entered. They were looking at each other in a dazed stare, the microfilm reader on the table in front of them.

"Thank God, Ken, maybe you can make some sense out of this," Lee said, jumping to his feet and shoving the reader to him.

The message film was from Codep and Ken scanned it quickly. Then he reread it slowly, word for word.

"Are they serious?" he demanded.

"You see?" Lawrence crowed triumphantly. "He's confused, too."

Hu Shih shook his head slowly.

"They say," Lawrence began in a mocking singsong, "this planet cannot possibly be populated. They say, the most thorough search was carried out according to strict Spacedep and Alreldep exploratory techniques. They say, see appendix." Lee paced up and down the room, swatting a closed fist into the palm of the other hand. "They say, make no effort to communicate with natives until trained personnel can be transported to the affected area. I love that, 'affected area.' What does he think natives are? A disease?

"Oh, and do you appreciate the next paragraph in this epitome of departmentalese?" Lawrence asked sarcastically, leaning his hands on the desk and rocking back and forth. "They say, compile language tapes for semanticizing. How'n'ell can you do that without contacting natives whom they insist cannot be here in the first place?"

Ken ran the message a third time and came to the final, thoroughly ridiculous section.

"I also notice that they wish us to retain the colony ship when it arrives and depart, bag, baggage and livestock, to avoid premature culture penetration with these same non-existent natives."

"Oh, how—how shall I explain? What can I say to justify our actions?" murmured Hu Shih. "What we have done seemed so logical considering our position."

"Shih," and Lawrence gave the conscience-stricken metropologist a gentle shake on the shoulder, "you did what any sensible man would do. And you can't tell me that the men—if they are thinking men—who wrote this contradictory garbage are sensible. They sound like dithering idiots, scared silly and looking for somewhere to hide. No," and Lawrence stalked around the room again. "We *have* made an impact on a sentient species, but in all my studies of cultures, e.t. and Terran, I have never heard of a race that absorbed that impact with less outward effect. They have met us as equals, and they had succeeded in counting coup—if I may inject an old Amerind simile—on us several times for all our culturally advanced level. No, Doctor, put away the sack cloth and ashes. Don't beat your breast or commit ceremonial suicide with remorse. The fault lies with Spacedep, or Alreldep or Codep; not with us. And I'll be damned if I'll take the blame for it—or if I will try to act on orders filmed on such a screw-up, illogical, inconsistent wisp of mylar. Besides," he said in an abrupt change, "the fat's already in the fire. We've done everything they said not to do and not done practically everything they said to do."

"Captain Kiachif should have waited," Hu Shih said to himself in an anxious tone. "I knew he should have waited."

Lawrence shot a glance at Ken.

"I doubt any of us could have persuaded him, short of physical restraint, once his radar screen showed the approach of the capsule."

A low hum filled the room, emanating from the equipment which controlled the homing device of the message capsules.

"Another one?" Lawrence demanded and leaned out the door, shading his eyes to watch the homing tower at the center of the landing field. Reeve joined him, scanning the sky with his binoculars until he caught the flash of metal in the sun.

"Sure is!"

This message was from the Alien Relations Department. It was more coherent than Codep's burble, but it too warned against the heinous crime of too premature an introduction of Terran culture to a less advanced race, with a list of the penalties attached to such illegal intercourse. It also demanded in official requestese that a detailed report on the 'observed' natives be forwarded by return capsule.

"In other words, we should never have so much as exposed a fingernail within their sight—which is long range," Lawrence snapped. "I'm not an alien relations expert but I *am* a sociologist and these people—well, they're people," he ended lamely. "Say, did we ever mention that we saw them first?" he asked.

"Well, as a matter of fact," Reeve answered after a moment's rapid consideration, "they advanced on me, not me on them," and he grinned, remembering the headlong dash of the two cubs in pursuit of their ball.

"All right then," Lawrence said briskly. "*They* found *us.* Particularly if this puts a different complexion on our culpability."

"Yes, yes, it does. Or does it?" asked Hu Shih, rising briefly to hope before plunging back into despair, washing his hands. "Oh, why, why?" he cried, rising wearily from his chair. "We had made a good beginning here in spite of that terrible long winter." He crossed to the window to gaze wistfully out at the vividly green Common, down to the river with its backdrop of the great mountain range. A prospect, a sweeping view no longer to be found on Earth even in the dozen carefully preserved Square Miles. "We must leave. And it would have been a better, cleaner break to have left this morning. Now, each day will make it harder."

He saw the rebellious expressions of his aides and shook his head sadly.

"And we must leave, gentlemen. If we cannot, in this difficult situation, uphold principles we have sworn to respect, then we are not one jot better than those barbaric, genocidal ancestors whose action toward minorities we have always deplored. We solved our own interracial problems only by Amalgamation. We solved the domination and destruction of alien species by the Principle of Non-Cohabitation. This is the first time that Principle has come to the test. This is the first time since the Siwannese Tragedy that we have come face to face with another sentient species. And our decision here on Doona is critical. We cannot fail this test."

Reeve and Lawrence stood silently before the little

colony chief. Never in their three years of association with him had they doubted his qualities of leadership or disregarded his gently given orders. But that had been as much due to conditioned respect for authority as for the man himself. Now they saw the inner firmness of moral rectitude that unmistakably marked him both man and leader.

"It has been said," Hu Shih continued, "that there is always a solution to every problem but not necessarily an agreeable one. One asks for wisdom and courage to accept the difficult solutions. For us, that is to return to Earth, stifling vain regrets, terrible disappointment, wrapping ourselves in the knowledge that, by our fortitude, we are redeeming the noblest aspirations of all mankind."

The metropologist took his aides by the arms.

"I look to both of you to support me as you always have done. We shall have trying days ahead of us. Both among ourselves and," he nodded toward the two messages, "with the departments that interest themselves in us."

Lawrence grunted but he gripped the metropologist's hand firmly. "Yeah, but I don't have to like it."

Reeve managed to nod and Hu Shih smiled wanly just as the air whistle blew the call to a belated breakfast. Silently the three went to join their peers.

Chapter XIV

THIRD MESSAGE

WHEN THEY REACHED the mess hall, they faced a silent, expectant group. Hu Shih gave his aides a shove toward their families. He stood by his wife for a moment, silently composing his thoughts. Reeve gave Pat's hand a quick squeeze as he seated himself, nodding to Hrrula where he sat by Todd.

"As you all know, we have had two messages today," Hu Shih began in his quiet way. "They are unusual." His wry smiled elicited a derisive snort from Lawrence. "In effect, we have already done what we are told *not* to do. And we have *not* done, with one exception, what we are told to do."

This was greeted by a ripple of nervous laughter. From the corner of his eye, Reeve noticed that Hrrula was watching him, not the metropologist.

"At any rate," Hu Shih said, "we have established some communications with our Hrruban friends." He bowed toward Hrrula. "In other matters, I fear we have bungled badly."

"*We've* bungled?" a voice protested. It sounded like McKee.

"We were asked," Hu Shih continued, "by Codep and Alreldep to send detailed reports. As you know, a full report of our actions of these past few days has already left."

Reeve was astounded at the amount of humor Hu Shih was able to inject into a humorless predicament. It was a very subtle flavor for such a bitter pill. Still, Ken reflected, if a guy didn't lose his sense of humor when the world was knocked out from under him, he might just somehow drag triumph out of tragedy.

"We were advised by Codep to embark on our already departed transport."

A grim mutter filled the hall.

"Our good captain has given us only a short reprieve from the inevitable, if you get what I mean."

"Yeah, we get what you mean, Shih," and McKee stood up. "It means we'll leave. This morning, next week, next month. What does it matter? We have to leave. We have to go back to Earth and *I don't want to!*"

A chorus of ominous agreement rose in support of McKee's sentiment. As one, Reeve and Lawrence rose and went to stand beside Hu Shih. Lawrence held his hands out for silence.

"Ken and I feel just the way you do. And, in spite of what you might think, Hu Shih does too. In fact, he's mad about it, if you can imagine Shih getting angry." It was a deft redirection of mood. "Mistakes happen even in our all-too-regulated world. Only this time, *we're* suffering for it—not some other guy down the Aisle! Yes, we have got a reprieve. We have a big beautiful world to enjoy while we can. And we can help ourselves, not by wallowing around in an it's-a-mistake self-pitying syndrome, but by enjoying every minute we're here— whether it's out souvenir hunting to improve our status when we're Earthside again, or getting to understand an alien psychology through our Hrruban friends." Then Lee grinned with mischief. "Who knows? Maybe Codep and Alreldep will spend so much time trying to figure out who's at fault they'll forget to take us off."

Hu Shih protested sharply but it occurred to Reeve that Lawrence's quip was not beyond the realm of possibility.

"I'd be glad to give it an assist," McKee shouted good-naturedly.

"Hey, Ezra, can't we suddenly get contaminated with a deadly disease?" Eckerd asked.

"Gentlemen," Hu Shih said severely. "I'm sincerely relieved that we can keep our sense of humor in this difficult situation but let us not speculate too vividly on future contingencies. We all have sworn to uphold the basic Principle of Non-Cohabitation. We *cannot* co-inhabit a planet with another intelligent species—and there is no doubt that our Hrruban friends are intelligent. We will leave when we must, because we must uphold these principles despite the terrible personal sacrifice. And," here the metropologist paused, sighing heavily, "to leave Doona is a great sacrifice!"

Pat, who had been listening intently, leaned over to Sally Lawrence and whispered something in her ear. Sally looked sharply at Pat and then smiled slightly in agreement. Reeve reminded himself to ask Pat what that interchange was all about.

"In the meantime . . ."

"In the meantime," Phyllis Hu broke into the pause that followed, "our breakfast is getting cold. And I really cannot see good food—real food—wasted, no matter what the crisis."

She injected enough of the plaintive into her cajoling tone to rouse people from their dejection. The children who had been quiet now broke the spell completely with subdued complaints of hunger. The clink of tableware against pottery and plastic and mumbled requests for platters and the replenishment of emptied pitchers resulted in a surface noise that bore some resemblance to a normal mealtime.

"What were you saying to Sally?" Ken asked his wife when he resumed his seat.

Pat's face was the picture of innocent surprise. "Oh,

nothing important," she replied too blandly and filled her mouth with scrambled *ssliss* egg. "Oh, but this is heavenly food."

Reeve's next question was forestalled by Todd who reached for berry jam and spilled his water all over the table. Hrrula swept the child up in time to save both of them getting wet. Before Ken could scold Todd, Dot McKee cried out that the message tower was lit.

"Another one?" Lawrence demanded, rushing to the window.

"Awh, for the love of little apples," Reeve groaned in exasperation, "whose finger's in the pie now?"

"The Royal Egyptian Society for the Preservation of—" Aurie Gaynor began.

"Aurie!" Kate Moody exclaimed, reminding her of Hrrula's presence.

Aurie was not the least bit abashed and handed her husband a couple of pieces of toast. "C'mon, Lightfoot. This'll give you energy, O Mercury," and she pushed him out the door.

"I'll wager it's Spacedep," Eckerd said to McKee.

"Naw, the Organization for the Prevention of the Suppression of Sentient Species," McKee countered.

"I told you—it's the Royal Egyptian—" Aurie began, undaunted, until she caught Hu Shih's stern look. She giggled but subsided.

Gaynor, panting from the round-trip run, deposited the message capsule and the reader in front of Hu Shih. He stood there, both feet firmly planted, while Hu Shih broke open the container and held up the space-blue, star-marked tube.

"My bet," Eckerd said with considerable malice in his voice.

Shih scanned the film, motioned to Lawrence and waited until the sociologist had read it.

"C'mon, Lee, forget the stupid protocol and read the stinking thing out loud," McKee urged. "We can take anything at this point."

Laughing softly, Lee lowered the reader.

"I was rather accurate when I suggested there'd be an interdepartmental wrangle over this. Spacedep's joined." He turned back to the reader and quoted in a stentorian voice: "'Soonest make survey determine alien landing site.'" He shrugged expressively. "That's a new way to evade blame; make our 'natives' 'aliens.' Ha!" and Lawrence bowed ceremoniously to Hrrula whose face was inscrutable.

"Hey, should he be allowed to listen to all this?" wheezed Gaynor, jerking a thumb at Hrrula.

"Why not? It concerns his future as much as ours," Lawrence replied. "And I doubt if his command of Terran is sufficient to follow all this."

As Lawrence continued to read the new message, Reeve watched the Hrruban surreptitiously. How much *does* he understand, Ken wondered. There was no tell-tale flicker of comprehension on Hrrula's calm face. He sat in polite silence, Todd nestled against him companionably. But, thought Ken, he is *listening* very hard.

"They forget, I guess," Lawrence was saying, "that we have only the one copter and not much fuel for an around-the-globe search. How long would you reckon, Eckerd, it would take to check on all continental masses for landing traces?"

Eckerd made a rude noise. "In a copter with an air speed of 150 miles top? Hmm," and he laughed. "Months. Assuming, of course, that the craft these so-called aliens used leaves a burn-off."

"What else would they use?" queried Ramasan.

"Hell, they could use magic for all of me," Eckerd retorted derisively, looking sideways at the imperturbable Hrruban.

"A broomstick?" suggested Pat with a giggle. "For a clean sweep."

"We're supposed," Lawrence went on, raising his voice over the ripple that followed Pat's remark, "to institute a search, soonest, until such time as a ship can be detached to aid the 'indigenous personnel.' Now, which personnel shall be considered to be the 'indigenous' one?"

Lee put the reader down carefully and looked around the hall until he came to Hu Shih. With a little bow, he gave the floor to the metropologist.

"We are causing quite a stir," Hu Shih remarked with a disparaging smile. "We certainly have had no clear orders from any of the departments interested in us. While we do know we must leave and Codep has so directed us, the only available transport refused to wait. Alreldep says stay and observe and now Spacedep tells us to beware of aliens." Hu Shih smiled benignly toward Hrrula, who gave no suggestion of hostility as he grinned down at Todd beside him.

"All right, so what do we do now?" Gaynor demanded bluntly.

"*I* want to move into the house you built me and start enjoying apartness," his wife said decisively.

Her feeling was unanimously seconded by all the women.

"I would like to know if there are more of these berries from which to make this jam," Phyllis Hu remarked when she could be heard.

"The Hrrubans know where to get 'em," Ramasan told her.

"Yeah, what do we do about *them?*" Gaynor demanded loudly.

"Why, we continue as we started," Hu Shih replied, "in honest friendship. Always keeping in mind that we are visitors and cannot abuse their hospitality."

Ben rose to his feet.

"Shih, we do have to make some provision for the animals. After all, there is a distinct possibility that we'll have to leave them here, which wouldn't be too bad a thing. It will keep their species from being extinct everywhere. And the Hrrubans may profit by it—call it a payment in kind for the rent of the colony estate. Hrrula has shown a keen interest in the horses and I'd say he would make a good stockman. I'd like to teach him what I can."

"I see no harm in that at all, Ben. What about you, Lee?"

"Hell, I can't see any harm. They've already domesticated the *urfa* and they milk them. They could sure use the cows. Why not? We can't do any more harm than we've done already!"

"I'll need more than just Hrrula to help with the stock," Ben announced, his deep voice filling the quiet room. "You, Ken, and Macy have just volunteered."

"And I'll need volunteers for the KP details. These dishes aren't disposable," Phyllis piped up in her clear light voice.

Chapter XV

INTERLUDE

▼▼▼▼▼▼▼▼▼▼▼▼▼▼▼▼▼▼▼▼▼▼▼▼

As KEN ROSE to follow Ben, Pat caught his arm, smiling up at him with an expression he knew all too well.

"Aren't you forgetting something?" she asked very sweetly.

Ken looked puzzled.

"Your son," she reminded him, indicating Todd with a dramatic gesture.

"He can help with the dishes," Ken replied firmly.

"Don't duck out, mister," Kate Moody said, sternly reinforcing Pat. Kate punctuated her remarks with her index finger jabbing at his breastbone. "He—is—now—*your*—responsibility, my friend. That boy needs a father's loving care."

Hrrula and Todd watched this exchange. Silently the two rose and joined Ken. Ken, who wanted nothing more than to have Todd out of his sight after the morning's antics, glowered down at the small serious face. There was nothing of apology in Todd's expression; no remorse for scaring his father or for putting Hrrula's life in danger, not to mention their relations with the Hrrubans.

To a child only the present and immediate future are relevant, Ken reminded himself.

Beyond them, other youngsters were clearing tables, their voices, as usual, subdued. Years of training in whispers held strong in a place where a shout died unheard. Even their walk, the mincing steps of those who learned the skill in small spaces and crowded sideways, reflected their earth-bound conditioning.

It occurred to Ken that Todd had never recognized such restrictions. His voice last night had been audible throughout the festivities. His clear requests at the breakfast table had stopped other conversation. On the walk back from the Hrruban village—until Hrrula had taken him pickaback—his stride had matched his father's when he wasn't dancing ahead or jumping over obstacles. He had not unlearned earthways overnight, Ken realized; he had never had them. And Reeve shuddered to think of Todd caroming off bodies and on toes on the city sidewalks, of his voice echoing through an entire level of Aisle flats, of Pat's desperate measures to control the rebel they had released on the world and to minimize the penalties exacted for such social misdemeanors.

Sighing, Ken held out his hand for Todd's. The boy's face lit up with a tentative smile and the small grubby hand curled into Ken's. The other hand, Ken noticed, was firmly gripping Hrrula's.

The three started for the barn.

Of the colonists only McKee and Ben had much experience with live animals. Once ticketed for Doona, McKee had been given extensive practical animal husbandry as the livestock allotted to Doona would have been partly in his charge. He would also have been responsible for the domestication of the *urfa*, the deerlike species of Doona. Samples of *urfa* milk proved rich in butterfat and calcium, and was not unpalatable; the Hrrubans used it to make cheese as well as for beverage. The short-coupled body of the *urfa* suggested that it would be uncomfortable as a riding animal—rather like the now extinct Terran zebra.

The major husbandry effort, however, was to have been the revitalization of the declining equine, bovine, porcine and fowl; the first two particularly.

Reeve had volunteered to learn horse breeding as one

of his jack-of-all-trades skills. He had studied the theories but had had no occasion to practice them. Vic Solinari, the second volunteer for this facet of the colony, was too busy with stores and supplies to help today. In fact, as Ken, Hrrula and Todd walked down to the plastic shed-barn, Vic was already busy with the forklift, directing his workers.

"Hrriss!" Todd's shriek of pleasure split the air and the boy shot like an arrow toward the bridge which the small Hrruban was crossing with a group of adults.

"Your people need not feel they must help us," Reeve protested courteously to Hrrula.

"There is much to do here and little of importance at our village now," Hrrula replied.

"Todd," Reeve called, realizing as he did that the child couldn't possibly hear that polite summons. "TODD," he bellowed. Everyone stopped work and turned to look at Reeve.

"YEAH, DAD, WHAT DO YOU WANT?" Todd replied in equal man-sized voice.

There was a second stunned silence until the newcomers realized that such volume was no longer a social sin but an asset.

Unsettled by the reaction to his stentorian call, Reeve beckoned broadly to Todd. Rope tail trailing behind him, half dragging the larger Hrriss, Todd scampered back to his father, absolutely oblivious to the curious looks turned on him.

Sitting firmly on his temper, Reeve resumed their walk to the barn with Hrrula and the two youngsters.

"They've already been grained," Ben told Reeve and Hrrula. He kicked at a grain sack and Hrrula, hunkering down, caught the slight shower of seed. He held it to his nose and inhaled deeply.

"They will need to be watered, however," Ben went on. "I'll demonstrate how to bridle a horse and then I suggest that you get your first lesson in equitation by riding the animals bareback to the river. They're still groggy enough not to be frisky."

Reeve looked dubiously at the horses in the shed.

"Ze big hrrss," Hrrula said softly in Terran, making the 'r' take the place of the vowel. "I am to learn to care them?" His eyes glistened with eagerness as Ben nodded solemnly.

"He understood?" Ben asked Reeve in a quiet aside.

"Evidently."

"I prefer that Hrrubans get them. It would be a pity to shoot them," Ben remarked.

"Shoot them?"

"They are unused to freedom, and it would be unfair to permit them to fall prey to *mda* after we left."

Ben ushered them over to the nearest stall and, taking a bridle from its peg, explained its purpose and use. He spoke next in simple but adequate Hrruban, although something he said caused Hrriss to giggle until Hrrula growled warningly. Todd then pulled Hrriss's head down to whisper something which made both boys laugh.

"You! Sit here," Ken said irritably. He picked up Todd, then Hrriss, and set them on the unopened feed sacks. "And stay there. These horses are nervous and we don't need you getting kicked. Watch."

The boys blinked rapidly, their eyes accusing Ken; they hadn't done anything wrong. He resolutely turned his back on them.

Ben gave Ken and Hrrula a bridle each.

"When you go into a stall, go to the left side and slap the horse smartly on the rump. Tell it to get over," and he demonstrated. The gray mare moved over obediently. "Horses like to be talked to in low reassuring tones. Now, release the halter strap from the manger, so. Slip the reins over the head, so; the headstall goes up over the ears. Hold the bit, so, in the hand, and open the teeth, forcing the bit within. So! Now, taking the reins behind the bit, so, and encouraging the animal with your voice, back it out of the stall. So!"

The procedure appeared remarkably simple and, determined to learn what he could, Ken advanced resolutely into a stall. It was not entirely by chance that he picked the ruddy red mare. He had admired her when she had come off the ship. She was a cheerful color, with white markings up to her knees on her front legs. Her name turned out to be Socks. Ken slapped her smartly on her rump, advising her to move her big warm rear end over. Socks snorted but obliged. Where Ben had smoothly slipped the reins over his mount's neck, Ken found he had too many lines and they got entangled. He had to stop and sort out the bridle again. This time he got the proper lines on the proper sides of the mare's neck. Fumbling, he got the headstall up on the ridges above her eyes. She blinked patiently. He put his fingers on either side of her mouth and was appalled at the size and quantity of her teeth. He inserted his fingers as he imagined Ben had done and discovered that her hard teeth could also hurt him. He got his thumb out of the way and tried to get her to open her jaws to take the bit. Socks snorted, ducked her head, the reins slid to her ears and the headstall crumpled over his fumbling hand.

When he finally got her bridled and out of the shed, he saw that Hrrula, with two small followers, was halfway across the meadow to the river on the stallion. Ben was already returning with the gray mare.

"I'll give you a leg up," the vet called cheerfully.

This recalled to Ken the fact that he was supposed, somehow, to get astride this now large looming animal. He patted her shoulder tentatively and she looked around at him, her big brown eyes politely questioning. Her hide was warm and velvety. And the rich aroma of her was oddly comforting to Ken.

Ben gave him a leg up as promised and there was Ken high up on the horse, his legs dangling uselessly down. Socks didn't seem to mind and Ken told himself that if she didn't, he shouldn't. But her backbone was very hard and pressed him in a physiologically vulnerable place. He adjusted himself.

"Now," Ben was explaining. "She has been trained to neckrein and this is what you do. You wish her to turn

left, you lay the rein, so, on her neck, turning her head.
You wish to turn right, you lay the rein, so, turning her
head the other way. You wish to back her, pull firmly
backward on both reins. You wish her to go forward,
ease up all pressure on her mouth and press your heels,
so," and his big hand took Ken's left heel and pressed it
firmly, into Socks's ribs "and she will move forward."
Which is exactly what the mare did so that Ken was
caught off balance and clutched at her mane. He was
glad Ben was too polite to laugh for he knew he looked
ridiculous.

"What do I do when I want to stop?" he asked, trying
not to sound frantic and pulling up on the reins. The
mare obediently stopped.

"She knows," Ben said encouragingly and led his horse
back into the shed.

Ken found he was pressing tightly with his knees
against her withers and that she didn't seem to mind.
Her ears cocked forward and her head came up. He let
up on the reins and she moved forward in a pleasant
rhythm. He got himself into a comfortable position although he felt he must look foolish with his feet flopping
around. She moved a little faster as she smelled the
water.

"Daddy, look at us," Todd's voice crowed, interrupting
Ken's concentration, and startled, he looked up to see
Todd and Hrriss, legs at right angles on the back of the
big stallion.

"Faster, faster, Hrrula," Todd said in Hrruban. Grinning, Hrrula urged the trotting stallion on. Todd had his
fists knotted in the black mane, bouncing happily.
Hrriss, his arms and tail around Todd's waist, wore a
grin of apprehensive surprise.

Reeve swiveled around in horrified concern for the children. The next thing he knew, he was spitting out black
dirt and grass, one arm pulled upward with socket-
wrenching jerks.

He realized he still had the reins in his hand and he
looked up at the green sky, the mare's pretty head sil-

houetted against it. She made a farrumping noise and
blew down in his face as if apologizing for finding him
there.

"You've the makings of a good horseman," Ben said as
Ken scrambled to his feet. "You held onto the reins."
With no more comment, Ben linked his hands to give
Ken a knee up. Before he realized it Ken was mounted
again and Ben, riding beside him, patiently explained
the elements of equitation just as if falling off a horse
was an everyday occurrence. As Reeve was soon to
learn, it was.

He took the bay mare down to the river next and
found that he preferred the sorrel mare Socks. The bay
mare minced her way in a bone-jerking fashion and had
an annoying habit of tossing her head constantly.

Back at the shed, Ben set about teaching his four pupils how to groom their animals.

"Todd's too small to curry a horse. He might get hurt,"
Ken said anxiously.

"I will not. I didn't fall off," Todd reminded his father
pointedly. "I'll stand on that," he added, indicating a
plastic crate, "and then I'll be tall enough."

"The child doesn't fear the horse so why should we? It
is good to catch them young," Ben said with a grin
which included Hrriss too.

It took Todd a little longer to finish but he worked
willingly and well. The little gray mare he had been assigned stood obediently throughout the ministrations.
Hrriss and Hrrula both had an additional hazard in that
their tails were painfully trod on several times by their
charges. Todd had merely wrapped his pseudo-tail
around his waist.

Bill Moody and Alfred Ramasan appeared at the shed
door, eyeing the horses nervously.

"Mr. Adjei," Bill began tentatively. Ben was crooning
to the horses and did not hear the boy's properly modu-
lated tones. "Mr. Adjei," and Bill blinked startled at his
own unaccustomed volume, "we were told to help you."

"We're finished here but we could use your help with

the cows," Ben declared, pointing to the placidly chewing beasts.

Fifteen minutes later his helpers were back to the original four. Alfred was being taken to the infirmary with a crushed toe and Bill willingly accompanied him. Bill was,—well, frightened wasn't kind—unaccustomed to livestock.

"I'll be back tomorrow?" he had asked and Ben, impassive, had nodded consent.

"At least he is willing," Ben remarked cheerfully after the boys had left.

"Ben, you'd never have made an animal husbandman out of me," Ken groaned. "Hrrula, Hrriss and Todd, yes, but not me."

Ben's eyebrows went up in surprise. "Do you think I made no mistakes the first time I met animals? I lost the thumb nail because I left my finger too long in a cow's mouth." Ben grinned reminiscently. "My foot was broken when a stallion reared and I've lost count of the bones I broke falling off horses before I learned." He gave Reeve a friendly shake on the elbow. "No, no, Ken, you'll do fine but it takes a little time."

"Yeah, but look at those," he said, indicating Todd and the two Hrrubans.

"Hrriss and Hrrula are used to animals," Ben replied with a shrug. "I'd be surprised if they behaved otherwise. And Todd, well, Todd is in a separate category altogether," Ben added with a grin.

"What makes you say that?" Ken growled.

Ben's grin widened. "Akosua has told me much about young Todd. No, do not frown. The boy sees things with different eyes than most children. I think, seeing him today, he sees more clearly. Plainly he was meant for Doona, not Earth."

"Yes, that is painfully obvious," Ken agreed.

"No, no," Ben said earnestly, "he is right. On Earth he took too large a step; on Doona, we do not step wide enough. Look at Alfred and Bill. On Toddy I can rely. And on Hrrula. Tonight," and his voice became busi-

nesslike, "you must return after the evening meal to help
bed the stock down. I shall require Toddy's help too."

Ken snorted with self-disgust. Ben laughed as Reeve
stumped off to Solinari's work gang.

Chapter XVI

BARN RAISING

▼▼▼▼▼▼▼▼▼▼▼▼▼▼▼▼▼▼▼▼▼▼▼▼▼▼▼

By afternoon, the cargo was all sorted and stored, and that which could be left for the Hrrubans put in one shed. The women and children spent the rest of their first full day on Doona in an orientation meeting. This, too, like most of the colonists' original plans, had been revised. But the newcomers were shown slides of the various animals—though they were unlikely to encounter a *mda* during the short time they'd be on the planet—and the flora, including live samples of the *rroamal* vine and the *ssersa* bush and berries. Although the children were sternly restricted to the Common and such wooded areas as were adjacent to their homes, *rroamal* was a creeping parasite, springing up everywhere, and so were the *ssersa* bushes.

Ken Reeve completed this truncated orientation with a lecture on what had been observed of Hrruban manners and customs. He made everyone learn by rote a few basic words and phrases and repeatedly emphasized the parallels of exceeding politeness and friendliness.

"A grin is the same thing for Hrrubans as it is for Terrans. If you don't know what else to do, smile!" he ended his comments.

That evening, after the women had struggled to cook real food on the unfamiliar apparatus in their private kitchens, the adults gathered in the mess hall for the next day's assignments.

"I'll learn how to produce an edible meal on that—that contraption," Kate Moody vowed, "if it's the only thing I do on Doona."

Sally Lawrence, who had been softly strumming on her guitar, struck a major chord and sang out a jingle:

> What can I do, do, do on Doona?
> What can I do, do, do on Doona?
> What can I do, do, do on Doona?
> Learn to cook, learn to cook, learn to cook!

Hu Shih stood up as the laughter and applause subsided.

"A very good introduction for me," he smiled. "However, we cannot spend all our time perfecting cooking techniques or collecting treasures. Now I estimate that we have about four or five days before one or the other of the three Departments send us transport."

"Not if the Spacedep wants us to search the planet for an alien touch-down burn-off," Eckerd remarked.

"One thing sure, Codep won't get Kiachif back here short of four-five *weeks*," McKee added, "and one of the crew told me his is the only transport in this Sector."

"Gentlemen, please!" Hu Shih called them to order and waited a moment until the murmuring died down. "In view of the emergency and our repeated requests for transport, I cannot hold out any hope to you for a prolonged stay. Particularly when Alreldep is so anxious for us not to complicate their contact techniques.

"As I said, I feel we have four or five days minimum. Lee and Ken agree with me that it is doubtful that the transport can accommodate the livestock which we had hoped to breed here. Ben tells me there is insufficient feed for their return journey. Pending subsequent approval, there is no reason why the animals cannot be given to our Hrruban friends who have already evinced considerable interest in them. It would be comforting to know that at least one facet of the colony's original purpose will be thus realized: the preservation of these all but extinct species.

"Therefore, it has been suggested that we begin the construction of a more permanent structure to house the animals, for the present accommodation is inadequate and the females will shortly reproduce.

"Ken has in fact suggested this to Hrrula who appeared excited at the prospect, if you can imagine Hrrula excited about anything." Hu Shih smiled tolerantly and won a few smiles from the audience. "Sam and Macy believe that a good-sized, snug barn, utilizing one of the heat converters, can be built in two or three days, thanks to the Hrruban *rlba* preservative. That would still leave us time for our personal enterprises. However, this is just a suggestion. The project is not compulsory. I will leave the matter open to discussion and suggest that it be voted upon."

"That heat converter? I'm not sure we should leave them such a sophisticated artifact," Lee protested.

"We'll bury it too deep to be found," Sam explained. "They'd never find it, but those stupid animals'll need more than walls during a Doonan winter. Ben says they'll need time to get acclimated."

"Say," and Lee Lawrence rose again, "have we ever determined whether these Hrrubans are hibernators? There's not much sense in leaving the horses in a warmed barn if no one is going to be awake to feed them."

Hu Shih turned questioningly to Ken who had increasingly discovered that he was considered the Hrruban expert.

"Don't ask me, Shih. I've had more evasions on that subject than any other. However, there are those southern villages. They may all go there in the winter."

"Then why do we build a barn for the horses *here?*" Aurie Gaynor asked with some asperity.

Ben was on his feet instantly.

"You noticed the chill in the air this morning, and

again tonight. It may be spring but the temperature still plunges down into freezing. Right now that could be fatal to these barn-bred air-conditioned beasts. Also the cows will soon calve, the sows farrow and the eggs for the fowl species will soon hatch. These young animals must be protected. The barn will not be wasted effort. It will also show the Hrrubans how much we value these animals. I intend to start cutting timber for the barn to-morrow whatever the vote may decide."

Akosua leaned toward her husband to whisper in his ear. He listened imperturbably and only shrugged in answer.

"Oh, what the hell," Gaynor exclaimed into the momentary silence following Ben's calm declaration. "I've never built a barn before. It'll only take a couple of days."

> What'll we do, do, do on Doona?
> What'll we do, do, do on Doona?

sang Sally in a laughing voice.

> What'll we do, do, do on Doona?
> Build a barn, build a barn, build a barn

most of the colonists joined in.

It took three days, even with the Hrrubans' help, to cut, trim, notch and stack the timber. The women prepared the sap, a less arduous but equally time-consuming occupation.

"Everything turns into a language lesson," Aurie Gaynor remarked the first evening when the colonists still had enough energy to congregate in the mess hall.

"If a language lesson is accompanied by such willing hands, I have no objections how many I take," Ben had replied.

Gaynor had rumbled a monosyllabic objection as he inspected the blisters on his hands. With massive anti-histamines he was able to associate with the Hrrubans, but the drugs made him slow and sleepy.

"At the rate we're going," McKee said, "we really will raise that barn in two more days."

Reeve eased his aching shoulder muscles, cramped from hunching over the wheel of the power sled. It took more skill than a man realized at first, to keep the drag load from jackknifing. He'd thought about it all morning and wondered if it wouldn't have been easier to drag the logs by animal team. He'd suggested it to Ben at the lunch break and received a long humorous look.

"Those horses and cattle have been pampered too long, Ken. They just aren't suitable for heavy draying, but their descendants will be."

"Well, one thing sure, we'll all sleep tonight," Ken remarked now, rising and gesturing to Pat, who was deep in conversation with Kate Moody. Still trying to apologize for Todd, Ken decided from the tense look of her face; not that it had been Todd's fault—exactly.

The Hrruban youngsters had come along with their parents that morning to play with the Terrans. Todd had pre-empted Hrriss's company and, with Bill Moody and another cub, had gone off to the village to play some Hrruban game.

Hrriss's mother, Mrrva, had brought Bill Moody home with a split lip, a black eye, and shaking with sobs. Todd, not bothering to hide his disgust, much less his own honorable battle scars, had listened unrepentantly to the bilingual conversation.

"I'm not blaming Todd, Pat," Kate had said. "But how can Bill possibly cope with a rough-and-tumble fight when he's never had a finger lifted against him in his life? But there's not a cowardly bone in Bill's body."

"Of course not," Pat agreed loyally, looking at Ken who hastily agreed.

"It just made matters worse to have Todd pitch in and settle the argument," Kate concluded grimly.

Ken groaned inwardly. Todd was seven years younger and at least forty pounds lighter than Bill Moody.

"I simply haven't understood how a fight started in

the first place." Pat frowned, perplexed. "The children were supposed to make friends."

"I was given to understand wrestling between evenly matched youngsters *is* a friendly sport," Ken said dryly.

Both Pat and Kate turned on him indignantly.

"Hell, don't look at me like that. I don't invent Hrruban customs," he protested.

"I honestly don't think we'd better let the children leave the Common, even in the company of the Hrrubans," Kate said thoughtfully. "For one thing, there's not much point in letting them spread out if we only have to box them up again. Yet I hate to see them lose the opportunity, no matter how short it is. Why, none of them has ever been to a Square Mile!" She turned to her husband who had just entered. "Where have you been?"

"Painting scratches, lacerations and numerous contusions, removing splinters, and aiding abused digestive systems." Ezra took things literally.

"I beg your pardon," Kate and Pat said with a certain amount of understandable irritation.

"Pat, let's go to bed," Ken said firmly and drew her away.

The second day was, in some ways, worse than the first. Everyone was sore from unaccustomed exertions, and tempers were short. Yet they were able to turn out an incredible amount of work. Ken, jouncing on the tractor-sled seat as he drove it back toward the barn site with the day's final load of logs, gazed out across the meadow where the horses were grazing. Hrrula, who had worked as hard as anyone, was stalking the stallion. Reeve grinned. Hrrula's fascination with horses was surpassed only by Todd's obsession with Hrruban tails.

Ken hoped there hadn't been another crisis involving Todd today. Kate and Ezra had been generous yesterday but Todd—Ken stopped that line of thought. It wasn't Todd's fault that he was different from the other children; that he refused to be conditioned to cramped spaces, to play games that required no space, that he made noise and could not be pressured into unchildish quiet.

When he reached the front yard, there was Todd, happily and dirtily erecting a series of twig houses. His arms and legs were scratched in countless places. The heel of one hand was skinned and there was dried grass in his hair. His coverall, fortunately made of an indestructible fabric, was encrusted with mud.

"Hey, Todd, how'd you do today with Patrick Eckerd?" he greeted his son cheerfully. The wary look he received in return braced him.

"Patrick Eckerd does *not* know how to swim," was Pat's opening phrase.

"Huh? You mean Todd does?"

"Evidently," Pat remarked with lavish sarcasm. She hastily turned down the heat under the pan she was tending and then devoted her entire attention to the day's episode. "As nearly as I can understand it, Hrriss and another cub joined Todd and Patrick in the calm pool below the falls at the village. Patrick was picked because he was too big for any of the other cubs to fight with."

Ken groaned and sank to the couch. "Go on."

"Todd caught a huge fish and was, according to him, doing great. However, the fish pulled him in although he says he wasn't in any trouble at all in such shallow water. Anyway, Patrick plunged in, thinking Todd needed to be rescued, only he lost his footing and had to be hauled out. Don't laugh, Ken, the boy could have drowned. And I don't know who'll go with Todd tomorrow. Everyone's scared to be with him."

It was clearly a problem and it was clearly to be his problem, Ken realized. It was also obvious that Todd, even though he was undismayed by his environment, could not be left alone at six years of age. Nor was he to be left with his mother.

"Okay, Todd will not go to the village tomorrow. He'll be confined to this side of the river with the rest of the kids."

Todd was not very happy about this because there was no way to tell Hrriss ahead of time. Nor could an adult go over and back with such a time-consuming message. One of the McKee twins was assigned to keep an eye on him around the Common.

The logging crews, Terrans and Hrrubans both, completed the cutting, peeling and notching of the logs by the end of that third day's hard labor. Ken, with thoughts of dinner only, wearily turned down the path to his cabin. No aroma assailed his hungry senses. The kitchen area was empty. Ilsa, hearing his step, came out of her room, round-eyed.

"Mother's at the McKees," she began, washing her hands in dry anxiety.

"Goddam, what happened this time? Todd duck out to the village?"

"Oh, no, daddy, he stayed here all day. But we all took a walk in the woods this afternoon to look for pretties—you said we should. Something bit Maria and her arm is all swollen up."

Reeve raced to the McKees' house, his heart pounding in his chest, wondering what poisonous thing it was. Pat and Todd were sitting, very stiffly, at the kitchen table. Ken could hear Moody's voice, answered by Maria's quavering whimper.

"Why didn't they send for Ezra earlier?" he muttered at Pat, limiting his communication with Todd to a fierce glare.

"Todd only got her here a few minutes ago. It happened about an hour back, he thinks."

"Todd, what was it?"

"*Rroamal*," the child replied with a perfect pitched vowel. "I told her it was bad stuff but it was blooming and she picked it. Can she yell!" He rolled his eyes expressively. "All the other girls ran away, screaming." His tone indicated what he thought of them. "And then she started to hurt. And cry. I had the worst time with her."

Pat groaned, shaking her head slowly.

Moody came out of Maria's room, also shaking his head.

"I've given her a massive antihistamine, I've used a poultice to draw out the toxic fluid but the edema in the hand is incredible. I never thought—" and he shook his head again. "These kids—they just aren't suited to such conditions. And we haven't time . . ."

McKee came out, his face dark. When his glance took in Todd, his lips tightened over clenched teeth.

"She says Todd warned her and we mustn't think it was his fault this time," and he emphasized the last two words slightly.

"I got her back as soon as I could, Mr. McKee," Todd said softly.

"I know, son. The others ran off and left you. They thought Maria was a *mda* screaming."

Reeve put his hand on McKee's arm, trying to convey the secondhand guilt he felt. He was mixed up, for somehow it still seemed as if Todd emerged as the guilty one.

"It's not your fault, nor the kid's," McKee muttered dejectedly, sitting down heavily. "Like Ez says, these kids—they're not used to this. Oh, we showed 'em films, pointed out the dangerous weeds and animals and stuff. But they've lived all their lives where things that snap and bite are behind bars or in books—" He trailed off. "She's never hurt anywhere in her life. How do you explain pain to her?"

"Doctor?" Dot's voice called. Ezra, roused from his thoughts by the panic in her voice, rushed back into the sickroom.

"I'll fix something to eat for all of us, Mace," Pat offered and busied herself in the kitchen.

They were ready to eat before Pat called their attention to the fact that Todd was no longer there. Full dark had settled when Ilsa knocked apologetically at the door.

"I waited and waited and I'm awful hungry, mother, and is Maria all right?" she asked tentatively.

"Oh, good heavens, I completely forgot we don't have an automat feeder," Pat cried, full of remorse for her neglect of the biddable child. Spoon half-raised, she whirled from the stove to her daughter, her eyes wild. "Isn't Todd with you?"

"No, mummy, I thought he was here with you."

Swearing words he didn't realize he knew, Reeve charged out of the house, up to the office for arms and power lights. Just as he reached the porch, he caught sight of torches on the bridge. Squinting, he was just able to make out a small group of Hrrubans. Three of them and yes—that smaller figure must be Todd. They were headed straight for the McKees.

When Ken joined them, Todd came to a halt.

"I broke my promise," he said in a defiant voice, "and we will have to leave Doona but Mrrva has something that brings down *rroamal* swelling." He pointed to Mrrva who carried a pottery bowl carefully in both hands. "Only you gotta use it as soon as possible."

Hrrula stepped out of the shadow. "He said it was a matter of life and death and too much time had already passed. That is why he broke his promise. He said he tried to tell his mother but she did not listen. We came as quickly as possible. Will your man of healing allow Mrrva to attend to the child?"

Christ, thought Ken irreverently, they have professional ethics, too?

"Mrrva has used it on cuts of Todd's so we know it will not have an adverse effect on a bareskin," Hrrula added after Mrrva fluttered a purr at him.

Reeve hurriedly ushered Mrrva on to the McKees, and into Maria's room, explaining quickly to Ezra. Dot McKee jumped up with a cry and pulled Mrrva to her daughter's side.

"Anything, anything," Dot cried. "Just look at her arm. What can I get you? Water, bandages?" she asked, peering urgently into Mrrva's face.

The Hrruban pointed to the pan in which cloths had been soaking. She gestured the level of water she wanted and Dot rushed out, muttering incoherent thanks.

Leaning slowly over the bed, Mrrva touched Maria's cheek gently with one soft finger. Maria was unconscious of her presence, moaning and restlessly turning her head from side to side, oblivious to externals. Her arm was immense with the edema, up to the shoulder. Mrrva took the pan from Dot and soaked a clean cloth, wringing it dry before dipping in the salve which she then began to spread generously on the child's shoulder. She motioned to Dot to imitate her. Side by side, the two women worked, laving the girl's arm in the yellow substance. Tenderly but firmly and ignoring the child's cries, Mrrva turned the hand so that she could see where the *rroamal* toxins had burned into the tender flesh of palm and fingers.

Then she repeated her ministrations, beginning again at the shoulder. The original application was already absorbed by the taut skin but it was obvious that the swelling had ceased its ominous spread.

"Well, I never," Ezra sighed as he examined the result closely. "I never." Then, because Mrrva looked up in concern, he hastily added in hesitant Hrruban, "This is good thing. We give you all thanks."

Mrrva's jaw dropped into a smile and she nodded her head in acknowledgment before she turned back to her patient.

Reeve and McKee left the sick room and joined the others at the table. Todd stopped eating, looked quickly at Hrrestan and Hrrula as if for reassurance.

"I'm sorry I didn't listen to you, Todd," McKee said, holding out his hand to the boy. "You *tried* to tell me."

Todd took the proffered hand and nodded solemnly. He immediately took up his fork and concerned himself with eating as much and as quickly as he could.

"I would ask a favor of you, Rrev," Hrrestan began as Ken sat down facing the Hrrubans. "A very great favor," he added, laying a hand on Todd's shoulder. The boy gave him a quick wide smile. "Concerning this very small one."

With a pang which Ken had to admit was jealousy, he

realized that Todd had never smiled at him with such spontaneous affection. Christ, what kind of a father was he, anyway?

"I'm sorry Todd is such a nuisance," Reeve began apologetically.

Hrrestan's upheld hand stilled his argument.

"No, he is not a trouble to us," Hrrestan continued, inclining his head in a courtly gesture that robbed his remark of any hint of discourtesy. "It would seem, however, that when someone is set to watch this young hayuman, it is the watcher who comes to harm," and Hrrestan's glance traveled from one adult to the next around the table. "Yet it is not the fault of Zodd. The Bill misunderstood a friendly contest between Zodd and another cub of the same age and received small injuries. The second day, an older boy appeared to believe Zodd was in danger when he stepped into the stream to land a very large fish," and Todd beamed up at Hrrestan. "Today, although warned, the watcher of Zodd plucked a flower that is poisonous. Are my facts correct?"

The Terrans grimly agreed.

"Already he speaks our not-so-easy-language. He understands what we say to him." Hrrestan paused, his eyes carefully examining the faces of each adult before he continued.

"My cub, Hrriss, has spent the day unhappily," he said with a sigh. "All morning he waited for the small figure of Zodd to come down the slope to our village. All afternoon he lay in his bed, sighing deeply and sad." Hrrestan's jaw dropped and he shrugged in a very human fashion. "After today, I think Zodd will have no one to take him over the hill to our village and Hrriss will continue unhappy. Hrriss has ever been a lone cub—which happens to some—but in Zodd he has found a heart that reaches to his, and a mind that understands all that is not easy to say in words. This is rare. It is too bad to part such friends. If you are willing, may Zodd come to our village each day? Mrrva has suggested it and is willing to assume the watching of this young cub. There will also be an elder who instructs our young in the traditions of the Hrruban. We hope that you will permit Zodd to listen to this elder who is wise and kind. I believe it will be of great benefit to both our villages that one of your young becomes close with one of ours."

Ken noticed that Hrrula was watching him intently, the green eyes of the Hrruban brilliant, the body unnaturally tense. Hrrestan on the other hand was relaxed and now smiled encouragingly at Pat.

"Ken, that would be the most terrible imposition," Pat temporized, but there was an incredulous hope in her eyes.

McKee broke the impasse by slapping his thigh and letting out a muted crow.

"Sorry, Ken," he apologized absently, "but it's an ideal solution. Honestly, I've got nothing against Toddy but . . ."

Pat grimaced. "There's always a 'but' when discussing Todd. Oh, I'm his mother but I'll be honest. I'm the first one to agree with you. After all, I've had to put up with him longer than anyone else."

"Now wait a minute," Ken said, feeling control slipping from his paternal hands.

"Hey, man," McKee protested, "don't refuse. They offered, remember, so it's their idea. And just think of it from the standpoint of colony relations."

"What colony?" snapped Ken. "He's my son. It's his good I'm thinking of."

"Then remember he's a natural at their kind of life," McKee said. "Furthermore, when Alreldep gets here, your Todd'll be an Hrruban expert compared to the rest of us. Man, your son might be your passport into improved status. Think of it from that aspect."

"Bargain my own son?" Ken exclaimed.

"You'd better," Pat said, her lips thin, her eyes anxious, "if you don't want to go back to Aisle 45 and Proctor Edgar with Todd!"

Inwardly Ken shuddered and looked across the table at Todd. The child had fallen asleep, his head resting against Hrrula's velvety arm, his dirty, scratched hands limp on Hrrula's encircling tail. Todd back in Aisle life?

"Please consider Hrriss." A soft purr fluttered behind him, and Ken turned to see Mrrva, her deep green eyes pleading.

"It is extra work for you—" his voice trailed off as Mrrva made an impatient gesture at that protest.

"Mrrva made the suggestion," Hrrula spoke up. "Hrriss will come with us in the morning to meet Zodd at the bridge. That way Zodd will continue to keep his promise to me."

"How do you say thank you, Ken?" Pat whispered urgently, trying to smile at Mrrva at the same time.

Shortly afterward, Ezra Moody appeared to reassure everyone that Maria's arm was appreciably better, so Ken and Pat excused themselves and left, Todd sound asleep in Ken's arms.

"I have to admit it'll be a relief to come home without worrying about what colony-shaking crisis Todd has precipitated during the day," Ken remarked.

"You don't think we should have discussed this with Shih, do you?" Pat asked anxiously.

"He's got enough to plague him and it isn't as if we were giving Toddy away or anything."

The moonlight touched her face, pensive and withdrawn.

Pat rebelled against putting Todd to bed without washing off some of the surface dirt. However, once he was tucked in for the night, Pat was, to Ken's delight, anything but pensive and withdrawn.

Chapter XVII

SEARCH

▼▼▼▼▼▼▼▼▼▼▼▼▼▼▼▼▼▼▼▼▼▼▼

THE NEWS of Todd's invitation was all over the camp by morning. Pat remarked acidly to Ken that she thought the general relief was almost indecent. After all, Todd wasn't a monster and he certainly was the only one of the children who got along on Doona. She felt as if she were paroling him to the custody of the Hrrubans instead of sending him as an honored guest.

"The Hrrubans wouldn't *have* any of their mealy-mouthed kids," she said, loftily maternal.

"Honey," Ken drawled warningly.

"Well, he *is* my child," and she glowered at Ken.

"And be honest, hon, you're the gladdest of all to get rid of him."

"It just isn't natural," she wailed, abruptly contrite.

He pulled her into his arm, kissing the end of her nose affectionately.

"I'll get you an appointment with the colony head-shrinker for those guilt complexes," he said. She gave a little sigh and leaned against him.

Once Ken reached the lumber team, he took so much teasing that he began to understand Pat's irritation. Before he reached the end of his patience. a minor emergency diverted everyone's thoughts from Todd.

That night Todd returned from the village, relatively

clean, two new cuts neatly bandaged. Proudly he handed over to his mother four brace of the small ground fowl the Hrrubans relished. He had trapped them all singlehanded.

"You should have seen his little face when he presented them to me, Ken," Pat murmured, her eyes misting.

"You should see yours," Ken retorted.

"Oh, you! Yipe!" because Ken had pinched her after the fashion of husbands who wish to prevent their females from waxing oversentimental.

"We'll be barn raising day after tomorrow right enough," Ken announced at the dinner table. "Todd, do you think you and Hrriss can catch a whole mess of these whacha-callums?"

"*Brrnas?* Sure!" Todd replied, his eyes snapping with pleasure at the challenge.

Ilsa regarded him with an expression akin to awe.

"How do you catch them?" Pat asked.

Todd launched into a blow-by-blow description of the process that made Ken's eyes widen. Pat's face took on an expression of horrified fascination.

"I think it's cruel, cruel," Ilsa cried out in anguish jumping up from the table and running from the room in tears. Pat, with an angry glare at Todd, rushed from the room to comfort her daughter.

Todd gave his father a what-have-I-done-now look. Ken shrugged his shoulders and, for a few moments, a bond existed between the two males of the house drawn together against the vapors of their women.

When the children were in bed, Pat settled down on the wall couch, and curled up against Ken. There was a pungent aroma emanating from her hair and Ken sniffed experimentally.

"Oh, dear, that *rlban* sap stink just won't go away," she apologized. "Did you know, they use it as a coating on their pottery before they fire it. That's why their pots have that high glaze we couldn't identify."

"Hmmm," Ken mumbled contentedly, settling his

cheek against her soft hair. God, it was good to have your arms around a woman.

"You know, I'd very much like to—well, do something for Mrrva."

"Hmmm."

"She had him all day and it's just—oh, you know."

"Huh?"

"But I can't think what to give her that she doesn't already have. I mean, she's got so much more than I have."

"What on earth are you nattering about, hon?"

"Nattering about? I like that!" And she struggled up and out of the comfortable position he had arranged.

"I like it too," he grinned at her. "It's so damned good to have you . . ."

"Just a moment, Ken Reeve. I'm talking about something important."

"I know, giving Mrrva something. Well, hon, we're kind of out of our element here. Seems to me the giving's all from them."

"That's exactly what I mean. Really, it goes against my pride to take all the time. But what can I give her?" Pat's voice ended on a mournful note.

Ken ran his finger down the side of her throat to the hollow of her collarbone, across her smooth skin to the top of her tunic.

"I tell you one thing you do Mrrva doesn't—you do fancy sewing. There's not a female in either village that doesn't like something pretty to wear."

"Of course!" Pat sat up, delighted. "Just the thing." But when she tried to rise, heading toward her small chest of treasures brought from Earth, Ken pulled her roughly back into his arms and silenced her protests with deliberately passionate kisses.

The next evening, when Ken got home from laying the barn's foundations and flooring, his house seemed to have sprouted wings. Small fowl carcasses hung in garlands from the branches of the sheltering trees. Todd,

Hrriss and two other cubs who had helped transport this plenty, were squatting in the front yard, consuming berry tarts with great gusto. They looked exceedingly pleased with themselves.

"My word is their command," Pat greeted her husband gaily.

"It looks as if he had organized the entire Hrruban youth for the dirty deed."

Pat looked at him curiously. "According to him, he did. And we'll need it. Todd also bears the message that the whole village plus some extra visitors from the south are coming tomorrow to help. The men to raise the barn; the women to cook."

"That's the plan," Ken agreed, stretching wearily out on the couch.

"Dinner'll be a few more minutes," Pat told him, bustling away toward the kitchen.

Ken closed his eyes and the sounds around him seemed to magnify. He heard the bubbling of boiling water in the kitchen, the clunk as Pat's spoon hit the pot, the noises of the birds outside in the trees and the chatter of the children. The Hrrubans burst into a purring laugh as Toddy corrected himself on some mispronounced word. The Hrrubans chanted it back at him until he got it right. This accomplished, the chatter subsided into a low purrish rumble and Ken drifted off into a doze.

The next day, an early morning thunderstorm threatened to postpone the barn raising. The Hrrubans arrived, despite the storm, and took shelter from the downpour in the mess hall. They assured the colonists that the storm would abate. Suddenly the sun came out and the skies cleared of the scudding black clouds.

By high noon, two sides of the barn were up and the skeletons of the others ready to be hoisted and joined. The womenfolk called the men to tables where steaming mounds of crisply browned *brrnas* awaited the hearty appetites.

Halfway through the meal, with a suddenness that left the Terrans speechless, the Hrrubans seemed to melt away, into the forest, across the bridge, out of sight.

"Well, howd'ya like that?" Gaynor exclaimed when the colonists realized what had happened.

"That's odd. I didn't think they took a siesta," Dot McKee said.

Reeve caught the patronizing expression on Todd's face.

"Okay, young man, so you know the answer?"

Todd assumed an innocent expression.

"Why did they leave, Todd?"

"You don't hear so good, do you, dad? Not like Hrrula." Todd grinned. He stuffed another berry tart in his mouth, detouring the overflow of the juices with a grubby fist. He wiped his hand carefully on his pants and pointed a berry-stained finger skyward. "Something's coming. Something big. And loud."

"Stop wiping your dirty hands on your pants," Ken admonished absently. "What's coming?"

In answer, the homing beacon lit up.

"A message capsule?" Lawrence murmured hopefully.

Ken felt Pat's fingers twine into his, press them fiercely.

Todd shook his head and squinted up. "Biggern that. *I* can hear it," he said and blithely reached for another berry tart, utterly oblivious to the consternation his announcement had caused.

"So soon, so soon," Pat cried.

"Alreldep?" Eckerd suggested tentatively and then cleared his throat hastily.

Someone had enough presence of mind to get binoculars, but by that time the glint of the sun on metal was already visible.

"Can't you distinguish the markings yet?"

"Too much reflection. But I don't think it's a big ship," Macy McKee remarked and passed the glasses to Gaynor.

"It's not a transport," Sam said after a long, long pause. There was an audible sigh of relief from the small bunch of anxious adults. "I think it's Spacedep. Here, you take a look, Buzz," and he handed the glasses to Eckerd.

"No, it's not a transport. It must be Spacedep. They're the only ones run that class ship."

"Codep said they were sending someone too," Hu Shih reminded them.

"Whoever it is, it's trouble," Gaynor grumbled.

"You won, Sam," said McKee when the markings on the ship were clearly visible.

"I can't call *that* winning," Sam growled.

"Why'd you suppose the Hrrubans left?" Pat whispered anxiously to Ken as Hu Shih and Gaynor got into the tractor to welcome the arrival.

"Ask our authority," Ken said, jerking his thumb at Todd who was slowly munching through his fifth tart. He seemed to be the only one interested in eating, although coffee was passed around while the colonists waited.

It took an unconscionably long time, Ken thought, for the tractor to make the return trip. Maybe that was why he felt apprehensive and uncertain when Al Landreau stood up in the back of the tractor sled to be introduced. He was a compactly built man, his close-cropped hair graying. His piercing glance swept over the scene, the bird carcasses, even Toddy munching stolidly away.

"Have you eaten, Commander Landreau?" Hu Shih asked politely.

"No, although the offer is appreciated," was the crisp reply. "I early learned to stick to my own diet. That way I don't experience any cravings for foods I can't have in deep space." It was not so much a criticism as a statement of the facts of his way of life, but Reeve was certain not a single adult missed the inference. The colonists would find it doubly hard to return to the pre-processed taste of Earth.

"Commander Landreau is here to conduct a search for signs of alien invasion," Hu Shih remarked formally, his expression bland.

"I'll require the assistance of all indigenous personnel," Landreau said, looking over the men and mentally picking out those he would recruit for the job.

"There's a little confusion over the exact definition of 'indigenous personnel,' Commander," Lawrence said with covert humor. "You see, we feel the Hrrubans are indigenous. Now I'm sure they'll be glad to help . . ."

A flick of Landreau's hand cut Lawrence off.

"You," and the finger stabbed at the colonists, "are the indigenous personnel as far as Spacedep is concerned."

"We—" and Reeve paused, imitating the spaceman's rhetorical style, "disagree."

Landreau's sharp glance swung around to isolate Ken from the rest. Reeve had the feeling that every nerve and sense in the man's body was concentrated on him and him alone. Unconsciously he straightened up.

"Yes, Landreau, we disagree," he repeated. "And you will have to too, Commander, no matter what official position you have been ordered to take. The Hrrubans are very much in evidence and their habitation is permanent. Consequently, *they* must be considered indigenous."

Landreau blinked his eyes once, the only sign of his reaction. The man's supreme self-assurance infuriated Ken but he kept a close hold on his temper. It would be intensely satisfying to witness Landreau's discomfiture when they showed him the Hrruban village.

"The Hrrubans have spent all week helping us cut and trim lumber for the barn here and, just before you arrived, they were joining us in lunch," Hu Shih said, determinedly pleasant as he indicated the tables which had obviously accommodated more than the number of colonists.

Landreau disregarded such evidence with a careless gesture.

"You realize, of course, that you have laid yourselves

open to severe penalties for unauthorized contact with aliens," he said with flat disapproval.

"Look, Landreau," and Ken stepped forward, "dump that alien bit. The Hrrubans are entirely too knowledgeable about this planet and its resources to be aliens. Your Department ostensibly surveyed Doona, and Alreldep searched it before they cleared it to Codep for our colony. Well, survey and search notwithstanding, the Hrrubans are here and you boys will have to admit to making a mistake."

"Prove it!" said Landreau expressionlessly.

"My pleasure," Reeve retorted, anger flaring unreasonably within him. He shook off Pat's warning hand. "Follow me." He started across the Common to the bridge.

"You've got a copter," Landreau reminded him in a curt tone.

Ken turned and looked the spaceman up and down as contemptuously as he himself had been examined.

"The village is in deep forest and inaccessible to a copter. We walk."

He and Landreau locked glances as he issued his challenge. The spaceman shrugged and gestured ironically to Reeve to continue. Lawrence, with a cryptic nod to Hu Shih, fell in with them.

As the three crossed the bridge, they could hear Gaynor's rousing bellow.

"Okay, okay, so we lost our helping hands but we've got to get the job done."

Once across the bridge, Reeve set out at a bruising pace that drew a startled exclamation from Lawrence. The spaceman, however, was imperturbable and lengthened his own stride to match. Before they had reached the midpoint of the initial slope, Reeve could see the shine of sweat on the spaceman's forehead. Lawrence, in the same keen physical trim as Reeve, was just beginning to breathe heavily as they topped the rise. Landreau was panting but he kept to the pace set.

The trio plunged down into the welcome cool of the

soughing forest. Reeve was forced to slow down or careen off tree trunks and boulders. At first, he attributed the absence of smoke to the fact that the Hrrubans had planned to eat with the colonists that day. They'd've banked their fire. But when he didn't see the bulk of the houses through the trees by the time they reached the edge of the clearing, a curious feeling hit him in the pit of his stomach.

"What the hell?" Lawrence demanded, turning around in the empty site, incredulous.

Where Reeve had first squatted under the needle tree with Hrrestan and the other elders of the village, there was no dust where restless fingers had made patterns; only an unblemished thick layer of tree droppings. No indentations were left to mark where the heavy trestle bench had been; no burned-over area where the fire had flared. Only the silence of the forest and the frantic scuttling of Reeve and Lawrence to find some scrap of artifact that would bear witness to the village's existence.

With a blandness that bordered on insolence, Landreau watched their hectic search.

"You've had your fun but I'll set the pace on the way back," he drawled at last. "And from now on."

Knowing that protestations were useless, Reeve attempted none and, shrugging helplessly at this unexpected development, he curtly motioned to Landreau to lead off.

Suddenly a small body erupted into the village site, round-eyed, breath coming in staggering gasps. A panic-stricken Todd dug frantically in the mulch where Hrriss's house had stood.

"They've gone. Where are they?" he sobbed, hysterically interspersing his gasping phrases with Hrruban wails of despair. "Daddy, where *are* they?" he demanded, darting to his father and tugging at his hand as if Reeve somehow could lead him to his friends.

"I don't know, son. I just don't know," Reeve admitted, looking about the clearing, anywhere except into the tragedy-filled eyes of his son.

Todd dropped his father's hand and whirled on Landreau, who was watching the scene with an expression of cynicism that deepened into a puzzled frown. The small wiry body seemed to coil like an overwound mechanism. And, with all the hatred of a loyal soul, Todd directed his righteous anger at the spaceman.

"You," and the force of the small boy's contempt made the spaceman take an inadvertent step backward, "*you* drove my friends away!"

Chapter XVIII

HEREAGIN, GONEAGIN, FINNEGIN

▼▼▼▼▼▼▼▼▼▼▼▼▼▼▼▼▼▼▼▼▼▼▼▼

REEVE WALKED PAST the half-finished barn, its bare studs pointing skyward like accusing fingers. He was going to report to the implacable Landreau the results of another day of fruitless searching. He had lost track of the number of drones he had launched and retrieved. As soon as one returned, a new trajectory was inserted, its film capsule was reloaded, and it was sent up again. He was now weighed down with exposed film which he hoped would keep Landreau up all night.

Only one burn had so far shown up. With a triumphant gleam in his eye, Landreau had taken off in the copter, to return—silent. Eckerd had reported sardonically that there had been nothing more suspicious on the scene than a natural forest fire, caused by the lightning storm the morning of the barn raising. Some of the larger stumps were still smoldering but the charred earth was cool and devoid of chemical traces.

When Landreau overheard someone mention the mountain caves, he had mounted a search party. To him they could easily harbor every variety of alien. All he found was dust, until Ben was attacked by a spider, the size of a dinner plate and extremely poisonous. But the spider was indigenous. And the necessity of getting the veterinary back to the camp cut short the expedition.

The fact that Moody attributed Ben's continued life to Mrrva's yellow paste did not register with Landreau at all after a chemical analysis proved the paste to be comprised of Doonan herbs.

Reeve was forced to admire the dogged determination of the spaceman. How the Hrrubans could have escaped the notice of such vigorous, intensive searching defeated Ken.

He mounted the steps of the mess hall, clumped wearily up to Landreau's neatly organized desk and tossed his load of reels down in front of the impassive spaceman.

"Care to try submarine probes?" Ken taunted. "This finishes the aerial series. And, incidentally, the fuel for those probes."

The clear quick eyes locked with his briefly and then Landreau snorted. His self-assured passivity reminded Reeve, oddly enough, of Hrrula.

"Switched sides?" Landreau asked. "Make up your mind, Reeve. Do you want indigenous personnel or don't you? Who do you want in the role? Yourselves or your—mass hallucination?"

Ken said nothing and withdrew, trudging up the path to his cabin. Suddenly he wondered who he did want in the starring role. The colonists or the Hrrubans? If the colonists were indigenous, they had not abrogated the Principle and could remain. But, and Ken shook his head sadly, the colonists knew the Hrrubans were indigenous and that they *must* leave.

Nevertheless, it was personally satisfying to see the haunted doubt flare occasionally in Landreau's eyes. And it was curiously gratifying, too, to find that the Hrrubans had been able to disappear so tracelessly. He knew the location of two of the other villages, and Dautrish and Gaynor had been at three others. No speck, spot or scorch could be found of any Hrruban habitation. A respect for them was mingled with a depressing sense of loss and frustration.

There had been quiet talk among the colonists, half-verbalized wishes to justify their initial reports by at least one trace of the vanished natives. Then oblique relief when the most careful search elicited nothing. But the colonists could not avoid the moral issue. They *knew* the Hrrubans existed and no matter how keenly they wished to remain on Doona, their conditioning on Co-Habitation was too strong.

"I'd like to know how Landreau can explain away those films we sent in of the first contact," Lawrence had remarked in a hurried meeting Hu Shih had called after the first day's fruitless searching. "And those artifacts we sent in after the bridge was built. We can't repudiate them. I admit it makes us look a little foolish right now but . . ."

"Landreau's looking for aliens, not natives," McKee had said.

"Yes, but goddammit man, where did *our* natives go?" Ken had demanded.

That question sang in his ears as he stopped to look down the sweep of the Common to the bridge. The wind from the mountains cooled his face and he sniffed it for any trace of smoke. Only the cinnamony odor of the porous wood trees filled his nostrils; nothing more. He trudged wearily on toward his house.

Under the needle tree that drooped over their roof stood what had lately been renamed the 'mourner's bench.' The central figure was the pathetically passive Todd, his hands for once limp on his thighs, his face immovably turned toward the bridge. He scarcely seemed to breathe. Beside him and on the ground at his feet sat several children, playing their endless quiet games, bearing him company in his sorrow in the curious way of the young.

"No change?" Ken asked Pat, indicating his apathetic son.

Pat hurriedly dried her hands to embrace him, her eyes sliding from his toward the child.

"Maria finally got him to eat something," and she gave a wry smile. "Some form of blackmail was used, I think.

Oh, Ken," and once inside the privacy of the house, her chin trembled and she dissolved against him, weeping.

Ken held her close, wishing that he were permitted to indulge in the therapy of tears.

"Ken, when I think how mean I've been to him—how mean we've all been—telling him to shut up, to sit still, to be quiet—and then to see him sitting there, hour after hour. Oh, Ken, I know he doesn't sleep. He just lies there, staring at the ceiling . . ."

"Honey, honey, it won't be long now. Landreau's about given up," and Ken tried to inject honest encouragement into his reassurance.

"Do you really think so?" Pat asked, looking up at him with watery eyes, sniffling back her tears.

"Looks that way. You know, in a sense, Todd brought this all on himself."

"Ken, how can you possibly . . ."

"Well, Pat, one thing that has kept Landreau here is the look in Todd's face when he charged into the clearing. *We* might have some motive for deceiving Spacedep, but not that six-year-old kid. Although why Landreau thinks we invented natives, or aliens, I don't honestly know. But it's Todd who's kept Landreau looking. God knows, there's not a stitch of evidence to support *our* story."

"Ken—will they come back?" and Pat's face began to crumple again. "I mean, after Landreau's gone, *will* they come back?"

"That's not as big a question as how and why did they disappear in the first place."

Toddy was still sitting on his mourner's bench when the rest of his family had finished dinner. Resolutely Pat had taken food out to him. Ken turned his chair to watch. Every evening that week Pat had advanced on her fasting son with the grim determination that food would pass his lips that night or else. An hour later, 'else' had been reached and Pat would trudge back to the cabin to seek solace in Ken's arms. Tonight Pat's pilgrimage was interrupted by the arrival of Landreau and Kate Moody. The trio stood looking down at Todd and something in Kate's face prompted Ken to join them.

"I don't care what your authority is, Spaceman," Kate said in a harsh, almost defiant voice. "I will not permit a minor in my charge to undergo such an ordeal. The lasting effects of such a treatment are too brutal to be considered."

"So you intend to be a party to treason?" Landreau demanded. He jutted out his chin until his head appeared neckless, drawn down between his shoulders, giving him a vaguely Cro-Magnon look.

Kate snorted derisively. "Don't be ridiculous and don't play the heavy militant with me. I will not risk warping a mind to ease *your* conscience or save your reputation; not on the grounds you supply."

Pat seated herself beside Todd, her arm thrown protectively around his shoulders. Todd paid no heed to their presence. He kept his eyes unblinkingly on the bridge. Reeve moved himself obtrusively into the spaceman's way. Landreau watched Todd through narrowed eyes. With a darting glance, he glared first at Ken, then at Kate, before turning again to Todd. Then he snorted, shrugged and, turning smartly on his heel, strode back to the office.

Deep night was broken by the roar of his ship's departure. The noise roused Ken and Pat, and Ken, a sheet clutched around him, rushed out to witness the bright lance of fire arrowing skyward.

"Just like him to take off in the middle of the night," he grunted when he was satisfied that the ship was achieving an escape velocity instead of veering off for an atmosphere flight. "But I wouldn't put it past him to double back and hide out somewhere," he added under his breath.

As he padded back to bed, he passed Toddy's room and heard a long-drawn-out sigh. Peering around the doorpost, he saw Todd turn over in bed. Slowly the child curled up into the tight little ball in which he always slept. Pat called it 'winding the spring for the next day.' Quietly Ken leaned over Todd and saw that the eyes were closed for the first time that week. A happy smile curved the childish lips. Infinitely relieved, Ken watched a moment longer to be positive. Satisfied, he tiptoed back to bed.

"Landreau's good and gone. And Toddy's asleep," he told Pat.

"Asleep?" Pat sat bolt upright, clutching at the sheet Ken was spreading back over the bed.

"Yes, my dear girl, asleep. Bet you anything the Hrrubans are back in their village tomorrow."

"How can you sound so sure?" Pat demanded.

Ken pounded his pillow into submission, dug his head into the depression and drew the sheet around his shoulders.

"I'm not sure of anything on this crazy, mixed-up world, but just wait until tomorrow."

Chapter XIX

THE WRONG SIDE

▼▼▼▼▼▼▼▼▼▼▼▼▼▼▼▼▼▼▼▼▼

"KATE MOODY, I will not pump my child," Reeve declared, pounding the table to emphasize his position.

"Kenneth Reeve, you're as wall-thick stubborn as he is," Kate flashed back.

"Good thing too. Seems to me though, Kate Moody, you're reversing yourself. I heard you tell Landreau you wouldn't . . ."

Kate flushed. "You know damn well I'm not asking your permission to drug the child and dig into his subconscious. I'm merely asking you to ask him to . . ."

"Get his best friend to give away trade secrets," Reeve finished for her. "And I won't. No sweat, Kate, I want to find out as badly as you do. But I will not ask my son to violate his friendship with Hrriss. It means too much to him. Why jeopardize it for a woman's simple curiosity?"

"That's just like a man, bringing sex into it," Kate snapped with trenchant scorn and exasperation.

"Bringing sex into it?" Ken gagged, trying to hold onto the shreds of his temper.

"You most certainly do when you use the noun 'woman' as a possessive adjective," Kate replied.

"Now, wait just a moment, you two," Pat said, stepping between them. "What makes you think, Kate, that

148

we could get Todd to tell anything he and Hrriss have talked about?"

Kate blinked at her in surprise. "What d'you mean?"

"I mean that Todd is monosyllable king. 'Honey, did you have a good day with Hrriss?'" Pat mimicked herself, turning her head one way. "'Yep.'" She approximated Toddy's oddly bass voice and turned her head in the other direction. "'What did you do?' 'Oh!'" and Pat's shoulders lifted in a childish shrug, "'nothing.' 'What did Mrrva give you for lunch?' 'Oh, nutty stuff.' You mean it tasted like nuts or it was nutty-nutty stuff?' 'Yep.'"

Pat regarded the two with amused tolerance.

"I absolutely defy either of you to get much information out of exchanges like that."

Kate had the grace to look sheepish and Ken straightened up, righteously redeemed.

"I did, I admit," Pat went on, "try to find out myself."

"What'd he say?" "What'd he say?"

Pat shrugged and laughed, spreading her hands wide in admission of her failure. "He said, 'they went someplace else for a while.'"

Kate sagged with deflation.

"Kate," Pat reminded the psychologist, "you were the one who told me Todd was unique and we'd simply have to let him 'dree his ain wierd in the world.' Mind your own advice." Then she turned back to her needlework, ignoring the other two.

Aimlessly Kate wandered out and finally sat down on the mourner's bench. Ken joined her.

"The ironical part of it all is that Landreau is right," she mused. "They *are* aliens."

Ken leaned forward, supporting his elbows on his knees.

"They must be, I suppose," he agreed reluctantly, "because I cannot figure out how else they could dismantle that village and the other five and hide them so effectively. Carrying houses through the forest? Up the mountainside? Throw 'em into the river?" He shook his head. "Even if they could have hidden the houses some-where—in the deepest caves, for instance—it just wasn't physically possible in the time between Landreau's touch-down and our arrival at the village.

"It just isn't possible, even with an advanced technol-ogy, to spirit away a substantial installation in a few minutes. I admit," he said generously as the two saw Todd appear on the far approach of the bridge, "that they had more time to take the other villages apart, but not Hrrestan's."

Kate sighed over the enigma. Todd scuffled toward the bridge alone, his step still jaunty after a long, busy day. He turned toward the woods, his figure alert, and tentatively raised one arm in farewell. Hrriss must be just beyond their sight, Ken decided. Todd turned homeward, kicking a stone out of his path as he trod across the bridge. His purring song was now audible in the quiet evening air.

"But I don't understand why they'd want to disappear in the first place," Kate remarked plaintively. "Particu-larly since they know we've taken films of them and taped their voices. I mean, why hide from Landreau?"

"I haven't figured that out either, but it's the nub of the solution."

"I should think that they would have shown them-selves to Landreau. I mean one man, in a small ship, couldn't constitute a menace to the Hrrubans, so why leave without explanation or clue?" Kate was saying as Todd passed them on his way to the house.

Todd halted and regarded them thoughtfully.

"Hrriss said things aren't ready yet," he volunteered.

"Oh," Kate drawled slowly, laying a warning hand on Ken's arm as she felt him stiffen attentively. "What things aren't ready?" she asked in the manner of the in-different adult.

Todd shrugged. "Oh, things." He looked down again at his bare dirty toes. Then he gazed off again toward the bridge, his eyes squinting in the last brilliance of the setting sun.

"So they had to go away to get things ready?" prompted Kate absently.

"You mean when *he* was here?" and Todd jerked a finger skyward.

"Hmmm," Kate agreed. Ken was awed by the control of her relaxed, semi-indifferent manner.

"Naww," Todd replied. "Mom, can I have something to eat? Hrriss and me missed supper."

"Certainly. Come in and wash first, though," Pat replied, unaware of what she was interrupting with her ready acquiescence.

Ken and Kate exchanged disgusted looks.

"What things?" Ken demanded in frustration when Todd had disappeared into the house. "Why must things be ready?"

"Well, if the confusion from our planet is any indication, they must be overheating their computer circuits for a print-out on their own colonial program," Kate suggested, sluffing off her own disappointment with wry humor.

"How much time do they need? And for what? And how can you extrapolate a computer science for the Hrrubans—" and Ken stopped, suddenly struck by the memory of Hrrula scratching in the dust on Saddle Ridge. Goddammit, the man had drawn samples of a binary-type computer print-out. That couldn't have been a random design, the odds were too much against it. Ken squeezed his eyes shut in an effort to recall the exact pattern of 0 and 1 which Hrrula had inscribed. The Hrruban had been trying to give him a message, perhaps. But why not speak it out loud? Oh, he had had the tape on, but what would that matter? All right, Reeve, think a little. Ken slapped his forehead.

"Inspiration?" asked Kate, amused at his distress.

"No, I can't remember something which might be important," he gritted out between teeth clenched at his own density. Kate would begin to believe he had gone bonkers if he voiced his incredible notion.

And suddenly Ken was certain that Hrrula had meant to reassure him by that curious method. He couldn't speak out because—Ken groaned inwardly this time—because Hrrula was also using a tape recorder, hidden somewhere on his person—which could be easy with such a mane of hair. Or secreted in that ornate knife handle. A race that could disappear in a flash could also have miniature recording devices. Again Ken writhed inwardly. What were the odds that the Hrrubans had bugged the colony, barn, mess hall and cabin? Very high, Reeve, very high.

Panic flooded him as he tried to edit every gathering, every conversation that might have any derogatory comments that would prejudice the Hrrubans against them. Well, that explained Hrrula's sometimes capricious use of good Terran. Was he perhaps the Hrruban semanticist? No, he'd been in the village when Ken had made the first contact. Or had the Hrrubans already known the Terrans were in residence and prepared for it? Why do that? No, he was positive that the Terrans were as much a surprise to the Hrrubans as they to the colonists. But the aliens—no, better keep the mental tag of 'natives,' he cautioned himself—the *natives* were far too familiar with the flora, fauna and dangers of Doona to have come *after* the colonists. But why the simple villages, the lack of sophisticated tools and equipment? Albeit, the Terrans had imported little automated mechanisms; mass had been their problem in Phase III, so they had brought in only the versatile tractor sled and heat converters. What was Doona to the Hrrubans then? And was the colony still faced with a test case of the Non-Cohabitation Principle? On what count had Hrrula wished to reassure him?

Kate was asking him something and he mumbled a meaningless agreement, relieved that it seemed to suffice. Resolutely he shoved the enigma of the Hrrubans to the back of his mind until she had left.

But it wasn't until that night that he could return to the intricacies of the problem. Friend or foe? Christ, what *had* they been discussing when Hrrula doodled in the dust? Oh yeah, about the colony leaving because the planet was already inhabited. And then he'd gone on at length about the long history of the Terranic aggression and genocide. Ohhh, he groaned at the memory of such an admission reaching Hrruban ears; ears unfamiliar with the Terran language. What on earth had possessed him to talk about that phase of Terran history in the first place? What an impression to be misinterpreted!

Oh God, and Ken rolled over, groaning with retrospective impotence. How far up the scale of civilization were these Hrrubans? Might they be powerful enough to wipe out the Terrans as unfit to spread through the galaxy? Would the Terrans suddenly become this century's Siwannah Tragedy? And why did they play at being simple souls?

Suddenly his sense of proportion overrode this wallowing in remorse. And he was put in mind of Todd, with the ridiculous rope tail dangling aft. Todd, whom the Hrrubans cultivated assiduously; Hrrula, fascinated by horses, secretly amused, and practising subterfuge to reassure Ken. Yes, by God, all instinct informed Ken that Hrrula had been reassuring him.

In the restless half-doze that finally overtook him, Ken was again subjected to his personal nightmare. It was so much a part of his sleeping pattern that he could enter the dream at any point of its familiar course. Any point, that is, except the ending, which eluded him always. Tonight he involuntarily started at the beginning. There was the gray street of towers, towers looming unimaginably far above him, defying geometric axiom by touching the tips of their parallel towers so that the desired sight of the sun was denied him. Onward he would dash, to the left, to the right, backward, forward. Then the mocking towers were telescoping into themselves so that there was the tantalizing glimpse of sunlight. Frantic, he would try to climb a tower, but as soon as he found a short stack, it would shoot up and its neighbors would crouch down into their bowels. Somehow, he would choose another tower, despite the eccentricities, and doggedly climb, while on either side other towers taunted him with diminished length. And it would be difficult to get hand and foot holds on the tower wall, for the surfaces would rearrange themselves. He would climb, panting, thirsty, weary, hot, desperate, climb and climb and climb. Suddenly the blessing of sunlight blinded him. Threshing he woke, trying to shake off the miasma of his dream, grateful that it was Doona's sun which had awakened him.

A homely clatter of dishes brought him to full consciousness. He staggered to the kitchen where Pat was busy washing dishes.

"'Morning," he mumbled, clearing his throat before he asked, "Todd gone already?"

"Yes, indeed, sleepy head," Pat assured him, pouring out coffee.

"Oh, I wanted to talk to him."

"You'd've had to get up very early then, dear. He was out and gone before I was awake. I let you sleep because you were so restless last night. That's the first time that old nightmare has bothered you since I got here."

Ken's agreement was lost against his cup. Pat laughed and combed her fingers tenderly through his hair. She massaged his neck and shoulders briefly, laughingly evading his encircling arms to return to her stove.

"I tried out a recipe on Ilsa this morning. It's called pancakes. The old film suggests serving them with 'butter and maple syrup.'" She laughed as she stuttered over the phrase. "I had to look that up in the dictionary. We've been getting butter from the cows, of course, but 'syrup' was made from sap drawn from the sugar maple. Ilsa thought it might be comparable to *rla* but I doubt it."

Ken did too.

"So," Pat rambled on, "we used some of that sweetened berry sauce Mrrva sent over with Todd the other day and the pancakes are heavenly."

Ken listened passively, sipping the hot reviving coffee as he watched his wife moving around the kitchen area. He had never seen her move with such a bounce nor her face so open and contented.

"Pat, you are happy?" he asked, interrupting her in midsentence.

She stopped and stared at him a moment. her cooking utensil poised over the pan. She blinked in the fashion she had when the focus of her thoughts was shifted abruptly.

"Yes," she said definitely. "Yes, Ken, I am happy—just as long as I don't think beyond the immediate task, beyond the day. I had never truly realized how empty and useless I was until I got here and started 'doing' things, not just programing machines to work for me. Oh, I guess it's all right for most women." She grinned maliciously. "Lord, one complained about the noises the machines made and having to wait days for repairmen and —all that. But here, no waiting, I do it. No noise, except what I make. No crowds. No crowding," she added fervently. "It's freeing. It's . . ."

". . . burning," Ken put in drily, nodding to the stove.

"Oh, damn," she said, whirling to rescue the burning pancakes.

No sooner had she started another batch than Bill Moody came racing to the door, catching himself against the post to get enough breath to gasp out his message.

"Mr. Adjei wants you at the corral on the run. Trouble."

Without further explanation, he disappeared. Ken was halfway to the door before Pat's gurgling laugh reminded him he was still in pajamas. She grabbed clean coveralls from the washbasket and threw them at him. Hopping from one foot to the other, he crammed his pajama-clad legs into the coverall pants and stamped his feet into boots.

At the barn, Ben Hrrula, Vic Solinari and McKee were already mounted as Ken swung up on Socks.

"Something has stampeded the *urfa*, Ken," Ben shouted the nature of the crisis. "They're making for the grainfields. Hrrula saw them from Saddle Ridge. The horses'll have to have that grain to live out a Doona winter. We've got to save it."

Infected by their riders' excitement, the horses started moving out of the stable yard at a nervous trot.

"We'll have to head off the leaders." With that, Ben kicked his horse into a gallop. Ken gritted his teeth as his mare, momentarily possessed of five legs, took her own sweet time settling into the easier gait.

Solinari, grim-faced, swung ahead of Ken, one hand on his saddle horn as he, too, tried to keep in the saddle. Ken, having only a little more experience than Vic, envied Ben and McKee their hip-loose conformation to the plunging motion. Hrrula, grinning from ear to ear in sheer delight, seemed to the saddle born, clinging like a vine to the back of his mare.

As the party passed Dautrish on the power sled, Ben shouted his warning and Ken, looking behind him, could see the botanist standing on the seat of the machine, scanning ahead of him.

The dust cloud was rising higher and the leaders of the herd soon became visible black heads, tossing in the forefront.

The herd was heading straight toward them, sweeping unimpeded toward the grainfields and the settlement, to the river beyond. The thunder of their hooves reached Ken's ears over the noise of the five horses. It seemed to Ken that his pulse raced to match the tempo of the onrushing menace. For the second time in his life he was frightened by events he could not control, order or ignore. So fascinated was he by the danger ahead that he narrowly missed careening into Ben's stallion as the animal was pulled to a straight-legged stop by his rider. Reining his mare ineptly around, Ken trotted back to the group as Ben explained the maneuver necessary to turn the herd.

It was a simple matter of crowding the leading *urfas* so that they were forced to veer in another direction. Ben cautioned the men that the *urfa* had never seen horses and the sight of unfamiliar beasts alone might turn them.

Before Ben could translate his direction to Hrrula, the Hrruban had already urged his animal onward. Considering his thoughts of the previous evening, Reeve wondered just how much Terran Hrrula understood. His friendly interest might well mask an unsuspected ulterior motive. Yet Reeve could not attribute hostility to the Hrrubans.

Ben's simple instructions suddenly became more complicated the closer Ken got to the horn-tossing, wild-eyed, froth-covered leaders. True, the *urfa* had never seen horses but they were too involved in their witless stampede to spook at another menace. The horses, on the other hand, had been raised as rare specimens of practically extinct breeds in ideal, protected conditions. Raw, raging wildlife in flight was more than they could take. Not only was Ken suddenly unable to carry out Ben's simple strategy, he was barely able to cling to the saddle of his terrified mount whose sole aim was to get herself as far away from these charging beasts as possible. Had Ken been a more experienced rider like Ben or a natural horseman like Hrrula, he might have anticipated the mare's attempt to seize the initiative. He had one fleeting glimpse of Ben, Hrrula and McKee, mastering their mounts and running with the *urfa* leaders, before his mare headed ignominiously into the dust cloud.

Swearing with indignation and frustration, Ken had the presence of mind to release the reins and yank back, repeating the process until he caught the mare unexpectedly and got the bit from between her teeth. Yanking furiously, he managed to turn her only halfway around. She backed obstinately away from the direction he wished to go.

Heaving and trembling, bloody froth foaming at her mouth, she sidled nervously. Ken belted her smartly with his rope. She bucked with a startled neigh. He nearly lost the rope, grabbing for his saddle horn. Furious at his own ineptness, Ken kept swatting and kicking her, barely managing to keep his seat but gradually getting her to move forward. With a resigned sigh, the mare walked, stiffly at first, then broke into her five-legged trot until finally Ken got her into a rough canter.

Squinting against the sun and into the haze of the dust ahead, Ken saw that the three men had managed to alter the direction of the *urfa* herd. Resolved that Socks must return to the scene of her cowardice, he kept whacking her forward, ignoring the raw patches of flesh at his knees and ankles, the ache across his shoulders and the abused muscles in his buttocks.

A smaller cloud of dust, rising at the far end of the valley, near the upper woods, caught his eye. He hauled the mare to a stop. Straining to see what caused this second cloud, it flashed through Ken's mind that he was not the only novice horseman. He had not seen Solinari with the other three. He turned the mare to investigate and, as she decided she was being taken away from the things which had frightened her, she accelerated willingly.

When Reeve got close enough to pick up the second trail, he was glad he had followed his hunch. A single horse had passed here at a frantic pace. The trail led east, at a tangent from the *urfas'* course, down to the end of the valley. The mare cantered easily now, her sweat-soaked neck drying, her gait smoothing out to a mile-eating lope. Each collect jarred the raw patches on his knees, however, and as the trail led farther and farther away from the settlement, it occurred to Ken that meant just that much more distance on the return journey. He was sure he would have no flesh left on buttock or thigh.

Apprehensive for Solinari's safety, he kept on. The

trail he followed changed its pattern and he guessed that the other mare had dropped to a trot. Solinari must have finally got her under control. Up the slope the trail led and down into the drier plain beyond.

Faintly on the wind was borne the sound of a scream, the like of which struck answering terror in both Ken and his mare. She came to a stiff-legged stop and began to tremble. Whinnying, she brought her head up in a painful collision with Ken's nose. Trying to control the mare and the nosebleed took all Reeve's attention for a moment. The mare danced as the scream sounded again and again and, as suddenly, died away. The mare snorted nervously and began her backward prancing again. With a determined whack on her rump, Ken urged her forward and to his surprise she complied.

She loped forward, snorting occasionally, as Reeve tried to convince himself that the scream had been animal, not human. The runaway mare had probably been attacked by a *mda*, or maybe slipped in a hole and hurt herself. To lose a brood mare in foal was bad enough, but it didn't necessarily follow that Solinari had come to grief at the same time. Reeve tried to ignore the growing physical discomfort of saddle galls.

As he rounded a rise, the plain beyond came into full view. With a scream very like the one they had heard, his mare reared, pawing the air. When her front hooves touched ground, she spun around. Reeve made no effort to stop her second mad flight. He had no desire to stay in the vicinity. Only the fact that there was no sign of Solinari near the apparition that seemed to be ingesting the mare whole consoled Reeve. If Solinari had been still atop the horse when the gigantic reptile had attacked, he was already dead.

In the interests of getting back to the settlement in one piece, Reeve gradually brought the mare down to a lope. He alternated reassurances to Socks with incriminations against the unprintable meat-heads who were supposed to have surveyed this planet. There had not been so much as a subheading or comma on reptiles possessing jaws wide enough to accommodate a full-grown mare.

His horse, weary from more hard riding than she had endured in all her short pampered life, gradually slowed her lope to a jolting trot. Ken kept trying to prod her back into the easier lope but finally gave up and let her walk. He followed his own outgoing tracks on the way back. Looking ahead, he saw that the now placid *urfa* were grazing far down the valley by the river, safely beyond the fields. Sentinel-like, he saw the silhouette of one lone horseman against the bright morning sky, the horse's neck drooping forward, the rider's body in a stoop-shouldered slant. The scene reminded him of a picture he had seen as a child in a museum. Once again the feeling of terrible loss assailed him as the unreceptive center of his soul struggled with the remorseful knowledge that he must leave this grandeur, this spaciousness, this thrilling recurrence of danger.

He pulled up sharply by Macy McKee, the lone guard.

"Solinari?" he asked, not able to add more to the question.

"Broke his leg. The mare tossed him. Did you find her?"

"More or less," Reeve admitted, heartily relieved that Vic had parted company with his mount long before her end.

"What d'you mean? More or less?"

" 'Natives' we got, and reptiles too," and Reeve could not control the embittered emphasis on the initial word. "I wonder what other unmentioned surprises the Scouts didn't discover are going to ooze out of this world to confound us."

"Reptiles?"

"Big enough to ingest a mare—in one piece."

He left McKee to mull over this comforting information at his leisure and turned the mare toward the stable.

The sun was at its zenith when he eased himself painfully out of the saddle at the corral. The mare farruped at him in weary recognition of home and rest.

Ben and Hrrula came striding out of the barn, both relieved at his appearance.

"Where did you disappear to?" Ben asked, automatically feeling the mare's chest as she greedily slurped in the water trough.

"I thought Solinari was on a runaway," Ken sighed, "so I took off after him."

"He's got a fracture," Ben said, unclenching Ken's fist from the reins. "Didn't you see him get tossed?"

Ken shook his head. He was so sore he was positive he'd never be able to dismount. He did not resist Ben's helping hand. His legs wouldn't straighten. The noises the mare made as she sucked in water were cool sounds. Reeve staggered to the trough and shoving her away from the tap, buried his hot face in the water. Coming up for air, he leaned against the edge, looking up at Ben, finally able to communicate his disgust.

"You—and your '*urfa* have never seen horses,'" he muttered sourly.

"I am sorry, Ken. I am sorry," Ben said fervently, his eyes devoid of amusement. "It never occurred to me the boot would be on the other foot."

"Hoof, you mean," Ken corrected caustically. "Oh, we got alone fine—after a while. That is," and he dragged out his syllables, watching Hrrula intently, "until the mare got wind of the snake."

Hrrula straightened, his body alert, his ears flattening against his skull as he threw his head up to sniff the wind.

"Snake?" Ben exclaimed, in the act of removing the sweat-crusted saddle pad, so he didn't see the Hrruban's reaction.

"Reptile, I ought to say, to give it full marks. One thinks of snakes as being small. This here now reptile had a jaw span wide enough to eat a mare—in one bite. I didn't stay around to note further details."

"There was no mention of reptiles of that size in the report," Ben protested, his face blank as he absorbed the full meaning of Reeve's news.

"There was no mention of Hrrula's ilk either," Reeve reminded him succinctly, shaking the water from his hair. The motion started the nosebleed again.

"Of all the misbegotten, unprintable days," Reeve swore. He felt like such a fool, standing there dripping water, blood and stale sweat, too saddle-sore to stand erect. "Scared mares, stamping *urfa* and starving snakes!" He caught the listening look on Hrrula's face as the Hrruban jerked his chin suddenly skyward.

Pressing his bloody nostril shut, Reeve limped bow-leggedly to Hrrula and grabbed his arm.

"Disappearing again?" he demanded roughly, not bothering to use Hrruban.

"These are our orders, Rrev, much as I would desire to stay," Hrrula grinned and, disengaging his arm, trotted away toward the bridge.

"What did you mean?" asked the perplexed veterinary. "What did he mean?"

"You'll catch on, Ben, you'll catch on," Ken assured him and staggered off in the direction of home.

Chapter XX

TURNABOUT

▼▼▼▼▼▼▼▼▼▼▼▼▼▼▼▼▼▼▼▼▼▼▼▼

"KEN," PAT called plaintively through the locked bathroom door, "Hu Shih wants to know how soon you can attend the meeting."

"When I'm damned good and ready," Ken replied, easing his buttocks into another position in the steaming tub. The damned plastic was slippery.

The ice cube at the back of his neck slithered into the water and disintegrated before he could locate it. He waited expectantly but the bleeding didn't start again so he resettled back into the warmth.

"Are you feeling any better?" Pat asked tentatively.

"No! Go away!"

When Hu Shih himself tapped politely at the door, Ken had finally emerged from lukewarm water and was drying himself with great care.

"Ken, I need your support at this meeting," the man began calmly. "The Hrrubans have disappeared again and, if it were not for the film evidence of their existence, I'm afraid the entire personnel of the colony would be reclassified as neurotics."

"Good!" Ken said savagely and then swore because he had inadvertently translated the forcefulness of speech into action and rubbed the rough toweling over a particularly raw place on the inside of his leg. "For Christ's sake, honorable and respected sir, send Ez Moody over with something for these unprintable saddle galls . . ."

"Did you say the Hrrubans are gone again?" asked Pat. The note of fear in her voice took Ken's attention away from his sores.

"Yes. When Lee took the—was Toddy there today?" exclaimed the metropologist.

Pat's horrified gasp answered him.

Wrapping the towel around his middle, Ken yanked the door open, barking his finger on the catch as he flipped it. "And there's no sign of Todd anywhere either?" he demanded, sucking the scraped finger.

"Oh, Ken, your legs!" cried Pat, her eyes widening.

"Damn my legs! When I get my hands on Hrrula, I'm going to yank his tail out and leave him a bloody stump!"

"Oh, Ken, you don't—you can't think they'd hurt Todd?"

Ken stopped midstride and stared down at Pat. Her face was white. She was scared breathless, her hand flattened against her cheek in the age-old gesture of feminine distress.

"No. Todd's safe. They set great store by honor," he said without explaining his remark. "But this whole bit is ridiculous. Ridiculous! *Ridiculous!*" he shouted, pounding his fist on the wall with frustration. "And, dear Shih," he continued, whirling on his heel to face the man, "if you insist on dragging me up in front of those half-baked, half-dozen, semimoronic xenophobes, I'll damn well tell 'em exactly what I think of their unprintable department."

"Kenneth Reeve!" Pat exclaimed, aghast at his explosion.

Reeve glared at her so fiercely that she stepped backward and closed her mouth with a snap on what she had been about to add. He gave the colony leader one more glance, unable to express his seething fury coherently, and stalked off to his room.

"What are you going to do, Ken?" asked Pat timorously.

"I'm going back to the bed I never should have left this unprintable morning."

"And Toddy?" she quavered, following him to the door.

"Todd is the only one on this whole unprintable planet willing and able to take care of himself."

With that, he slammed the door in his wife's face and did exactly as he said he would.

Stewing to himself and unable to get comfortable even in bed, Ken could hear the low mumble of a hasty conference between Pat and the metropologist. He ignored it. Silence fell. Still muttering under his breath, Ken twitched his resisting body this way and that. Never in his life had he experienced more than momentary discomfort. The events of this notable morning had heaped indignity after indignity upon him. Wallowing in the totally new emotion of physical self-pity, Reeve wondered what the hell was keeping Moody. They must have sent for him. They must know how painful these galls were. Why didn't Moody arrive? It was inexcusable that he was allowed to suffer so when relief lay in a hypospray. Where was Moody? What was keeping him?

He was ready to storm out in search of the doctor when there was a quiet knock at the door.

"Come in!"

The door swung open but there was no greeting, no sound of anyone stepping into the room. Irritably Ken swung around, but at the sight of Ezra's expression, he had to laugh.

"I've a good idea what Pat said to you but for Christ's sake, man, make with the salve. I hurt deep."

Moody grunted as he entered the room. However, when he had flipped the towel away, and surveyed the extent and condition of Reeve's sores, his attitude thawed considerably. He immediately administered a shot. With unexpected gentleness, he sprayed a salve on thighs, knees and ankles and motioned Ken to reverse.

Already relieved by salve and painkiller, Ken grinned as he flipped onto his stomach, displaying the ultimate indignity horse can perpetrate on man.

"I'd better take a look at the mare's back," Moody chuckled.

"As far as that pigheaded, pigmy-brained mare is concerned," Ken began, gritting his teeth against the exquisite tenderness of his rear, "she can——."

"You're nowhere near as inventive as Vic was," Moody remarked. "Now this is what he suggested would be fitting." And by the time Moody had finished Solinari's theory on the care and treatment of recalcitrant mares, Reeve was restored to good humor.

"You really had better get up to the office," Moody said to Ken seriously when he had finished. "The chief is getting a hard time he doesn't deserve and he's too much of a gentleman to retaliate in kind. A little plain speaking is required. By some incredible semantic gymnastic, it seems that we, the colonists, are at fault."

"Are you kidding?" and Ken reached for his coveralls.

Moody shook his head gloomily as he handed Ken his boots. As they made their way to the office, Ken noticed the columnar shape of the Codep ship on the landing field. It was larger than Landreau's, for Codep was in the habit of sending delegations rather than single officers.

"They give the distinct impression that we created the Hrrubans to annoy and embarrass Codep," Moody said.

Reeve quickened his steps. His physical discomfort was numbed but his mind was honed to such an edge he'd have tackled the giant reptile confidently.

"So, instead of showing the Spacedep these misbegotten natives and thrusting the blame on them," Moody said, "we allow—get that, 'we allow'—the Hrrubans to decamp; heaping coals of ridicule on Codep's collective head."

"And how in the hell do they think *we* feel?" Reeve

muttered angrily, stamping up the steps injudiciously, jarring his sore body even through the analgesia. He slapped the door open with the flat of his hand and stood on the threshold, surveying the scene coolly.

At one end of the large room stood Hu Shih, looking harassed; Gaynor and Lawrence appeared about to explode, while Dautrish was overenthusiastically showing the four Codep officials various artifacts of Hrruban manufacture.

In the light of his suspicions, Reeve found himself wondering if the Hrrubans had run these items up especially for Terran benefit. The rest of the adult colonists were grouped at one side, a tension of sullen, stunned silence emanating from their environ.

Pat half-rose when she saw Ken enter. Dautrish, noticing her movement, saw Ken and trailed off in midsentence, causing the Codep men to look around incuriously.

"Ah, Ken, I deeply appreciate your coming in in view of your injuries," Hu Shih said.

"I'll live," Ken assured him expressionlessly as he limped toward the delegation.

"Gentlemen, may I present Kenneth Reeve, our jack-of-all-trades and our Hrruban expert," Hu Shih began politely. "These *ranking* officials of Codep . . ."

"Is this the man who reported seeing a giant reptile?" asked the short, plumpest member of the group. Showing no more courtesy to his confreres than toward Hu Shih, the man pushed past intervening bodies until he stood alone, eyeing Reeve patronizingly.

Pointedly waiting until a name was supplied him, Ken remained silent.

"Now, Chaminade," a tall, skeletal man began, touching his superior's arm deferentially, "I'm well acquainted with Reeve's father-in-law; you know Masaryk in Detailing and . . ."

"Yes, Chaminade," Ken interrupted, "I reported seeing a giant reptile. It was not particularly interested in me as it was busy eating a mare at the time. I didn't wait to be introduced then, either."

Ken heard Pat's indrawn gasp of astonishment.

"The mare was being ridden by one of your so-called cat natives?" asked Chaminade contemptuously.

"No. And Hrrula is a natural horseman, unlike us poor ill-equipped ill-trained fools who landed here on an unexplored, improperly surveyed, inhabited planet, expecting by the sweat of our brows and the galls on our asses to make it our home."

Ken ignored Hu Shih's frantic gestures.

"Furthermore, I'll take you to see my giant reptile that is not listed among the things that walk, swim, fly and crawl on idyllic Doona. Of course, it too may have disappeared, like our natives and our villages. And my six-year-old son. But spare us the contemptuous glance and the patronizing sneer. We could easily have denied ourselves the pleasure of your charming company but we thought that a certain basic principle was involved and in all innocence reported the violation. However, the matter is no longer your concern, but Alreldep's and I just hope the hell that that omniscient, omnipotent agency stirs itself to do more than try to pass the buck again.

"Eckerd, warm up the copter. I insist on showing these gentlemen," and Ken larded that courtesy title with venom, "another of our own special, personalized, Doonan hallucinations."

Turning on his heel, Ken strode from the hall, not really caring if the Codep men followed but knowing they would.

Despite an overload, the copter made it to the plain in considerably less time than it had taken Ken to cover the distance. Coldly he pointed out the swollen body of the immense reptile. It lay, torpid with sun and satiation, the mare's carcass straining the skin of its midsection coils.

Chaminade alone maintained his composure. When no one asked Eckerd to make a second pass over the reptile, Buzz opened the copter up, leaving the scene in haste. Ken sadistically noted the varying reactions of horror, fear and active nausea.

"I cannot understand, however," Chaminade remarked coolly, "why you have allowed a child of such tender years to wander unprotected with such menaces as this in the vicinity."

"You don't know Todd," Eckerd answered him nervously when Ken kept silent. "Besides, Mr. Chaminade, as Ken pointed out, we didn't know there were such menaces as gigantic reptiles and catlike natives on Doona. Not that the natives are menaces, mind you."

"*We're* the menaces, Chaminade," Ken snapped. "Or rather, *you're* the menace because you won't look at something you don't want to see: at something that threatens your oh-so-comfortable niche; your oh-so-comfortable theories and procedures, and your all-important status—which Doona threatens with its reptiles and its natives. Well, you all have to admit you saw a reptile back on that plain, with an undigested mare carcass midsection . . ."

"Mr. Reeve, is that necessary?" the skeletal man demanded, his complexion tinged with green.

"No, not necessary but true. Or are you going to erase that from your tapes too, because, like us, it's too much for your overcivilized mental digestion to cope with?"

Chaminade did not waste energy sputtering with indignation as did his colleagues. But his eyes narrowed and he bore a striking resemblance to the fat reptile under discussion.

"You know, Chaminade," Reeve continued inexorably, "I know why Codep made up that Non-Cohabitation Principle. And don't give me that nonsense we've all been so carefully conditioned to accept. Do you know the real reason?"

"Perhaps you'd better tell me," suggested Chaminade very quietly and very gently.

Eckerd shot Ken an appealing look, a halfhearted attempt to restrain him.

"Because we Terrans would make such a miserable showing compared with the most barbaric tribes in their own environment that the myth of Terran superiority would be exploded forever. We're not trained, as barbarians are, to survive no matter what the odds against us. Last winter three of us damn near froze to death because we didn't have sense enough to recognize the danger of a blizzard. I won't count the number of near fatal accidents with the most primitive of implements until we mastered them. And it was sheer good fortune that we had enough pre-processed foods to last us through the long cold because we couldn't have killed a *brna* if it had sat down to be killed. It took us months to be able to butcher what we did manage to kill, and a few more months to get hungry enough to eat it because of our conditioned revulsion to natural foods. All we'd been trained to do—in spite of all our book learning—was to exist—stupefied, spread out Hall by Corridor, by the Aisleful—stale, stupid, stagnating."

"Why, this is preposterous!" Skinny exclaimed, shocked. "When I tell your father-in-law . . ."

"Tell him anything you want," Reeve snapped, not taking his eyes from Chaminade. "He'll listen to you. He has to. I don't."

"You ought to," Chaminade reminded him softly with a slight smile.

"You mean because you're Codep?" said Ken as the copter landed. "Oh, Chaminade, we're not under your jurisdiction any longer. Nor is this problem, you'll be relieved to know, on your backs. The Hrrubans are not native to this planet. So we are officially, and by the fine print in our contract tapes, part of Alreldep. And the sooner they get here and attend to the business at hand, the better. Not that I expect any more intelligent treatment from their hands than we've had from you and Spacedep."

Ducking his head, Ken jumped from the copter, brushing past the anxiously waiting colonists and striding across the bridge.

Chapter XXI

RETURNABOUT

▼▼▼▼▼▼▼▼▼▼▼▼▼▼▼▼▼▼▼▼▼▼▼▼

ALTHOUGH HE KNEW a search would prove futile, Reeve
went directly to the village site. Grudgingly he admitted
that the Hrruban disappearing act was thorough. He
stood on the site of Hrrestan's home, in the spot where
Hrriss's room ought to be. He kicked and prodded
through the mulch and uncovered not the slightest trace
of habitation.

Whatever their motives, he was positive that the
Hrrubans intended no harm to Todd. The boy was safe
with them and probably far happier than he had been in
his own settlement, among his own people. That thought
no longer rankled. Ken had come to realize that he
would have to wait until Todd bestowed his friendship
and affection on his father; it did no good to chase after
it. If Ken didn't force himself on Todd, Todd would
someday decide to trust him.

Ken sat gingerly down on the cushiony mulch and
tried to draw some rational conclusion from the present
disappearance. Actually, the Hrrubans could have es-
corted Todd to Saddle Ridge. The kid've been safe.
Why had they taken Todd along with them? And what
kind of time did they need? Their technology must be
considerably more advanced than the Terrans to effect
such a total withdrawal. Ken snorted to himself; it had

171

taken them no time at all to develop those convenient artifacts, all of bona fide Doona origin.

The quiet glade calmed him and the sweet cinnamony perfume of the forest soothed his overburdened senses. He relaxed enough to fall asleep, until the orange eye of the sun glinted warning of day's end. Reluctantly, but feeling refreshed, Ken rose and went back to the settlement.

Pat raced across the bridge as soon as she saw him. Knowing how anxious she must be, Ken felt conscience-stricken for his delay, and ran to meet her.

"He's with them all right, but I'm sure he's safe, Pat."

She buried her face in his chest and sobbed. He comforted her gently, letting her cry it all out. After a few minutes, she pushed him back, snuffling and fumbling in her jacket.

"Damn," she stammered, realizing she had no tissues. She sniffed and wiped her eyes with her fist. "Landreau's back," she announced. "He wants to see you."

"I'm not surprised. He was probably lurking on the further moon."

"He was," Pat said in surprise. "And do you know what?" she added angrily. "They found out we're collecting things to bring back to Earth and *they're* going to decide what we can take. At the rate they've been vetoing anything that would bring a decent credit, we might just as well forget the whole idea. And another thing," Pat's eyes were flashing now. "Remember that sapphire Mace spent hours cutting? Well—it just happened to disappear."

"And so the exalted are tempted, hmmm?" and Ken felt sick with the bitterness of additional disillusionment. "The sooner we get off Doona, the better. We don't deserve its bounty."

Pat's sigh was half a sob. He put his arm around her shoulders, wondering how much more defeat they would have to endure.

"Landreau's at the mess hall, Ken," Pat said, halting as

he guided her in the opposite direction, toward their cabin.

"So? If he wants me, he'll find me at home."

"Ken, I can't tell him that," Pat objected.

"Pat, honey, you're telling him nothing. You're going to cook my dinner. They can't take that away from me—yet."

"Oh!"

He could feel her resisting him ever so slightly. He turned her toward him.

"Pat, I'm tired of deferring to this department and that manager. I'm tired of apologizing for my right to exist, for what I've seen, for what I know—for what I am. If Landreau has anything to say to me, he can find me. This morning was the last time I trotted obediently in answer to an official summons."

He opened the cabin door, then saw Pat looking at him, scared and uncertain. Relenting, Ken took her by the shoulders and gave her a little shake.

"Don't you see, Patty? It isn't a question any more of culture, it's a question of courage. With that theft, Codep has lost the right to command our loyalty. Landreau lost it by refusing to believe us or Todd." He sighed. "I'd give anything to believe Alreldep has one brain in its collective head, but the odds are sure against it."

"Alreldep doesn't enter the picture, Reeve," said Landreau who had quietly approached the house.

"Oh yes they do. The Hrrubans are not native to this planet."

Landreau snorted contemptuously. "Don't try that on me, Reeve. I won't credit it. Your so-called native-aliens are gone again, all right, because they never *were* here! And I've got proof. I planted satellite guards all around this planet. Nothing could have got through. And according to those sentinels, nothing did. Except Codep's ship."

"I'm not going to argue with you, Landreau."

"You can't," and Landreau's expression was openly scornful. "And I'll tell you another thing. I'm onto your little plot. Oh, I don't know how you managed those films—mighty clever, I'll say that."

"What are you talking about?"

"No skin off my teeth, pal, if you Tee Effs can't take the life. Open space is too much for you, isn't it? You all want to go back to your nice comfortable closets on Earth. Go ahead. I'll help. Then we can open this planet up to some real men!"

Reeve reached out and grabbed Landreau by the collar, jerking the shorter man off his feet.

"I've had my bellyfull of insults today, Landreau. You want to retract that statement?" and Ken poised his right fist right under Landreau's chin.

"Ken, don't!" Pat cried out, grabbing at his raised arm. "You can't fight with everyone. Not when we have to go back . . ."

When Ken saw Landreau's eyes flicker briefly with triumph, he thrust Pat back and purposefully tightened his hold on the spaceman's jacket.

"Give this planet a clear slate in your Department, remove Chaminade and his farting company and just see if you hear us pleading to leave Doona!"

"But we've got to leave, Ken. The Principle of . . ."

"Shut *up*, Pat. That damned principle's not even involved."

"Make up your mind, Reeve," Landreau sneered and wrenched himself free.

When Ken took a menacing step toward him, Pat threw her arms around her husband.

"Ken, stop it!"

"Where's your son, Mrs. Reeve?" Landreau demanded curtly. "This time you and that Moody woman won't stop me from probing that kid. I'll prove this is a phony scheme to get home."

Pat cried out in alarm, but Ken threw back his head and laughed at Landreau's request.

"Find him, Landreau. You have to find him first!"

The spaceman marched angrily down the short corridor to the bedrooms, slamming open doors to peer into the empty rooms.

"All right, where is he? He wasn't with the other kids in the mess hall. Where is he?"

"He was in the Hrruban village when the Codep ship arrived, Landreau, so wherever the Hrrubans are, Todd is."

Landreau's sharp eyes bored into Ken's for one long minute as though he could penetrate this suspected evasion by sheer will power.

"I'll find him. Believe me, I'll find him. Then we'll get to the bottom of this!" And he stalked out.

"Oh, Ken, why are you doing this?" Pat sobbed. "You've antagonized Chaminade, and now Landreau and—what are we going to do when we get back to Earth? We'll be pariahs and . . ."

"Pat, don't you see why I had to stand up to them? For everyone's sake." He held her a little from him so she had to look into his eyes. "They've been pushing us around to suit themselves, and as long as we let them, they'll push us further and further down."

"But we know the Hrrubans exist—and they've got Todd. Oh, Ken, if Landreau gets Todd, I'll know he'll do a probe and . . ."

"Landreau will get Todd over my dead body, Pat. But for the time being, he's safe with the Hrrubans. Bless 'em."

He could not reassure Pat. She had suffered too many disrupting shocks in the past two weeks. And although his thoughts about the Hrrubans and the reasons for their disappearing act were beginning to crystallize, he didn't dare hold out such a vague hope to her. Not in her state of mind.

The sound of running feet penetrated Pat's soft crying and she clung to him tightly, breathlessly.

"It's only Bill Moody, Pat. Todd's light on his feet."

But her body remained expectantly taut in his arms until Bill's reedy voice called out.

"Mr. Reeve, Mr. Chaminade wants to see you immediately."

"Oh, Ken," and Pat's voice held a world of entreaty.

"Thanks, Bill. Please give my compliments to Mr. Chaminade and tell him I'll receive him here."

Pat gasped and Bill's eyes went round and wide as rocket tubes.

"Bububut—he wants to *see* you," the boy repeated.

"Yes, so you said. Well, he can *see* me here."

Bill stared at him a moment longer and then took to his heels as if a *mda* were after him.

"That boy's going to make a good runner, by God."

"Kenneth Reeve," his wife broke away from him in horror. "Can you imagine what will happen to that child when he repeats such an insolent message to an official like Chaminade?"

Ken dropped his hands to his side and returned Pat's accusing glare.

"Nothing will happen to the child. Let me point out that my message was more polite than Chaminade's. But I'm not going anywhere else today unless it's back to the bed I never should have left."

Pat was instantly contrite. "I forgot all about your—wounds."

"My galls," he corrected her. "Well, I haven't," but it was not the galls on his hide he was thinking about as he sank gratefully down onto the couch.

He had barely settled himself in as comfortable a position as the nature of his injuries allowed before he heard the subdued murmur of many people nearing the house. He sighed resignedly. Well, this ought to be short and sweet, he told himself; just like my frame of mind.

"It was so kind of you to come, Mr. Chaminade," Pat began obsequiously as the Codep man, followed by his delegation, strode in. "My husband is in a good deal of . . ."

"That's enough, Pat," Ken interrupted her sharply. His wife wasn't going to suck up to Chaminade either.

"I received your message," Chaminade said acidly,

brushing by Pat as if she didn't exist. His little eyes, narrowed in his fat face, glittered with a dangerous intensity. The others ranged themselves behind him, every one of them socially scrawny. Then Landreau entered, standing slightly to one side of the Codep contingent, his face expressionless save for his mocking eyes.

Hu Shih and Lawrence came in next, their faces set. They nodded to Pat as they took positions behind Ken's couch, facing the officials. Outside the cabin, quiet in the twilight, the rest of the adult colonists stood about anxiously.

"Won't you sit?" Pat suggested in an inane attempt to restore social behavior.

"We shan't stay long," Chaminade said. "We have already delayed our departure, waiting for the return of *Mister* Reeve. Where did *you* disappear to, *Mister* Reeve?"

"I went to the village," Ken replied evenly.

"Village!" Chaminade contemptuously dismissed that with a flip of his pudgy hand.

"Yes, the village," Ken repeated firmly. "My son, Todd, was visiting the Hrrubans today."

"I have had enough of your son and your village . . ."

"And enough of our reptiles?" Ken interrupted coolly.

Chaminade exploded. "That's enough from you, young man . . ."

"And that's quite enough from you, old man," Ken retorted in a loud firm voice. He got to his feet, cursing the awkwardness of his sore body. "Now, *you* listen to *me*, Chaminade. Because we've been listening to you, listening until I'm nauseated by the sounds you make as you blame us for the Hrrubans, the reptiles, the whole smelly mess. But we're not at fault and all the official double talk you can dream up cannot put the blame on us.

"What in hell *were* we supposed to have done when we found Hrrubans? Ignore them because that Godalmighty report said they didn't exist? Ignore the reptiles too, until we get eaten by them? Or is that what you really want, Chaminade? Yes, there's your solution to the whole fiasco.

"We're just twenty-two adults, Chaminade, and a handful of quiet kids. You can write us off completely. Just leave us here. Forget about Doona. Write it off as inimical to human life. Then you can forget about Hrrubans that don't exist and reptiles that shouldn't be. You won't be embarrassed by the Doona predicament and the insolent, recalcitrant behavior of its indigenous personnel.

"Forget us. But don't patronize us. Don't call us liars. Don't rob us. Get off our backs and get off this planet."

"Are you quite finished, Reeve?" Chaminade asked in a deadly cold voice, his emotions now sealed behind his small white mask of a face. He even managed to look a trifle bored.

"No, I haven't heard your ship take off. Oh, and as you go, return McKee's sapphire. *We* won't ask questions but the Poldep back on Earth certainly will."

A flicker in the watchful eyes told Ken that the theft was news to Chaminade. But at this point Hu Shih stepped forward, gripping Reeve firmly by the elbow.

"If it were not for the Principle of Non-Cohabitation, Mr. Chaminade, I could in all conscience second Ken's solution." Hu Shih's voice, firm and loud, was polite, without trace of apology or appeal. "However, in my capacity as leader of these people who are all conscientious citizens of Terra, I must deny us that dearest wish of remaining here. I demand that you provide us transportation away from Doona so that we do not abrogate the Principle which has dictated our actions from the beginning of this unfortunate situation. We have been treated disgracefully: our efforts discredited; our integrity torn as you turn us into official scapegoats; while our futures have been jeopardized by the dishonesty and covetousness of members of your delegation. I insist that you allow us what honor remains to us and arrange for transport off Doona."

"You'll get your transport all right," Landreau interjected, his sharp eyes never leaving Ken's face.

"See here, Landreau, Codep is quite able to take care of its own problems," Chaminade assured him crisply, the pose of the bored official abandoned.

"Yeah, you've sure proved that with this bunch of fake-outs!"

With an angry curse, Ken leaped toward Landreau and knocked him to the floor with a savage and well-placed blow.

"There's a place for social incorrigibles like you, Reeve," Landreau snarled, wiping blood from his split lip as he got to his feet. "And that's where Spacedep is taking you. All of you!" He lurched out of the house, barging through the watching colonists.

"We'll see about that, Landreau," Chaminade shouted after him. Chaminade spared the colonists one more fierce look before he beckoned his delegation to follow him into the night.

The colonists crowded into the Reeves's living room, speechless but anxious.

"What did Landreau mean?" someone asked in a tight voice. "Where would Spacedep take us?"

"To one of the mine planets, probably," Lawrence replied, shrugging indifferently.

"I'm sorry, Shih, Lawrence, all of you," Ken said, suddenly cognizant of the likely repercussions. "I was speaking for myself . . ."

"Hu Shih spoke for all of us, Ken," Moody interrupted him and gestured around as tense, grave faces echoed the agreement. "None of us had the guts to say it, not even when we knew one of those pompous farts had stolen Mace's sapphire."

"Well, if I get the sapphire back, maybe it'll buy us all some extras in the mines," McKee remarked.

"Could they really send us to the mines?" Pat asked tremulously. "Could they? We've done nothing wrong."

There was no answer.

"Say, what did Landreau mean by calling us a bunch of fake-outs?" Lawrence suddenly demanded.

Reeve let out a bark of laughter. "He thinks we faked evidence of natives because we're afraid to stay on Doona; it's too much for us. In short, we're cowards, agoraphobes, Terraphiles, social slobs who want to get back to safe lives on Earth."

The colonists burst out with angry, indignant denials, releasing some of the terrible tension that had been building up all day. Reeve let them rant for a while before he quieted them.

"You've all realized by now that the Hrrubans are not natives; not when they can disappear instantly without a trace."

"Hey, nothing passed Landreau's sentinels, Ken. I know the type he used, so they—they—" Gaynor hesitated, perplexed. "Well, how the hell *did* they disappear?"

"Matter transmitters," Ken replied.

"Teleportation makes just as much sense," Lawrence suggested slyly.

"Ah, come on, you guys!" Gaynor groaned.

"Just because our scientists haven't been able to develop matter transmitters, it doesn't mean some other culture hasn't," Ken told the skeptical engineer.

"I prefer matter transmitters to teleportation," Hu Shih said solemnly. "Logically speaking, that psychic ability is coupled with telepathy of which we have had little evidence."

"What kind of evidence do you need?" Lawrence asked, his eyes dancing.

"Well—" Shih floundered a moment.

"Let's stick to the point," Gaynor suggested sarcastically. "Our futures are at stake. So they use matter transmitters, Reeve? Then why the hell do they live in forest villages, using the most rudimentary tools and no mechanical equipment at all? That doesn't jibe."

"But it supports my theory of teleportation," Lawrence chuckled.

"How can I know the why's or wherefore's?" Reeve said quickly, forestalling an angry rebuttal from Gaynor. "Let's assume, until we know better, that the Hrrubans are as alien to this planet as we are. Then neither Spacedep or Codep have any further authority over us. Alreldep does!"

"And that makes everything A-okay?" Lawrence demanded cynically.

"No, but the contacts we have already made with the Hrrubans and our grasp of their language gives us a bargaining point with Alreldep for better status," Reeve pointed out.

"But if the Hrrubans are aliens, then we have not offended the Principle of Non-Cohabitation!" Hu Shih exclaimed, his face lighting with a joyous relief.

"Oh, for Christ's sake." Gaynor threw up his hands in complete exasperation. "We're right back where we started!"

"If the Hrrubans are alien—" Hu Shih looked keenly at Ken. "Are you sure, Ken?"

"Hu Shih, I'm not sure of a damned thing. But if the Hrrubans are alien to Doona, it'll explain a helluva lot of inconsistencies," and Ken ticked them off on his fingers; "Their intricate language with pitch inflections; their sophisticated attitudes; the whole bit about the bridge, from their forcing the idea through over our protests to its design and construction. The whole damned situation falls into focus if the Hrrubans are alien."

"Except this nature-loving bit," growled Gaynor in the thoughtful silence that followed.

"And what kind of a colony did we plan to start?" Ken asked.

"A very good point," Lawrence agreed softly, "but it leads directly to another unsettling question. How much *more* advanced are they?"

Ken started to chuckle, he couldn't help himself. In the light of Lawrence's remark, the irony of the past weeks of association with the Hrrubans struck him as enormously funny.

"You know," he said, suppressing his amusement as a more important consideration occurred to him, "it might just be possible that they are advanced enough, ethical enough, sophisticated enough not to feel the need to absorb, dominate or manipulate us." Ken caught the dawning comprehension in Hu Shih's startled eyes. The metropologist seemed to expand as he grasped at the implication. "Wouldn't it be a relief to know that *we*," and Ken included all the colonists jammed into his living room, "that *we* can also be big enough, intelligent enough, maybe even wise enough to accept them for what they are without trying to question or change or impose our values on *them?* Can't we have learned enough from the terrible tragedies of history, from the Siwannah incident, to *cohabit* the universe? Mutually at peace with each other?"

"And I'm supposed to be the socio-psychologist," Lawrence remarked in quiet awe.

Hu Shih embraced Ken, his dark eyes brimming, unable to speak. His action released the others from their stunned reflections and everyone began jabbering at once.

"You believe that this is what the Hrrubans have in mind?" asked Ben Adjei, his deep voice cutting through the chaos. "They want peaceful coexistence with *us?*"

"I don't know what they have in mind, Ben," Reeve answered honestly.

"Oh, but it is now obvious to me that they do," Hu Shih interjected excitedly. "They have shown us no hostility, although our presence on Rrala was undoubtedly a shock to them. Immediately they began to help us; even against our better judgment, as witness the bridge. They insisted that we learn their language even as they willingly learned ours. Even when they offered to—excuse my bluntness, Ken—help with the care and protection of Todd. And the fact that they would not abandon him, alone and frightened, far from his own people in a dangerous forest simply adds further weight to this theory." Hu paused for a split second and then rushed on. "In fact, I shouldn't be the least bit surprised if the Hrrubans have not been testing us in adroit ways to judge our cultural ethics and maturity. Truly, Ken, your hypothesis is valid."

Ken looked startled. "For Christ's sake, peaceful coexistence is not new!"

"Yes, but never was it more applicable," Hu Shih beamed.

The night was cut by the crackling roar of a take-off ignition. A moment later the sound was augmented. The tail flames of two ships punctuated the dark spring evening and the colonists watched until the fiery columns had dwindled to a star spark in the sky.

"Ah, but will we be allowed time enough to find out if this is what the Hrrubans had in mind?" Lawrence asked softly.

"God, I hope so," Ken murmured, thinking of Todd.

Chapter XXII

DELAYING TACTICS

▼▼▼▼▼▼▼▲▼▲▼▲▼▲▼▲▼▲▼▲▼▲▼▲▼▲▼▼▼▼▼▼

KEN AWOKE the next morning, sore and stiff. Gradually he became aware of the unusual silence at a time when Pat should be bustling about. He slid carefully out of bed and padded quietly down the short hall to the kitchen. Pat was sitting at the kitchen table, her shoulders sagging in an attitude of hopelessness.

Suddenly he regretted yesterday's rebellion and the bright hope of coexistence. He wondered how many others were uncertain in the clear light of day. Then he pulled his shoulders back. Damn it, he'd've been a coward to knuckle under either to Landreau or Chaminade. If he'd believed in himself—and the Hrrubans—last night, he had better not vacillate today.

He cleared his throat to give Pat a chance to collect herself.

She turned with a smile of determined cheerfulness. Ken bent to kiss her and her responsiveness communicated her pride in him.

As he straightened up, he caught sight of a familiar figure racing up the path.

"Oho, here comes our little harbinger of bad news," he declared as Bill Moody skidded to a stop at the door. "You'll make a long distance runner yet, Bill!"

"Mr. Reeve," Bill gasped, trying to grin, trying to grab enough breath to get his message out. "Snakes!"

"Oh, Christ, not before coffee," Ken groaned. "Where?"

Pat was already galvanizing into action, handing him her full coffee cup, sliding a dish of bread his way.

"You're going to eat something first," she scolded as she picked up the dish of *brna* eggs and made for the stove.

"Mr. Eckerd spotted giant snakes on the plain beyond the valley," Bill panted out, slipping into the empty seat.

"On the plain? Then the snakes aren't close enough to stampede the *urfa?*"

"Mr. Adjei wants to herd the *urfa* across the bridge to the other side of the . . ."

Bill broke off, gawking at Ken's black expression.

"Across the river? Christ!" Ken swore savagely. "Ben ought to know better!" Even if he had to straddle a horse—Ken shuddered at the thought—and herd the *urfa* himself, they were *not* going across that river!

Bread in one hand, coffee cup in the other, Ken stormed down to the barn, his rapid strides jolting sore flesh and muscle.

"Ben, what's this about crossing the river?"

Ben turned, eyes wide with surprise.

"We can't have the *urfa* stampeding through the grain. The horses'll need it next winter."

"And we can't encroach on the Hrruban's domain. Not one jot or tittle. Particularly *now!*"

"What's the matter?" asked Gaynor, appearing from inside the barn. "Why can't we move the herd across the river? It's mutual defense against a common enemy—those snakes."

Ken groaned but the veterinary nodded slowly with comprehension.

"I understand. We will move the herd far down the valley. The prevailing wind sweeps away from there and they will be unable to smell the snakes."

"Well, I don't get it," Sam replied sourly.

Ben put a restraining hand on Reeve's arm as he began to answer Gaynor hotly.

"Sam, it has been understood that across the river is Hrruban territory. Ken is right when he believes that it is an act of aggression for us to cross the river with our possessions."

"Hell, we don't own the *urfa.*"

"It's the principle of the thing," Ken exploded, slopping half the coffee out of his cup with his emphatic gesturing.

"Not another goddam principle to foul things up?"

"The *urfa* stay on this side of the river," Ben said in a flat non-arguable voice. "Besides, the grass *is* better on our side." The big veterinary waved his team out of the stable yard.

Ken watched Lawrence, taking his place for the day, awkwardly hunching in the unaccustomed saddle, bouncing ignominiously as the mare's gait accelerated. For Lee's sake, he hoped the horses were adjusted to the sight of *urfa* today.

Unfortunately, the other cattle and Socks, who remained in the corral, were not downwind of the snakes. And Socks had had enough experience with that scent to become hysterical. She raced round and round the high corral, communicating her terror to the cows and the bull, the pigs and the people. The neighing and lowing brought out the rest of the colonists. That was fortunate, because Ken immediately suggested reinforcing the corral which Socks was trying to kick down. They couldn't get near enough to her to get her back into the barn where, presumably, her panic might lessen.

By noon she was foam-covered and so exhausted she could barely stagger. So Ben led her into her stall, tying her tightly just as the other horses took up where she left off.

By late afternoon, the men called a hasty conference.

"My wife's scared stiff," Macy admitted. "She's got visions of us either being swallowed by the snakes, beds and all, or yanked aboard a transport for a quick trip to the mines."

"The stench is terrible," Gaynor said, rubbing his nose in a piece of toweling, sniffling uselessly. "God, it's everywhere; even makes the food taste snake. Ugh."

"Look, that pass is narrow and it's the only entrance to our valley," Eckerd suggested. "Let's just blast it closed and be done with it."

"The Hrrubans might not want us to alter the landscape," Ken protested.

"Look, Reeve, I'm all for peaceful coexistence while Earth plays pass-the-buck," Lawrence said, "but I'm not anxious to be eaten by a snake as an interim project."

"And how in hell do we know those Hrrubans are coming back?" Gaynor demanded, then blinked as he noticed Reeve's tense look. "Yes, I know they've got your kid, Ken, but you'd better face the alternative."

"I am firmly of the opinion," Hu Shih stated, rising to his feet, "that the Hrrubans will return. The alternative is not consonant with the ethical standards they have exhibited, nor with our logical extrapolation of their future course. Had they not wished to continue to associate with us, they would have remained away the first time."

"Have you logically extrapolated why they disappeared at all?" Gaynor inquired. "Let's face it—the traffic in and out of Doona's atmosphere has been congested. If they are so scientifically advanced that they can leave as they choose, maybe they have left for good this time. Maybe we've already failed those tests of theirs."

"Yes, we may have," Reeve agreed slowly, aware that his throat was dry. He had stubbornly refused to consider that the Hrrubans might not return—this time. "It boils down to a question of faith. Nothing in our relations with the Hrrubans so far can make me believe that they won't return—if only to bring Toddy back."

"Do you think they know of the reptiles?" Ben asked.

Ken swore volubly. "I know damned well they do because I was watching Hrrula. Then that farting Codep ship homed in and he left."

"You don't suppose their policy of peaceful coexistence extends to the snakes, do you?" Lawrence asked.

"They did settle across the river here, away from the reptiles' accustomed trek," Dautrish remarked. "And if these creatures follow the pattern of reptilian life on Terra, they would most certainly have territorial imperatives. My studies of the *mdas* prove that that species does. One can assume it applies to the reptiles as well."

"Yes, but *we* are now in the snakes' back yard, and we've got to do something. Those things are too big for any weapons we have here."

"I would prefer not to risk the Hrrubans' good opinion," Hu Shih began.

"Let's not carry that Principle too damned far," Gaynor growled.

"However," Hu Shih went on, "as the Hrrubans are not loth to protect themselves from *mda*, as proved by Hrrula's slaying of the one that attacked Todd, we may take that as precedent. Eckerd, survey the pass with blasting in mind. How many men will you need? Ken, would you please go to the village in case the Hrrubans have returned?"

Ken was bitterly aware of Sam Gaynor's skeptical expression as he left the mess hall.

Goddammit, why had Gaynor brought up the alternative—'if the Hrrubans return'? And what about the more unsettling corollary—'if we're still here when they return'? Everyone had ignored Landreau's threat. Spacedep had precedence over both Codep and Alreldep. Yet Spacedep had turned Doona over to Alreldep which had cleared it for Codep—and the colony.

Ken gave a mirthless bark of laughter as he pounded across the bridge, grateful for the physical exertion as a release from the frustration, doubt and anger boiling up inside him. Christ, could they pull anything out of this fiasco besides the misery and anguish?

If the Terrans had failed the Hrrubans' test and they never returned, then the Terran colony could stay—*if* they could eliminate Landreau's threat. And *if* they

could re-establish cordial relations with Chaminade and
if—what if Todd . . .

Ken resolutely jogged up the slope of Saddle Ridge,
unable to dwell on anymore if's.

The Hrrubans had not returned. The forest clearing
was empty of any trace of them. Ken hadn't really expected anything else. He was used to hope deferred. He
considered hanging around the site until it occurred to
him that his very presence might possibly be inhibiting
their return. He got as far as the edge of the forest before a second notion struck him so forcibly that he raced
back to the clearing. It was not outside the realm of possibility that they had some kind of monitor system
rigged in the clearing.

"If anyone is listening," he called out, carefully pitch-
ing the Hrruban accents, "please tell Hrrula or Hrrestan
that the colony may be taken from Rrala at any time.
We are also in danger from the giant reptiles and must
take steps to protect ourselves." He paused, turning in a
slow circle, willing his eyes to find some evidence of
Hrruban reception. "Tell Todd—tell Todd we'll stay as
long as we can. If you could just send him back—no,
Todd's better off with you," and Ken broke off, running
halfway to Saddle Ridge.

He reached the mess hall in time to see the women
helping Buzz Eckerd load the copter with the plastic ex-
plosive.

"We've got to seal that pass tight," Eckerd told him,
all the while swallowing nervously. "I did a sweep down
that plain and snakes are all of a sudden everywhere."

Pat came out of the stores shed and raced up to her
husband, her face mutely appealing. He shook his head
slowly and hugged her tight when she burrowed into his
arms for comfort.

"Ken, what *if*—" she mumbled.

Ken gave her a little shake. "Look, hon, *what if* isn't
doing us any good. Let's start thinking in terms of *and
when*. If we trust the Hrrubans, we trust them; up to
and including Todd."

She turned tear-filled eyes up to him.

"Pat," he said sternly, "you let Todd go to Mrrva, right here on Rrala, didn't you? Because you liked her and trusted her, right?"

"Yesss."

"Then continue to trust her. She hasn't changed just because she's removed from the village."

"Well, if you put it that way," Pat conceded, straightening.

The homing beacon lit up.

"Who could be coming now?" Pat wondered.

"Well," Ken drawled, scratching his head, "we've got quite a choice: Hrrubans, Alreldep, Codep, Spacedep and who knows who all else is interested in Rrala-Doona?"

"Whoever it is is not going to be comfortable with snakes in their laps," Buzz said. "I'm going to get the plastic out to the pass, Ken. You make like a welcoming committee until I can bring Hu Shih back."

The copter had long since dwindled to a speck by the time the incoming ship was visible. It was a much larger vessel than the previous visitors; in fact too large to comfort the watching women.

"You don't suppose Codep is actually sending transport to take us off," Kate Moody remarked, shooting an anxious look at the Reeves.

"That is a possibility," Ken heard himself answering calmly. "And if it is transport to take us off Doona, we got more to worry about than the snakes."

"But why do we have to leave Doona now?" Kate exclaimed. "The Hrrubans are aliens, and the Principle of Non—"

"Yeah, Kate, but we don't happen to have a few Hrrubans around as proof. And no one trusts us!"

"Maybe it's Alreldep!" Pat suggested with simulated cheerfulness.

Ken shaded his eyes but the ship was still too high to make out more than the imposing size of her rocket flares.

"Kate, be a good kid and go get the binoculars and keep that thing in sight. If it is Alreldep, we're okay. If not, we've got to delay."

He raced to the mess hall ahead of Kate, pulling aside the panel that contained the com-unit. Frantically he signaled for Buzz to come in, cursing fluently when he realized that Buzz probably hadn't bothered to turn the copter's set on. They hadn't used it much.

If he could just get the men to scatter, on the chance that this was Spacedep or Codep, that would delay departure. Recklessly going on his theory that they were being observed, Ken spoke in a loud, clear voice.

"Hrrubans, if you're watching, there's a big ship landing and it may mean trouble. Please put in an appearance. Please bring back my son."

Then he left the hall, at a run for the stable. He had to get to the blasting party. Socks, however, was not about to cooperate, tossing her head away from the bridle, dancing and heaving when he tried to cinch the girth. By the time he was able to lead her from her stall, he was ready to brain her.

"You can turn that beast loose," a familiar voice ordered him as he emerged from the barn.

Ken whirled to see Landreau, leading a squad of space marines, approaching from the Common. Beyond them, Ken could see additional squads rounding up the women and children.

"Where're the rest of the men, Reeve?"

"You have no jurisdiction over us, Landreau," Ken replied, glancing quickly at the marines. All they carried were the riot sticks, heavy-duty plastic clubs which had become all that was necessary to quell masses of apathetic citizenry. Was Landreau that confident of himself, of authority, of conditioning? Or was Landreau cautious?

"On the contrary, Reeve," Landreau assured him arrogantly. "Spacedep has resumed its initial responsibility over Doona. The matter has been taken away from

Codep *and* Alreldep. *I* have full authority to deal with the matter. Where are the rest of the men, Reeve?"

"Off on a visit."

"Don't give me that, Reeve. Where are they?" Landreau advanced menacingly, his shoulders hunched forward so that he appeared neckless and, Reeve thought, rather stupid.

Socks snorted suddenly, tossing her head nervously as a fresh breeze brought the unmistakable rank stench of snake. Distaste for the odor was reflected in the expressions of the stern marines.

"Smell that, Landreau? That's snake stink."

"Cut it, Reeve. *I* made that initial survey. There were no snakes, no natives. And I've been over every inch of that Phase II report which happens to include the forest you claim is inhabited by Hrrubans. *Hrrubans!*" Landreau sneered.

"Then explain that stink to the mare. She smells it. Care to probe her? She's seen Hrrubans too. Been ridden by Hrrubans in fact. Probe her!"

The mare was neighing and cavorting in full panic now, requiring all Ken's attention.

"Where are the men?" Landreau bellowed above her shrill complaints.

Ground shock rumbled underfoot, followed by the sound of explosion, the sight of a dusty cloud roiling up in the distance.

"Why are they blasting at the pass?" Landreau demanded.

"To block the non-existent snakes, Landreau."

The spaceman fingered on a wrist radio.

"Launch the boat to the Pass and secure all colonists."

In the instant Landreau had his eyes turned away, Ken, yanking hard on the bridle, brought the mare between himself and the spaceman. With an agility that amazed him, Ken swung into the saddle and dug his heels into her ribs. She took off with a squeal of rage, knocking Landreau aside and rearing away from the upraised clubs of the space marines. Fortunately, her wishes and his coincided as she raced in the direction of the river, across the open field.

As Ken shot a glance over his shoulder, he saw Landreau's wrist raised to his mouth again and had no doubt of the orders the spaceman was issuing to the ship. Instinct as well as pain in his buttocks made him crouch low against the mare's straining back. And when he felt the hot breeze of a laser bolt, he began to neck-rein Socks in zigzag patterns, all the time urging her to greater speed.

A bolt boiled the waters of the river just as the mare plunged into the swift current at a dead run. Ken let momentum carry him over her head, down into the water, safely ahead of her threshing hooves. He felt the sudden spots of warmth from other bolts and dug deeper into the current, hoping to get far across and down the river from his point of entry.

He derived what comfort he could from the notion that none of the three departments could write Rrala off until he and Todd had been recovered.

Lungs bursting with fire, he thrust for the surface, restraining the panicky urge to shoot up high into open air. It proved difficult enough to keep his head above water in the rapid current which bounced him around. He realized he was well past the landing field but far too close to the first of the lower falls. There was no sign of the mare; Ken hoped she'd had wit enough to get to shore safely—if she hadn't been bolted into roast meat.

The water was icy, its source the distant snow-clad mountains, and while it numbed saddle galls opened in his rough escape, it also began to numb arms and legs. Fearful now that he might become a real casualty, Ken struck out for the far shore.

When he had finally dragged himself up into underbrush, he was bruised, freezing and exhausted. Shivering, he worked his way back into the thick woods, wondering how he was going to survive the chill of a spring night on Rrala.

By the time he reached the wooded ridge that ran

parallel to the river, it was growing dark. He shivered almost continually now, worried, hungry and angry! There were lights on in the mess hall but in none of the cabins set back in the woods. Landreau was presumably keeping all the colonists together. Ken thought he made out the angular silhouette of the copter in its parking space but he couldn't be sure, the usual Common fire had not been lit. But there was no mistaking the ominous bulk of the Spacedep launch.

He had to do something—besides wait and pray for the Hrrubans to return. He had to find some shelter for the night or risk illness. Where would he be least expected to go?

The answer was so ridiculous that Ken chuckled between spasms of shivers as he made his way farther up the river.

Chapter XXIII

INTERVENTION

▼▼▼▼▼▼▼▼▼▼▼▼▼▼▼▼▼▼▼▼▼▼▼

THE DUTY OFFICER, Hrran, who was monitoring the closed-circuit screens on Rrala happened to be acquainted with Hrrula. He was not a Barred Stripe himself, but he had great respect for that clan. Furthermore, the poignancy of the Terran's faltering plea made an impression on him. The moment he was relieved of his watch, he disobeyed stern directives and trotted over to Hrrula's quarters.

When Hrran had finished recounting the events he had witnessed but not completely understood, due to lack of language, Hrrula began to pace the floor, his tail twitching in wide, snapping arcs.

"Yes, it was only a matter of time before the reptiles finished laying their eggs on the plains and sought the river route to their swamps. However, the Trrans have the means to blow up the Pass and protect themselves." His tail gave a long lash.

"You know how some parties will construe that development," Hrran remarked discreetly.

Hrrula's tail gave a vicious swipe through the air.

"Hrran, why did you breach security? You are Third's appointee!"

Hrran nodded slowly. "I am—I was, I should say—because I find there is much to be said for the honorable conduct of these creatures. Oh, I do not understand the half of what is said but when this Rrev spoke of leaving Rrala without his cub—" Hrran shrugged his shoulders expressively. "I have cubs of my own. And I have met the young Zodd with his rope tail!"

Hrrula purred deep in his throat and his eyes moved restlessly, his nose and ears twitched, signs of deep perturbation for the usually composed Hrruban.

"How soon before these latest tapes are reviewed and translated?"

"They'll be in processing now, but as to when the Speakers will schedule viewing in their so busy days—" Hrran shrugged again, his expression ironic. "Third has many ways of deferring issues."

"He fouls his own lair with obstructive indecisions— oh, my pardon, Hrran. I have no right to insult your patron."

Hrran stood, his jaw dropping in a reassuring smile. His tail tip idly curled this way and that.

"There comes a time when the larger loyalty must be considered. I believe I see a way in which this matter may be put before Third immediately. I'll do my best." He rose.

"Hrran?" Hrrula stopped the officer on the point of leaving. "Who is duty officer now? Will he have wit enough to report an evacuation? We cannot let Rrev and the others suffer from the timid vacillations of lair loafers and we cannot in conscience separate Zodd permanently from his own kind."

"The duty officer is Hrrirl of the small mind but the technician is one Mrrim who, I hear, actually knows some Terran from close study of the screens."

When Hrran had left, Hrrula immediately changed into formal attire. He was determined to bring this news to the ears of the First Speaker. For such a crucial message, Hrrula would not trust public sources of communication. As he trotted quickly through the traffic on the Concourse, he wondered if he should stop for Hrrestan. No, he couldn't face Zodd at the moment and the sooner he got to the First Speaker the sooner action could be taken.

Yet what action could be taken until Council had deliberated? There had been uproar enough when Hrrestan had returned with Zodd, although Fourth had mitigated that by monopolizing the cub with his tests and intensive language training. And Zodd himself was his own enchanting advocate right down to the tip of his frayed rope tail. He also insisted on wearing the *mda* jacket and loincloth—though *mda* fur was shades darker than even the oldest Hrruban's. The cub's grasp of Hrruban was nothing short of miraculous, and his willingness to purr and growl with Hrruban intensity and accuracy won him many adherents.

However, they were bound by the Laws and the Laws said that all Speakers must be unanimously agreed on major policy changes. And this Terran incident definitely was a major change—no, upheaval. And that was the problem.

Hrrula, in the heat of his thoughts, was inexcusably rude in passing a lagging group of dark stripes and, but for his excessive speed, might have been severely detained. However, he reached the Great Compound safely and, once inside the Executive Shaft, used his security card to get him transmitted to First's suite.

Fortunately for him, not only was First in residence, but a personal friend was duty officer and Hrrula was ushered in at once. He began the proper ritual of entreaty, only to be cut off by a peremptory wave of First's hand.

"You would not importune me with nonsense. Come to the point, young Hrrula."

Quickly recovering from the surprise of such a compliment, Hrrula outlined the new developments, adding Rrev's pleas at the village site and in the hall. For a long moment First sat deep in thought, even his tail still. Finally he sighed.

"I was afraid of just such an occurrence," he murmured with a sad smile and sadder eyes. "These Trrans are so much like ourselves. So much, even to the fear of change and the prevalence of petty ego-centricities. And yet—in honor what can I do?" The last was a bare whisper, heard only because Hrrula was breathless, every sense alert.

Suddenly First propelled himself from his couch and paced to the window wall, flipping off the opacity and gazing sadly down at the gleaming miles of structures that marched up to the horizon itself.

"If they leave Rrala, we are not positioned to follow. Even if they leave Rrala, we shall not be able to continue the reeducation program there; not with Third and Sixth in their present fog. We are no longer programed to act quickly," First growled. "Nowadays even dire emergencies take time! However," and he spun back to his control panel, tapping out sequences with a deliberate claw ticking against the metal keys, "we can at least set all in motion—slow motion, that is," and Hrrula was unsure of whether he should have laughed in response to that or not, although First did not seem to take offense.

Then he realized that First was staring at him intently.

"There must not, young Hrrula, be any incidents of violence among the Trrans; that would certainly prejudice the uncertain. Yet, as you describe the events, Rrev has already evaded custody."

"Only to be sure that no one will be taken from the planet until Zodd returns," Hrrula added hastily.

"No matter. There can be no violence."

"And what of Zodd?" Hrrula pressed anxiously. "What will become of the cub if his people do leave without him?"

First's grizzled head came up sharply and the old Speaker looked intently into Hrrula's eyes.

"You are right, my clever stripe. It *is* a question of honor! A delicate question of honor. And on that rests our case, I believe."

First ushered Hrrula with hasty ceremony to the door,

offering his open hand to the scout, an unexpected civility from such an august personage.

"There must be no violence on Rrala among our new friends, Hrrula," First said, his voice charged with excitement. "Do nothing rash but proceed."

Hrrula found himself outside the suite, the Speaker's peculiar farewell ringing in his ears. "Do nothing rash but proceed?" Hrrula murmured. "Proceed—where?"

"This film is proof," Hrrula heard Third's truculent voice down the corridor, "that all their fine talk is windblown. They do not respect each other. They will not respect us. They are landing ships in force on Rrala."

Hrrula jumped for the transmitter pad, slapping at a random station to avoid being seen by Third. When he emerged at the Transmitter Base, deep below the sea, he was startled by that coincidence to his subconscious desire. Even as he cleared the pad and approached the floor officer, he knew where he was going. 'They are landing ships'—Third had used the plural. He had to know if that second ship was Alreldep or Codep, and since Mrrim was on duty, fortune was favoring him. Mrrim would know what to do.

Chapter XXIV

PROOF POSITIVE

▼▼▼▼▼▼▼▼▼▼▼▼▼▼▼▼▼▼▼▼▼▼▼▼▼

THERE HAD BEEN a guard stationed just off the path to the Reeves' cabin but Ken had had no trouble working his way around back. And no trouble removing the window frame from Todd's room. Fortunately, Pat had left the clean clothes in the washbasket in the hallway, so Ken had not had to risk entering his own bedroom in the front of the cabin.

He was also able to sneak around the kitchen and get himself some ration packs. Thus, warmly dressed, with a blanket thrown over his shoulder and food in his pockets, he retreated the way he had come.

If they searched the cabin again, they'd find his soaked clothes in a heap on Todd's floor. That would jar them.

He worked his way cautiously through the woods; he wanted no encounter with *roamal* vines or *ssersa* bushes. There was a rough lean-to back in the woods where they'd been logging and that would give him a night's shelter. He was exhausted when he finally made his destination and was asleep as soon as he stretched out, rolled up in his blanket.

The unmistakable thunder of rockets jerked him out of a deep sleep. He untangled himself quickly from the blanket, ripping it in an effort to get to his feet. The deep woods prevented a clear view of the sky and he charged recklessly toward the colony, desperately afraid he would see the exhaust flares of the Spacedep ship.

He had almost argued himself into the specious logic that at least he would be here when Todd got back, when he reached a clearing and saw that a ship was descending to the landing field.

He caught only a glimpse before the tree tops obscured it but he halted, sagging wearily against the nearest trunk until his heart stopped forcing adrenalin through his trembling body.

As far as he was concerned, it didn't matter if the ship was from Codep or Alreldep. Either would disrupt Landreau's nasty little plans for the colonists.

He opened a package of rations and broke the heat seal, gulping down the metallic-tasting coffee, munching the nutritional wafers, oblivious to their cardboard taste. Once again in command of his energies and emotions, Ken carefully worked his way thru the woods to the colony. He had to get within sight of the field and the Common and figure out what was happening.

Ken finally positioned himself behind a thicket on the edge of the Common, in full sight of the mess hall and the landing field. The Codep blazon was plainly visible on the second ship, a comfortingly smaller craft than the Spacedep one; it was not an obvious transport vessel.

He could smell breakfast being prepared, but the presence of guards, wearing both Spacedep blue and Codep green, was not the least bit reassuring. He could only wait, hunched up under the thickly crossed branches, passive when his nerves strained for action.

Suddenly the main door flung open and guards marched smartly down the steps, followed by Hu Shih, Phyllis and his two children. Hu Shih's profile was set, his chin high, his shoulders back, but the children were weeping. All Ken's half-allayed fears returned forcefully and, regardless of exposure, he jumped up. Lee Lawrence, one arm around Sally, came next, turning his head to look searchingly around the Common.

Ken could see the sociologist start with surprise as he caught sight of Reeve. Lawrence gestured to him to take cover, then immediately jerked his head around. But one of the guards had noticed his action and whirled toward Ken's position.

"There he is," he gave the alarm.

Ken took to his heels, knowing what he had to do now. Once they had seen him, they would delay until they caught him. So he made a plain dash up the river bank, crouching when he broke into the open because someone was already firing lasers above his head.

He took Todd's route to the village, along the river bank, leaping underbrush and fallen logs, and digging his heels into the mulch when he hit the deeper forest. He had reached the clearing where Hrrula had killed the *mda* when he heard an ear-piercing whine and saw the misty cloud appear in the center of the village site.

The mist dissipated and Hrrula appeared, clad in an ankle-length pale red robe, with jewel-studded harness at waist and across his chest, and highly polished black boots.

"I've only a moment, Rrev. Delay, but with no violence. Delay as long as you can."

"Delay?" panted Reeve, trying to regain his breath. "How? Why?"

"Our ruling Council must be unanimous and there are two rabid xenophobes in high position with much influence. Our First Speaker has some plan to force their cooperation but it will take time."

"Time, Hrrula, is the one thing I haven't got. Listen!" Ken pointed back the way he had come; the shots and shouts of his pursuers were clearly audible. "Stay, Hrrula. Prove to Spacedep and Codep that there are Hrrubans and we'll have all the time we need."

A mist was already surrounding Hrrula. Startled, the catman glanced wildly around as if this phenomenon were premature.

"Something's gone wrong. I'm being drawn back. Under the mess hall tables, Rrev, and up over Hu's—"

the last word was a bare whisper from the depths of the mist.

Christ, what's under the tables? Up over whose? Ken wondered frantically as he took off, up the clearing, kicking up mulch to show his passing. The first dip he crossed he scuffed up badly, then he cut suddenly to his left executing a wild jump over a thicket. He ran more carefully now, on his toes, although his leg muscles ached with the unaccustomed strain.

As he doubled back, he couldn't resist chuckling as his pursuers went tearing on past the dip.

With luck he could make it back to the Common before they realized they were following a dead trail.

'No violence,' huh? That was asking a lot of him—with no hope held out at all. God, but Hrrula looked magnificent in that outfit.

He crossed the river again, falling and splashing in but getting across and into the woods above the Common without being seen. He returned to his previous thicket and settled down with the problem of how to get into the mess hall and look under the table and above whose what?

He saw the searchers straggling back, infuriated by their failure. He watched the consultation on the porch between Landreau and Chaminade and wished lip reading had been one of his skills. He was certain they were discussing him. It was then that the animals began to shriek and bellow, raising such an uproar that it disturbed the conference. Reeve watched Landreau beckon a guard and send him off to locate the cause of the commotion.

Grimly Reeve spotted the source—the roiling clouds of dust from the direction of the pass to the plains. Not *urfa* this time—reptiles; and undoubtedly in the force that had panicked Eckerd yesterday. Was it only yesterday that the colonists had tried to blast closed the pass?

The guard came back and his report caused Landreau to shrug with indifference. Ken saw the guard hesitate, glance to his left and address Landreau again. The

spaceman's answer was sufficiently curt to bring the
guard snapping to attention, make a crisp about-face
and resume his position at the perimeter of the Common.

Regretting the lack of binoculars, Ken kept close
watch on the growing cloud, aware of the increasing
odor on the light morning breeze. The thin whine of a
com-unit alert penetrated the placid scene.

Landreau lifted his wrist up, his whole attitude one of
sudden alert. Lowering his arm, he addressed a few crisp
remarks to Chaminade, whose disagreement was cut
short by Landreau's peremptory gesture.

Instantly the guards quick-marched to the mess hall
and began herding out the colonists. At the same time,
Ken saw the ship's launch rise from the landing field and
head toward the ominous cloud in the valley.

Going on a reccy, Ken decided, and then wondered
why in hell the colonists were being marched away from
the Common, away from the landing field. That didn't
make much sense. Even from this distance he could hear
the frantic thud of hooves against wooden stalls, as the
now hysterical animals tried to free themselves from
their tethers.

Cautiously Ken rose to a crouch, crept sideways for an
unobstructed view of the barn. Alarm began to grow in
him as he watched the colonists herded into the corral.
A flash in the distance caught his eye. The flash was repeated, stabbing through the dust cloud.

The launch was shooting laser bolts at the snakes.
First sensible thing Landreau had done since he got
here! Ken tried to relax but his apprehension did not
dissipate. The guards now had their lasers aimed at the
colonists and were moving back from the corral. Ken
saw Lawrence waving his fist, make a move toward the
high corral fence, saw the laser bolt dig a clod of earth
right at the man's feet, saw Lawrence pull back with an
angry yell, the words indistinguishable above the commotion of the horses.

Two things Ken realized simultaneously: the lasers

were not killing the snakes, they were herding them *toward* the barn. The second was that no one was guarding the mess hall. Ken dashed toward the hall, running low and fast, leaping the railing with an agility born of desperation. As his feet hit the porch, he saw that the hall was not entirely empty. But he barged right in, clobbering one startled Codep man across the head and felling the other with a crack to the jaw.

With a fluid motion he overturned the tables nearest him, forcing his trembling hands to move slowly, searchingly across the underside. Nothing! One of the men groaned and Ken kicked him in the head with unexpected ruthlessness. He flipped over the next table. There was no way of telling at which one Hrrula had sat at that first breakfast; all had been moved many times. The third table was the jackpot. Where the center brace joined the legs, Ken felt a half-sphere. He heard the faint pop of a seal breaking as he pulled the hemisphere loose. It was the size of the first joint of his thumb, a dull brown metal covered with minute screenlike patterns. There was a small circular seam in the base which was of a softer material.

Please God let this not be made of Rralan metals, Ken prayed. He weighed it in the palm of his hand; it was heavy for its size. A frantic screaming penetrated his reflections. He glanced toward the window and saw a terrifying sight. The monstrous heads of the great snakes were all too identifiable as the creatures undulated closer and closer to the barn.

"Hide, will you, Hrrubans?" he cried at the device. "Look what's happening because you won't meet us! In honor help us!"

Whirling, he jerked the laser guns from the belts of the two unconscious Codep men. Another quick glance out the window showed him that the colonists had taken refuge in the barn itself while their guards, still firing sporadically in the dirt around the barn, were pulling back across the wide sweep of the land to the Common and the mess hall. Ken positioned himself to the side of the window and waited till the squads had drawn into sight, their tempting backs toward him.

He lobbed off several quick shots into the dust at their feet, got off another which twisted into uselessness the gun of the man nearest him. The man cried out as the overheated metal burned his hands.

"Drop your guns. Raise your hands," Ken shouted, "or the next shots get Landreau and Chaminade." Then he barked some unintelligible phrases in mock Hrruban, as if he had brought reinforcements. "The Hrrubans' weapons are heavier than ours, Landreau. Don't try anything."

A trigger-happy marine attempted to turn in the act of dropping his rifle. Ken dropped him with a bolt through his leg and no one else tried to turn.

"Okay, Landreau, let me see you order those snakes herded away from the barn. Now!"

Ken could imagine the expression on the spaceman's face, but at that moment one of the guards let out a startled howl, jabbing his hand frantically toward the barn.

The main door had been flung wide and from the barn charged every head of the stock—horses, cattle, pigs. Leading them on the bull, a pitchfork carried like an archaic lance, was Ben Adjei, his wife clinging to him on the back of their improbable mount. The guards were overrun by this unlikely cavalry before they could recover their rifles.

Ben leapt from his bull, pulling down the spaceman. Even before Ken could reach the scene, Ben was ordering the launch to turn back the reptiles or hear a laser bolt sear through their commander's skull.

In the subsequent confusion, no one immediately noticed that the homing beacon was lit; everyone was too busy helping the wounded and recapturing the stock. By the time someone did notice the beacon, an uneasy truce existed between the colonists holding hostages and the remaining crews aboard the two spaceships.

"Hey," Kate Moody cried out, returning from a trip to

her cabin for more medical supplies, "the beacon's lit—and you can already see the ship."

"It had better be Alreldep," Ken growled and suddenly remembered the Hrruban bug in his pocket.

"See this, Landreau," he held the metal object right under the spaceman's nose, although the man was still groggy from Ben's stunning leap on him. "Here's proof of the Hrrubans' existence. And watch what you say, because the whole thing's being transmitted back to them. In fact, everything, since we made first contact, has been relayed to Hrruba. And, man, just think how that makes you look."

As the spaceman thrust it away, Chaminade intercepted the object.

"Truthfully, I would like to see your allegations substantiated."

"Is that why you were so eager to agree to Landreau's scheme of having the snakes destroy us?" Lee Lawrence demanded. His head was bandaged but the arm that cradled a laser rifle was steady on the hostages.

"An extraordinary situation requires extraordinary measures," Chaminade replied in a bland voice.

"The appropriate measures were laid down close to two centuries ago," Hu Shih remarked in a crisp stern voice, cutting through Lawrence's outraged roar. "We followed them when we asked for transport which was denied us. We filed reports which were disbelieved. *You*," and he pointed at Chaminade, "and you," he swung on Landreau, "have complicated a very simple incident and you shall not escape its consequences."

"It's an Alreldep ship," someone yelled from the porch.

Ken activated the com-unit.

"Doona colony calling Alreldep ship. Come in."

"Sumitral speaking. What has been happening there? What's that armed launch doing? Where is Shih? Why are Codep and Spacedep ships reporting a state of siege? They have no jurisdiction here."

"This is Shih, Admiral Sumitral. An unusual situation has developed . . ."

"You're damned right it has. Any of the aliens in hearing distance?"

"I only wish they were, sir," Hu Shih replied fervently and then saw Ken gesturing wildly to the bug Chaminade still held. "I mean . . ."

"If you've driven them from Doona, we've lost the chance of a lifetime." Sumitral's voice, charged with angry frustration, was cut off by the fury of retro-blasts.

Ken reached over and flipped off the unit to lessen the echoed roar. He took the little recorder button from Chaminade's hand.

"You got here too late, Sumitral," he murmured. "Too late."

"What do you mean?" Lee asked.

"All the sound and fury is what I mean," Ken replied, waving at the sullen marines. "When I tried my delaying tactics earlier today, I got to the village just as Hrrula appeared. He started to tell me what was delaying their return; they've got troubles with their own government. He managed to warn me about avoiding violence of any kind, then he started to get yanked back and told me about the bugs in the mess hall."

"Yanked back? How?" demanded Landreau, suddenly alert. "Where'd you say he was? In that village of yours?"

"They use matter transmitters," Ken told him.

"Matter transmitters?" Landreau turned pale under his tan. "Then they are much more advanced than we are," he groaned.

"You're damned right they are," a new voice agreed. A tall thin man, elegantly attired in deep maroon coveralls with the diamond-sand stripes of an admiral, stood in the doorway an instant before striding purposefully across to them. "Landreau! Chaminade," he jerked his head with scant courtesy at the two men, his keen brown eyes falling at last on Shih. "Hu Shih? Now, where are those Hrrubans?"

"Well, it sure is a relief to hear someone admit they exist," Ken remarked sardonically.

"Of course they exist. Who're you? Reeve? We've found traces of their explorations on half a dozen planets. Just missed them on 87-SN-24C. You remember that incident, Landreau, yours was the Phase I Ship."

Again Landreau blanched, sinking back against the table.

"But there were burn-off marks, traces of chemical deeply imbedded in the soil. No matter transmitters . . ."

"You got to get *to* a place to install a receiver," Ken said and was rewarded by Landreau's groan as the spaceman buried his head in his hands. "What I don't understand, Admiral, is why, if you knew the Hrrubans existed, you wasted such a helluva long time getting here?"

Sumitral blinked at such open criticism.

"A confrontation of such importance to the future of our Amalgamated Worlds is not made without thoughtful preparation," he answered. "I've spent hours in a sleep tank, learning Hrruban. Those tapes you people sent were excellent, by the way. My compliments. Now," and steely authority entered his voice, "kindly take me to the Hrrubans."

"I wish I could," Ken replied sadly, tossing the bug button to Sumitral. "Our—friends here," he gestured at Landreau and Chaminade, "never took our reports seriously because we couldn't show them any *proof*. In their efforts to change our minds for us, things got a little rough. I have it on good authority the Hrrubans don't take kindly to shows of violence so I don't think we'll be seeing much of . . ."

"HEY, DAD!" The volume as well as the cry was heart-stoppingly familiar.

Ken whirled. There was a rapid thud of racing feet and then Todd, improbably dressed in *mda* fur, rope tail jerking behind him, came charging into the hall.

"TODD!" Pat shrieked, racing for her child.

"Hey, mom. Hey! Lemme go. DAD, I brought some-one who wants to see you!"

Ken had taken one step forward in Todd's direction before he halted, staring at the imposing figure framed in the doorway.

Face-fur grizzled to white, mane hair long and very dark, the Hrruban appeared to tower above the tallest man in the hall. His brilliant green eyes, slowly moving from face to face, were oddly gentle and very search-ing, as if they had long since penetrated life's ironies and weird humors. The glowing ivory of his robes which fell in ornate folds to his booted feet, were dappled with the flashing colors of the brilliant green and red stones in his jeweled harness. It was the Hrruban's inner maj-esty, rather than the sumptuous richness of his dress, that evoked the reverent bows which acknowledged his entrance. As he approached Ken, Todd's small hand tugged at his father's.

"Dad, that's Hrruna." Todd's idea of a whisper pene-trated to the hushed spectators on the porch. "He's First Speaker and that's as high as you can get on Hrruba. He brought me home so I wouldn't have to break my prom-ise to Hrrula. That means we don't have to leave Rrala —I mean, Doona!" And Todd smiled trustingly up at his father.

Ken swallowed hard as he realized the First Speaker's gaze had settled on him.

"Gracious noble sir," Todd said in stentorious tones, "may I be permitted to introduce my father, Rrev." And he bowed very low, craning his head back toward his fa-ther as he remained stooped. "You gotta be awful care-ful to speak right to him, Dad. He's real important! Just *look* at him."

"I will also listen very hard to him," Ken murmured, under his breath.

"We better," Todd agreed, straightening up as Hrruna nodded.

Out on the Common, someone began to cheer. Ken distinctly heard Terran voices calling out Hrruban greetings. Todd broke the tableau and rushed to the window. "Hey, here comes Hrrula and Hrrestan! And lots of other guys!" he crowed and made for the door.

A single quiet trill from Hrruna brought him up sharp. He flushed, murmured an apology, bobbed a bow and then returned to his father's side.

"Gracious First Speaker," purred a smooth voice in reasonably accurate Hrruban at Ken's side.

Admiral Sumitral stepped forward, palm open and outstretched toward Hrruna.

"We of Terra are immensely honored by your presence in this humble hall. I am called Sumitral . . ."

"He won't shake hands, sir," Todd hastily warned, his eyes a little scared. "It's not done to him."

Ken admired the way Sumitral was able to keep right on smiling at Hrruna as he casually changed his gesture from a proffered handshake to one directing Hrruna toward the alcove which Hu Shih used as office.

"Clear the hall, Reeve," he muttered as he turned.

Hrruna, inclining his head graciously in acceptance, beckoned Todd to him, laying a dark brown hand lightly on his shoulder. "Will you be my messenger, please, and request Hrrestan and that young stripe, Hrrula, to join us?"

As Todd ran off, very solemn, Hrruna gestured Ken and Hu Shih over. Ken could see that Sumitral was not at all happy that they had been included among the select group in the alcove, but the Alreldep official was too good a politician to countermand Hrruna's express invitation.

Ken's mind raced frantically, trying to understand why Hrruna had incredibly appeared on Rrala, with his son in tow. If Hrruna was First Speaker and the most important man on Hrruba, what in hell was he doing walking into the disputed, discredited, all but disbanded colony? Had the differences been settled? Was it customary for their first citizen to announce such decisions? Ken could understand only that something unforeseen had occurred; something unprecedented in such a highly stylized culture as the Hrrubans. Could it be turned to advantage? To *mutual* advantage?

Hrruna was settling himself gracefully in Hu Shih's swivel chair, automatically compensating for its nimble action.

"It is with deep regret that I find myself unable to reply in your language, noble Sumitral," Hrruna was saying. Sumitral bowed, but a slight flexing of Hrruna's finger stilled ready diplomatic reassurances. "I come only as an escort for young Zodd, to be sure he returned safely to his people."

Ken stared at Hrruna, aware of a slight frown on the Admiral's face, relieved that the diplomat must have caught the significance.

"With your permission, noble sir." Sumitral turned to Ken. "Did I understand correctly what he just said?"

"That he only came to escort Todd through the forest. That's what he said."

"I didn't understand but two words."

Ken blinked; tried to rephrase Hrruna's words in Hrruban, only to come up with an entirely different sounding phrase. Hu Shih leaned over to the two men.

"He's using different inflections but I understood what he said and what he means. This is a *purely social* visit."

Ken licked his lips and anxiously glanced toward the door. Lawrence had cleared the hall but there was too much congestion on the porch to see the Common. Suddenly Lawrence stepped aside and Todd squeezed through, imperiously beckoning someone to follow.

Hrrula appeared, still gorgeously clad in red, although now Ken realized how much richer Hrruna's finery was. Hrrestan followed closely and it was obvious both had been running hard. Hrrula hung back a little for Hrrestan to precede him. Both bowed with precision to Hrruna, made shallower bows to Sumitral, Ken and Shih.

"I suspect your deep maroon is a fortuitous choice for Alreldep, Admiral," Ken murmured under his breath.

Sumitral raised his eyebrows slightly and opened his mouth to speak.

"Dad," Todd's stage whisper was audible to the Common, "Hrrula says *I've* got to do the talking to Hrruna." Todd hurried forward, glancing apprehensively up at Sumitral, flinching at the admiral's expression. "You can't sit either. He'll be thirsty. He isn't used to walking so far," he added as an afterthought, and then asked Hrruna if the gracious noble sir would like some refreshment.

Ken fumbled in the kitchen cabinets, came across a glass goblet that Mace McKee had blown as an experiment that winter. He put it on the nearest tray, added a pack of coffee, some chilled *urfa* milk and ice water in a pitcher. Hrruna smiled his gratitude and murmured a question to Todd, who was curiously at ease with Hrruna despite his formality.

"This is the cold milk of the *urfa* beast of Rrala, gracious noble sir," Todd said clearly and Ken suddenly realized that the boy was using the same unusual pitches that Hrruna had employed. "This is very cold water and this is a drink from our home world which is hot but everyone drinks it often. I'm too young."

At that moment there was the sound of heavy boots thudding up the porch steps. Ken caught sight of half a dozen Hrrubans filing quickly into the mess hall with the unmistakable dispatch of trained soldiers.

Hrruna looked up calmly, nodded and gestured them to keep their distance before he smiled with great affection on Todd.

Todd's eyes were wide and he gulped before he spoke. "I think Mr. McKee made the cup. He's very clever."

"McKee's sapphire," Ken whispered, his voice carrying to Shih and Sumitral. "I've a feeling a gift of value is indicated."

"Can we leave here, though?" Shih asked and then inhaled sharply.

Ken turned to see Todd raise the goblet of *urfa* milk to his own lips. He then carefully wiped the lip mark from the goblet edge, rotating it before he presented it with a respectful bow to the First Speaker. When the man accepted it, Ken and Shih both let their breaths out with relief.

"Who in hell taught the kid all that protocol?" Sumitral's muted voice reached Ken's ears.

Ken rolled his eyes toward Hrrestan and Hrrula. They both wore expressions of intense interest and deep amusement.

"The *urfa* milk is very refreshing. A new taste for an old mouth," Hrruna remarked, smiling benignly around. "There is much of value on this beautiful planet, is there not?"

"Most gracious First Speaker," Ken began, trying to remember the pitches which Todd had used, "may I be permitted to withdraw? There is another example of Rralan riches which you might like to examine."

Hrruna graciously dismissed him and, with a second nod, indicated Hrrula might join him.

Ken could barely wait to get the Hrruban out of earshot but he had to wait until they had passed the obvious bodyguards, poised unmoving around the hall, before he felt it safe to speak.

"What has been happening?" he asked in Hrruban.

"Too much," Hrrula answered in easy Terran, "but do you mean to get the big blue stone of Mace? Blue is very prized on Hrruba."

Ken looked around for Chaminade, somewhat bewildered to find that the Common was also crowded with Hrrubans soldiers.

"Where'd they all come from?"

Hrrula hissed out his chuckle. "Something like this has never happened. I cautioned you against violence. No, I understand it was impossible to avoid it with a man like Landreau, but the instant it was reported to the Speakers, all hope of an alliance was lost. Then the messenger arrived, saying you had called out in Hrruban that we were in honor bound to help you. Zodd started to cry that he wanted to go home. Hrruna remarked quietly that this was no longer a time to hide cowardly: honor was at stake. He took Zodd by the hand and left—with all the Speakers staring after him. He had himself transmitted back to the village before anyone knew what he was about to do." Hrrula wheezed in another paroxysm of laughter. "Hrrestan and I leaped after him, vowing to protect him with our lives; the bodyguard was right behind us but got lost in the forest and all this is being seen throughout Hrruba right now."

Ken spied Chaminade as Hrrula talked, and beckoned him over, deriving a small satisfaction as the fat figure waddled obediently to his summons.

"Remember that sapphire someone snitched from McKee? I want it *now*, Chaminade, for the Hrruban leader."

The little eyes narrowed speculatively. "It does belong to the Hrrubans, I guess," the Codep man agreed and snapped an order to his wrist unit. "Those bare-chested catmen are armed, Reeve," he remarked, looking Hrrula directly in the eye.

"We are protecting our First Speaker from you barbarians," Hrrula replied in his fluent but oddly accented Terran.

Suddenly Ken realized that Hrrula accented the wrong Terran syllables at times and retained his own pitched inflections. If you missed his first words you missed most of the sentence.

"Let me explain quickly, Rrev. Zodd must remain by Hrruna. No talk of treaty or anything, for this is a social visit," and Hrrula wheezed briefly. "Zodd has been trained in the protocol of formal Hrruban and, since every circuit on Hrruba is turned onto this scene, our people must receive the best possible impression of yours. It can still reverse opinion in *our* favor!"

"But a kid—" Chaminade protested.

"Already that Sumitral has made several errors—understandable, because no one in our village used the formal tones, but few on our planet will make that allowance. They will only see discourtesy toward our First Speaker. I agree it is wonderful that Sumitral tries to speak Hrruban but he does not speak well enough yet."

"From the mouths of babes," Chaminade sighed.

Unexpectedly Hrrula grinned. "It is a saying on our world that if one wishes to hear the truth, let him ask a child. That child of yours may deliver us this planet. He is the best advocate you possess. However, while we have the view-screen coverage we have tried so often to secure, let us use every argument. I saw only part of that unfortunate stampede. Was the black hrrss injured? Very good. Please will you ask Ben to bring him and the pretty red mare here, saddled and ready to be ridden. They are an important argument because on our worlds we have sacrified every living species but our own. Now it is regretted."

Ken called Bill Moody over and gave him the message just as the guard brought the jewel which Chaminade immediately passed to Ken.

"Be sure to give the jewel to Zodd," Hrrula whispered as they re-entered the hall.

"Sumitral is going to hate talking through Todd."

"Is not expediency a diplomatic thorn on Terra?" inquired Hrrula mockingly.

Ken awarded him a long look before he followed his example and bowed low as they re-approached the First Speaker. Sumitral was evidently relieved by their reappearance.

"Todd," Ken began in low-voiced Hrruban, "would you present this properly to the gracious noble First Speaker? Say it is a poor example of what else is to be found on Rrala."

Todd grinned broadly at his father as he took the sapphire. He bowed very low to the First Speaker to gain his attention, then carefully folded back the cloth in which the stone had been wrapped, presenting the gleaming jewel on both hands.

"Oh, noble sir, my father asks that you accept what is humbly offered."

With an exclamation of unfeigned delight, Hrruna held the sapphire up so that the sunlight caught in the facets which Mace had skillfully cut into the huge blue stone. It was not of a perfect water, having a tiny flaw which cutting did not entirely excise, but it was a brilliant color.

"This is much prized by us. Old eyes hunger for blues," Hrruna said to the beaming child. "Truly Rrala has many hidden riches."

Why, the old showman, Ken thought, he wants his people to stay on Rrala.

"Rrala is good for things from Terra too," Todd remarked, suddenly peering excitedly outside.

"Indeed?"

"See? Hrrses!" and Todd pointed just as Ben, leading the black stallion, disappeared around the corner of the hall.

"Gracious First Speaker," Hrrestan interjected, bowing deeply, "you once expressed a deep interest in the animals which the Terrans brought with them."

"They are perhaps nearby?"

"They await your inspection at the door, gracious noble sir."

Hrruna rose with an alacrity that displayed his keen interest.

Hrrula quickly stepped to one side, gesturing Todd to fall directly in behind the old Hrruban.

"Every time I try to talk, either Todd or the other old one shuts me up," Sumitral complained in a low voice. "Why?"

Thank God for a reasonable man, Ken thought gratefully. "He's been taught their formal speech. You've already insulted Hrruna by using vulgar Hrruban—not your fault, just their crazy customs. Hrrula says everything's being beamed back and their whole world is watching."

Sumitral paled, swallowed hard.

"Then I can't get him to talk any treaty?"

"Uhuh. This whole thing is completely unexpected, unprecedented and incredible. Hrruna *wants* an alliance and he took this tremendous chance to force publicity. We've got to make sure it's all good!"

Sumitral's mouth formed an 'o' of surprised shock but he had recovered himself as they stepped out onto the porch and watched Ben and Hrrula display the horses' paces. Hrrula, on the stallion, was grinning like a fool and taking extraordinary chances.

By the time the exhibition was over, the sun was lowering in the west. The First Speaker gestured to one of the Hrruban guards who nodded solemnly and barked orders in a staccato howl. Hrruna turned to the Terrans, inclining his head in an expression of deep regret.

"I have too long absented myself from the duties of my office, gentle friends. I must take my leave. My thanks for the courtesies of refreshment, and entertainment, and for this beautiful product of a lovely world." He held up the sapphire which scintillated in the afternoon sun. Politely his eyes lingered briefly on each face. Ken was sure the man was amused and pleased with the outcome of his outrageous visit. But he was already sweeping down the Common with Todd his obedient shadow. Hrrestan signaled Hrrula peremptorily to leave the stallion. Ken hurried after them, but before he could catch up, the Hrruban guards cut him off politely but firmly.

"What's going to happen now?" Sumitral exclaimed, joining him.

"Maybe Todd will know."

They watched, frustrated at the enforced passivity, as Todd stepped out of the procession at the bridge. The First Speaker and his guards crossed over. They saw him step onto a metallic grid that had been placed on the far side of the river at some point in the afternoon. A misty envelope hid him and then dispersed, leaving the bare grid.

"So that's their matter transmitter," Sumitral murmured.

"And that's how they removed the village so quickly. I'll bet their whole site is laid out on a huge grid."

"Think of the economy of such a system, let alone the convenience."

Four guards removed corner posts and rolled up the grid. Then the whole column, Hrrestan and Hrrula in its van, marched off into the forest, Toddy waving sadly after the disappearing backs.

Chapter XXV

VIGIL

▼▼▼▼▼▼▼▼▼▼▼▼▼▼▼▼▼▼▼▼▼▼▼

"And still we don't know to go or stay," Lee Lawrence remarked with a wry grin.

The weary, confused colonists had asked the three departmental representatives to a meeting on the Common. It had been decided not to remove any of the Hrruban devices although most had been located. It seemed wiser, however, to hold the meeting on a 'blind' spot.

"The Hrrubans are technically the owners of this planet," Sumitral pointed out, "until we can assume, by their continued absence, that they have abdicated their rights. In either case, an apology is owed these fine people," and he gestured to the colonists, "for the discourtesies, inconveniences and insults they have suffered." He glared at Landreau and Chaminade. "They have earned their right to remain on Rrala."

"Yes, indeed," Chaminade agreed easily, staring pointedly at Landreau.

The spaceman rose, his manner truculent. "There were neither reptiles nor aliens when I landed here."

"Indubitably. According to Hrrestan, they are deep-sea creatures," Dautrish put in. "They were quiescent at the time of the two surveys. And we know now that the Hrrubans are only in residence during the warmer seasons."

Landreau shrugged and sat down again but Ken hoped they would never require favors of Spacedep.

"However, if the Hrrubans release Doona," Chaminade clung stubbornly to Terran nomenclature, "to *my* colonists, they are under Codep authority," and he had the gall to smile.

Sumitral's objection was indignant. "On the contrary. These people have made a fine, favorable contract with a highly civilized, technically advanced species. They have learned not only the language but its rigid and complex protocol." He glanced briefly at Ken. "There is every chance that although the Hrrubans withdraw from Rrala now, events may bring them back at a later date. We have overlapped too often in our mutual space explorations. Some agreement, now or later, will eventually come to pass. Therefore Rrala, by edict of the Congress of the Amalgamated Worlds—check it if you must, Chaminade—is under Alreldep aegis."

"Now wait a moment, Sumitral," Landreau began belligerently. "Alreldep handles *alien* relations, but Spacedep handles defense and . . ."

"Shut up, Landreau," Ken snapped, rising. "We'd've been at a treaty stage if you hadn't acted like a horse's ass with your snake drive . . ."

"See here, Reeve," and Landreau advanced menacingly.

"That's enough," Sumitral bellowed, staring the spaceman down. "And frankly, Landreau, if I thought we weren't in danger of being observed, I'd let Reeve take you apart. But get this: *defense* is not indicated, a difficult distinction for your space boys to make. The Hrrubans aren't the cotopoids of Lyrae or the plague carriers of Zeta Algeiba. And they're not Siwannese either. We've still got a chance to form a mutual coexistence pact with the Hrrubans and I will do everything in my power, including the use of a six-year-old boy as my chief of protocol, if that can be achieved."

Sumitral looked a little startled when the colonists, led by Ken, began to cheer him.

"My chief informed me—before he went to bed," Sumitral continued with dry good humor, "that we'll know tomorrow. That boy's remarkable, Reeve, and I regret I had to monopolize him when he's been away from you so long, but he was able to give me some valuable insight into Hrruban thinking. However, since their civilization makes full use of mass communications, we can assume that a popular vote can be computed overnight. *If* a popular vote was forced by the First Speaker's superb strategy of this afternoon.

"Now I'm for bed. I'm an optimist by nature and I want to be ready for tomorrow's demands."

He departed, adroitly taking Landreau and Chaminade with him back to their respective ships.

"How'd we ever turn up lucky with Sumitral?" Lawrence asked.

"Third time?" Ken tendered.

"No," Hu Shih answered. "I know his reputation. He is a shrewd man but an opportunist. Our circumstances give him an unparalleled chance for promotion into the Executive Echelons—if he can bring off a treaty with the Hrrubans. He may not *like* the expedients but he is clever enough to use them. However," and Hu Shih's unexpected cynicism dissolved into a more characteristic smile, "he is forced to be as candid as a child and *that* is to our advantage—and Hrruba's."

"I'm so tired, Ken," Pat whispered plaintively. "They kept us up all night last night."

"I didn't sleep much myself, hon," he replied, "and if our shrewd admiral is seeking the sack, so will I." He slipped an arm around her and, bidding the others good night, led her off toward their cabin.

"Ken," she murmured as they passed Todd's mourner's bench, "what will Toddy do if the Hrrubans leave us?"

"Rrala wouldn't be the same, would it," he mused, glancing back to the Commons. "But Todd's done more than any of us to prevent their leaving. And he may well have pulled it off."

"What do you mean?"

Ken was so tired the words did not come easily to his tongue. He half pushed, half dragged her to their room, sinking wearily to the edge of the bed.

"Nothing's more appealing than a cute kid and that crazy rope tail of Todd's—" he stopped to yawn. Pat was fumbling with her shoes and stretched out with a groan. He forgot what he'd been trying to explain and lay back, pulled both legs up onto the bed and was asleep.

"Daddy—Dad. Hey, dad, wake up. Dad!"

"Huh?"

Even that monosyllable took tremendous effort. Ken's mind seemed to grasp that someone wanted him awake, but his body could not be convinced of the urgency.

"*Dad!*"

The sound was accompanied by the touch of a small hand, warm where it rested on his chilled shoulder in an effort to move his rebellious body.

"DAD!"

Ken's eyes flew open. Todd's anxious face swam into focus. Ken could still only blink and wish the hell that Todd would leave him alone.

Surprisingly, that was just what Todd did. The reprieve, however, didn't last long. This time Todd brought coffee and the smell was the necessary catalyst.

Groaning because his muscles were slow to function, Ken swung his legs over the side of the bed. The lower part of him was warm, the upper frigid. Then he realized that both he and Pat had fallen asleep fully dressed on top of the covers. He gestured to Todd to pull the blanket over Pat. Then he saw that Todd was fully dressed and in his best coverall, over which he wore his *mda* fur vest, a Hrruban belt with modestly carved knife dangling down and, of course, a rope tail. A new piece of rope, with the frayed end fluffy and neatly tied off to prevent further raveling.

"Are the Hrrubans back, Todd?" he croaked.

Todd's face took on a closed look and suddenly Ken understood.

"I'll dress, son, and we'll go wait at the bridge together."

The look in Todd's eyes made Ken feel nineteen feet tall. The lump in his throat prevented him from saying anything until he'd melted it with coffee.

"Make me some more, huh? And grab up some food. We'll need our energy today."

Dawn was just tinting the sky a pale green, Ken noted ruefully as Todd skipped ahead of him down to the bridge. Well, if the First Speaker of Hrruba would see that Todd kept his promise, he could lose a little sleep to do the same. Unbidden, Pat's words leapt to mind. 'What will Todd do if they leave us?' Ken felt chilled with more than cool morning air.

He had thought to bring a blanket and they wrapped that around them, sipping their coffee, eating stale bread and cold *mda* steak in a companionable silence.

"How'd you get to learn the formal language so well, Toddy?" Ken asked at length.

"Oh," Todd scrunched his face up expressively, "Hrrula told me I had to. Hrriss helped. So did Mrrva," and he giggled. "She'n' Hrrestan took turns pretending they were very broad Stripes. And then some always turned up at the flat. Dad, they have aisles and corridors like ours only they call 'em 'narrow trails' and 'wide trails.' Then Hrral—remember the old white-face in the village—well, Hrriss told me he's way high in govment. He'd come and make me talk and talk. Me and Hrriss didn't get that much time to play but I didn't mind—too much. We'll have all summer to play. Hrrula promised."

Fervently Ken hoped that promise would be kept.

"Toddy, sometimes adults aren't able to keep promises, no matter how hard they try or how much they want to."

Todd let his bread drop back into his lap, staring at his father with penetrating accusation.

"I know I did everything right. Hrruna told me I did and he used village talk. He said I remembered everything. And that it'd be all right!"

Fleetingly Ken thanked the First Speaker for his kindness. How could he tell Todd that Hrruna, too, might have to break his word?

"Son, you did so well everyone in this colony is bursting with pride. And the admiral called you his chief of protocol . . ." Ken couldn't continue.

"We're staying on Rrala, aren't we, dad? Aren't we?"

"Yes, Todd," Ken had to agree, looking away from him, down at the rushing river, "Yes, we're staying on Rrala." He made his mind blank so he would not communicate his fears to the child.

The sun came up over the edge of the pass, slanting down into the valley, touching the exclamatory shafts of the three ships before lighting the lower colony buildings. Animal noises drifted up to them. The lights in Ben's cabin came on. They watched as the veterinary made his way into the barn to milk the cows and grain the stock. The lights in Hu Shih's house lit too, but the rest of the cabins were dark, inert. Ken envied them their respite, yet he would not have traded this vigil with his son for anything.

The decision to be made on Doona, Ken decided as his mind refused to ignore its uppermost concerns, was more than the justification of the colonists' reports of the Hrrubans or which department had jurisdiction over their futures; or whether the colonists could pursue their interrupted dreams. It was more important than the terms written into any treaty, more than a symbolic expiation of the terrible Siwannah tragedy. Yet it was all of these and more. And it was two small boys of different races, listening very hard to each other's words, and wanting to grow up together on a world with plenty of space to run and shout in. Mutual coexistence already existed on Rrala—between Hrriss and Todd.

Suddenly Todd's body stiffened, his head jerked over his shoulder. Ken was sure he saw the boy's ears twitch. They were both on their feet, both eager for the sight of tall, tailed figures on the ridge.

There are too many of them, was Ken's first thought.

It's the guard come back. And he caught Todd by the shoulders for fear the boy would run forward to disappointment.

"It's all right, Dad. It's all right," Todd screamed. "They've got the grid with them. See. Lots and lots of grid!"

Chapter XXVI

TUMULT AND SHOUTING

▼▼▼▼▼▼▼▼▼▼▼▼▼▼▼▼▼▼▼▼▼▼▼

WHEN THEY TRIED to recapture the events of Decision Day, none of the participants had any coherent recollection. However, as the proceedings were fully taped by both Hrrubans and Terrans, the sequence was not distorted. And everyone had curious fragments that remained personally vivid.

Ken remembered receiving innumerable cups of coffee and being unable to drink one. He remembered finding and losing Todd a dozen times, exhausting all patience but managing somehow to produce Todd as needed. For the boy had to do a great deal of interpreting at first.

Pat recalled being yanked out of bed by her exultant husband, the only detail she grasped from his garbled phrases being that the Hrrubans were back and it looked as if they'd stay. The next thing she remembered was Mrrva arriving, almost unrecognizable in filmy jewel-dusted robes, a retinue of purring Hrruban women in her wake. She had acquired a startling fluency in Terran overnight—at least that's what it seemed like to Pat—as she outlined the day's incredible schedule and asked Pat's assistance.

"Then I cooked for *fourteen* solid hours," Pat would sum up the remainder of her day. Ken would grin indulgently.

If Todd were in the room, he would wrinkle his nose at her and twitch his ears—a habit which was beginning to pall on his parents—and remark with utter disgust, "I didn't get to play all day long! I had to *talk!*"

Hrriss would counter, "Well, I had to stand *without* talking."

"As for myself, I was glad to be silent for I had talked myself hoarse the night before," Hrrula said, grinning at Ken.

"All in a good cause," his friend would agree.

Even as the Hrruban technicians crossed the bridge with the grid panels, Ken had sent Todd to blow the air whistle. As the Hrrubans passed him, they peered at Ken with a mixture of curiosity and interest but there was no doubt of their underlying excitement. Their leader was a tall dark-maned female who told Ken in faltering Terran that her name was Mrrim. She immediately lapsed into middle Hrruban.

Mrrim offered him a tape, printed on the watery blue plastic film which Ken later realized was used for all governmental declarations, sealed with many odd designs which were the official signatures of the various participating or endorsing Speakers. Mrrim spoke Hrruban slowly, her eyes on his, and Ken understood that the Hrrubans wished to set up a grid installation on the Common near the mess hall for a meeting to be held several hours hence—*after* (and Todd arrived in time to translate) very important details had been satisfactorily completed. As soon as the grid was in place, other officials and dignitaries would arrive to direct preparations. Therefore, would the noble Rrev assist her, Mrrim, to complete her assigned task speedily?

Now Hu Shih came running across the Common, followed by Ben and Lee. The air whistle's shattering summons had also roused the three ships and a land vehicle raced up from the field, necessitating more explanations and delays while Mrrim waited with growing impatience. In the back of his mind, Ken swore that whatever government existed on Rrala, it would stay small enough to be manageable. However, while Ken was trying to explain matters to the Alreldep messenger, Lee and Mrrim locked glances. With a jerk of his head, Lee indicated that Mrrim should follow him. By the time the Alreldep messenger had returned with the clearance for the installation, it was already completed and misty with the first scheduled transmission.

From then on, Hrrubans poured into the Common: soldiers first, carrying supplies and flags and bales, their side arms secured at the back of their belts. Shih adroitly ordered all Terran marines to do likewise.

Hrrula arrived with the first contingent and quickly separated Ken and Shih for a hurried conference. Ken noticed that Hrrula's eyes were enlarged and that he had difficulty controlling his tail. He didn't know then that Hrrula had been up all night organizing this meeting.

"The popular vote favored the resumption of the Rralan project—for the time being and subject to review," Hrrula told them, purring as he talked. He kept lapsing into Hrruban but Ken and Shih were able to follow him. "Oh, that Zodd!" he exclaimed fervently. "He did the trick with that rope tail. No one could fail to see the compliment of imitation. And his manners were perfect. 'Just like a well-brought up cub,'" and Hrrula mimicked some high quavering voice, his eyes gleaming wickedly. "You can just imagine the panic when the rest of the Speakers realized where First had gone with Zodd. Ha! Well, Third did exactly as First hoped he would when he threw the circuits wide open on Rrala and pre-empted all communication channels.

"Then we shall be permitted to stay?" Shih asked, adding when Hrrula nodded, "Then our problems are over."

"Oh, no," the others disagreed in chorus, "they've just started." But no one appeared to object to the challenge.

"Now," Hrrula began again, briskly, "these are the things which must be accomplished before the meeting can start, and these are the details which must be observed." He pulled out two tapes. When he had finished them, the colonists were apprehensive.

"Sumitral's not going to like that at all," Shih remarked slowly.

"He will have to," Hrrula replied with a shrug. "True, we never meant for Zodd to be burdened with such responsibility when we taught him high formal Hrruban. And true, it would not take long to instruct Sumitral in the proper usage, but we have no time. We must catch the interest of the people now, with yesterday's scene fresh in their minds, or suffer endless, ridiculous delays. Believe me, never has any major decision been made with such speed before. Middle Hrruban can be used among us," Hrrula indicated the crowd of Hrrubans busy in the Common, "but not to our highest officials at such an important table. Zodd is the only one who can cope with the necessary language tonalities."

"I think Sumitral's reconciled to Todd," Ken said thoughtfully. "He hasn't got any choice."

"No, he hasn't," Hrrula agreed drily. "I have a child's ceremonial dress for Zodd to wear. It's a shame to take him out of the *mda* fur and the tail but it is expedient."

"If you promise Todd Hrriss, he'll move mountains."

"He has. He moved the High Council here. Now, do you men have more formal clothes than these?" Hrrula asked, indicating their utilitarian coveralls.

"I believe there are sufficient Alreldep uniforms for most of the men," Sumitral remarked, joining their conference. "Will that suffice?"

"Red is an excellent choice," Hrrula said. "Now, to save time, Admiral, may I continue? Someone can bring you up to date on the background. Now these are the things you must *not* do." The list was, as Sumitral agreed readily, not inconsonant with the highly circumscribed Hrruban culture.

"But a damned bore and time-waster," Ken added with an apologetic nod to Hrrula.

"We shall dispense with that here on Rrala, but remember, Rrev, there is much time to be passed and accounted for on Hrruba. Ceremony helps."

"Coming directly to the nub of the matter, Hrrula," Sumitral broke in crisply, "just what can we expect as terms of the treaty?"

Hrrula's face and tail were still. "I do not know. My people need time to think beyond themselves. We considered ourselves to be unique in the galaxy, you realize. Time is needed for them to learn to accept the startling concept of a race their equals—if not their superiors—to grow used to the sight of your bareskins, to understand that their comfortable apathy is not threatened, but enriched."

Sumitral gazed thoughtfully around, pursing his lips slightly and rocking back and forth on the balls of his feet. If he had a tail, Ken thought irrelevantly, it'd be a-twitch.

"Do not press for any commitment that robs both our races of time to adjust. The rest will follow when the time is ripe for further change."

Sumitral nodded slowly.

"You do realize, Admiral," Hrrula went on gravely, "that you must speak through Zodd as he is the only one of you who can handle formal Hrruban."

Sumitral raised his eyes skyward, shaking his head ruefully.

"Yes, I got that message loud and clear yesterday, but I somehow feel that that will improve the Treaty rather than hamper it. 'Out of the mouths of babes,' you know! By the way, that's going to be quite a strain on young Todd, Reeve. Is he up to it?"

"Just threaten him with no Hrriss," Ken suggested and was suddenly conscious that he hadn't seen Todd lately. "Hrrula, Hrriss hasn't sneaked in, has he?"

"Probably. Anyone who understands Terran was ordered here."

By the time Todd and Hrriss were located, in the hayloft of the barn, Ken was ready to threaten Todd with a good deal more than the lack of Hrriss's company. For the Council was all set to convene and here was Todd, filthy with hay dust. He was unceremoniously dumped in the horse trough, roughly washed clean, and jerked into the pale red robes that had been supplied. He was scared and sullen by the time Ken manhandled him to the Common in time to see the Council arrive.

Soldiers from each race were interspersed at parade rest around the Common, brilliant with flags and banners. On one side the mass of Hrruban workers were now ranged; on the other, the Terrans and the original Hrruban villagers. The day was brilliant and clear, the air heady with the sweet smells of spring and cooking, and electric with excitement. The huge grid was wreathed with the familiar transmission mist. Solid forms coalesced within the mist, which suddenly dissipated. On the rectangle of the grid appeared an assembly as awe-inspiring as the most pagan heart could wish.

Centered on the rich pale blue rug which covered the metallic mesh was a magnificently carved table of a gleaming silvery wood. In equally ornate chairs sat seven male Hrrubans, dark-furred and heavily maned with age, their face hair grizzled. On their shoulders were clasped jeweled neckpieces holding colored capes in place. From the waist down they were clad in the long kilts of the Stripes, each man wearing a different shade. Regal they were as they appeared enthroned on their side of the gleaming table. Seven empty chairs faced them, each one as beautifully contrived as those occupied.

"God, you guys set quite a scene," Ken whispered to Hrrula. "The natives are awed."

"Which ones?" retorted Hrrula in a soft purr.

"Who's Third?" Sumitral whispered as he glanced down the row of Speakers.

"Second from left, by Hrruna, and he's scared. See his tail?" Hrrula replied.

Ken grimaced because he couldn't see from where he stood without bending, which he couldn't do. Todd's hand twitched in his and Ken suppressed the inclination

to squeeze it admonitorily. The kid would have enough
to contend with today.

At that moment the Hrruban herald called the meeting to order and, as rehearsed, the Terran delegates took
their places in front of their chairs: Lawrence, Landreau, Shih, Chaminade, Sumitral, Todd and Ken.
Hrrula stood beside Todd, Hrrestan by Shih, for they
would act as auxiliary interpreters. Todd, however, was
the only one who could address the Hrruban Speakers.
He seemed to know the Hrruban directly opposite him
at the table, and even to Ken the man looked slightly familiar. Todd tried not to fidget during the long peroration in Hrruban announcing the background and circumstances of this momentous occasion. He squirmed a
little during the monotonous recital of the previous day's
popular vote. Then everyone was allowed to sit down.
Sumitral rose immediately to give a résumé of Terran's
history on Rrala which he kept to short sentences for
easier translation by Todd.

Ken began to relax a little as he realized Todd was
handling the narrative beautifully, including a polite but
boyish preface of his own, begging pardon in advance
for any mistakes. Several of the Hrruban Speakers
smiled at that. The Third Speaker stared expressionlessly
ahead of him during both summations.

Hates the whole bit, Ken thought, and he isn't even
listening; afraid he'll hear something good.

Hrruna then proposed that the meeting consider a
joint tenure of Rrala, and the hassling began.

It went on and on, particularly because the Third
Speaker now roused himself to join battle, complaining,
protesting, objecting to every constructive thought ut-
tered. Despite his obstructionism, a framework emerged,
with Sumitral obviously bearing Hrrula's words in mind,
and suggesting waiting periods, tentative arrangements,
options on everything except the coexistence of the two
races on Rrala. Each time, Sumitral took the sting out of
the Third's violent restrictions.

Time and again it was Todd, growing more and more

weary, stumbling occasionally on complicated phrases, who channeled the discussion back to coexistence on Rrala. He was simply unable to translate the subtler tricks of such trained politicians as Sumitral and Third.

"You aren't saying what you mean, and I wish you would—sir," Todd said once to Sumitral. "We'd get through faster."

Although Sumitral's patience was strained as compromise and concession were whittled or discarded, he also realized that Todd was performing the same curious veto with the Hrrubans and that the Third Speaker's designs suffered far more than his. As it became obvious to the other Hrrubans that the Terrans were acting with great candor and understanding compared with the fierce suspicions and covert aggressiveness constantly underlying Third's objections, Third began to lose control of his supporters.

At that point, Todd helped Sumitral win a very important concession. The admiral particularly wanted a transmitter station from Terra to Rrala to facilitate communications. He had specifically stated the grid need be no larger than would accommodate six men, that it ought to be manned by Hrrubans at all times, and that all transmissions would be cleared through the Hrruban colony chief. Third had ranted on and on about the dangers of such a concession, then glared at Todd to make the translation of ten minutes of rebuttal.

"Noble gracious sir," Todd had replied with a deep bow, "I will tell Admiral that you are afraid that we shall send big weapons to Rrala and forbidden things and all that. But it's silly. And I guess you think our scientists are smart enough to look at those grid posts and figure out the whole idea of transmission from them. But that's silly too. I'll just tell him you don't like the idea at all and see what he says."

Ken caught the sight of Hrrula's tail standing straight out in shock, but when he was about to reprimand Todd, Hrruna leaned across to Third.

"Third, the boy is right, you know. It is impossible to

extrapolate the mechanics of the matter transmission from grid posts and mesh. A small grid is therefore no danger and certainly an easier way to transport the hrrses and other interesting animals of the Terrans from there to Rrala."

Third glared around but he found no support from his previous adherents and had to withdraw his objections.

By midafternoon the basic points of the Decision had been formulated. The Treaty would remain in effect for no more than fifty Rralan years, no less than twenty-five; during which interval sufficient mutual understanding was to be achieved so that a more lasting agreement could be drawn for matters beyond Rrala.

Both races agreed to uphold scrupulously the Principle of Non-Cohabitation with an intelligent species on its native planet, while pursuing their independent explorations of space. Both space arms were to be provided with recognition signals and orbiting buoys which were to broadcast warnings of posted systems. There was to be no differentiation between systems posted for inimical life, conditions, or previous and present colonization. In that way, neither race, assuming they abided by the restrictions (and there would be telltales to record violations, the penalty for which would be tantamount to war), could penetrate systems of interest to each other. Or their home systems. Rrala would be the only contact point. No Hrruban was to visit Terra in any circumstances; no Terran could go to Hrruba.

A large land mass situation in Rrala's southern hemisphere was to be set aside for the neutral control force which would record and broadcast all posted systems. Exploration teams were to file all projected journeys with this central agency to prevent overlapping. A trade organization would be admitted at a later date once it had been established which commodities might interest the other race, but the Rralan colony was to be separate from the commercial interests even though they contributed Rralan products to it for sale.

The autonomy of the colony was the hardest problem,

but here Sumitral remained adamant: only the colonists directly involved could ascertain what regulations would be required for the smooth functioning of this joint colony. Third insisted the colony must be self-sufficient of either planet. Sumitral agreed wholeheartedly; that had always been a fundamental premise for Terran colonies. Third pounced on that by saying that an agricultural community was always a drain on its home world. Sumitral pointed out that the mineral and metal deposits of Rrala, slight though they were, should be the colonists' to control and that the profits would be more than adequate for their off-world requirements. Third replied that if this world was to be agricultural, there would be no need for sophisticated machinery. Sumitral smiled and permitted Third to limit all heavy machinery, all automated equipment—except medical supplies of any kind —because Third forgot that hand shovels and incentive were used long before mining machines and printed circuits.

He did not protest when Third insisted that the government of Rrala—whatever government there was, Third added sourly—must prove itself by showing a balance of credit and smoothly running departments in all the proper phases of government within five Rralan years, or the project would terminate. All Rralan citizens attaining physical maturity must be permitted to return to the planet of origin on request. Any Rralan found guilty of committing an act of physical violence against any other Rralan within that five-year period would render the Treaty null and void. Sumitral immediately countered with a demand that the government of Rrala could exile any member of either race considered dangerous to the community for any reason; that person to be remanded instantly to the control island in custody of the neutral force.

Third insisted that all minors were to be taught high formal Hrruban as well as middle. Sumitral agreed, if Terran were taught and if middle Hrruban was considered the official language of Rrala.

Sumitral pointed out that the Hrrubans had five village sites on Rrala at this point whereas the Terrans had only one, causing a disparity of population. He requested that sufficient Terran family units be added to equalize the inhabitants from each planet. Third adamantly insisted that no more adults could then emigrate to Rrala. Unless there is a vacancy caused by an exile, Sumitral countered.

By now Todd was showing unmistakable signs of strain, stammering and fumbling for words, but struggling gamely along. Hrruna began to frown with concern. At this point Landreau's wrist unit beeped and he looked around for permission to answer it just as a Hrruban technician stepped forward to whisper to Hrruna's first assistant.

"A ship comes." Todd announced the obvious with unadulterated relief as he saw a reprieve.

Third half-rose, his eyes starkly apprehensive. Todd gave him a faintly contemptuous look. Ken pinched the boy's leg under the table and Todd subsided with a sullen glare at his father. The Hrrubans were conferring in low undertones. Then the homing beacon lit.

"Are we expecting anyone else?" Ken demanded in a whisper of Sumitral, who shrugged and glanced toward Chaminade.

"An evacuation order was issued for you people," he remarked softly, flicking his eyes toward Ken and smiling slightly. "Of course, in the light of today's proceedings, it will be canceled. Unless, of course," and the grin widened maliciously, "you elect to return home?"

"You gotta be kidding," Ken exclaimed far louder than he intended.

Chaminade leaned back in his chair, his expression smug although his rotund belly appeared afflicted with a curiously rhythmic inner motion. In that moment, Reeve mellowed toward the Codep man in a way he would not have thought possible even three hours earlier. It occurred to Ken that if Landreau had been thoroughly frustrated, Sumitral stymied, Chaminade had come off rather well. Although now a separate entity, his colony was still in residence and sanctioned. Landreau's department would have to take official reprimands for his actions, but Chaminade might now move on to bigger and better things. Well, Ken decided, not until Chaminade had compensated the colonists—in minor but vital ways —for *his* earlier condescension.

"Toddy," Sumitral was saying, "please tell them that the ship is a transport vessel, ordered here to prevent further violation of the Principle we both uphold."

Toddy frowned. "But we don't need the ship. We don't have to go. Isn't that what this is all about?"

"Oh, don't worry, you're staying, lad. You deserve it!"

Toddy glanced skyward again and then grinned. He couldn't stop grinning even as he translated.

Abruptly, Hrruna rose to his feet. Everyone scrambled hastily to theirs as the First Speaker adjourned the meeting—over Third's spluttered objections—and arbitrarily nominated certain members to pursue minor details with their Terran counterparts at another time. He trusted that a finished document would be presented to himself and Sumitral within three days, Hrruban time; no significant changes to be contemplated or acceptable on matters already discussed. He then bowed ceremoniously to everyone and, beckoning to Todd, stepped away from the table.

Instantly the Second Speaker, dressed in deep gray, left the Council table to say a few quiet words to his first assistant, who immediately approached Sumitral and Landreau.

"We may leave now," Hrrula murmured to Ken. "They'll be transmitting those who do not care to remain for the rest of the day."

"Should Todd be left with the First Speaker?"

Hrrula grinned broadly, wheezing a little as he flexed muscles stiff from long standing.

"Intimate pitch is being used. It would be an insult to interrupt without invitation."

"Got acquainted, I see." Kiachif's booming tones penetrated the still subdued conversation. Ken turned to see the inimitable captain, followed by his supercargo, striding toward them across the Common. "Seems to me, though," he growled, glaring in Chaminade's direction, "that my ship's a bit superfluous with all that sitting idle on its tails. How do, sir?" and he nodded affably to Hrrula.

"Chaminade will cancel that order personally, Kiachif," Ken assured him. "We drew up a Treaty today with the Hrrubans and we're staying."

"Did right to disappear then, didn't I?" Kiachif grinned expansively, winking at Ken. "Having another one of those dry do's of yours?" He jabbed his pipe stem toward the groups setting up tables under the trees of the Common.

"You do get here at feast time, don't you?"

Kiachif eyed him speculatively, rubbing a grimy hand through his beard. "Seeing as how you're friends with the cats now, you haven't by any chance discovered if they've a—I mean . . ."

"An alcoholic beverage? No. Things have been a little confused here lately."

Hrrula wheezed.

"He understand Terran?" Kiachif asked in mild surprise, favoring Hrrula with a thoughtful look.

"If I listen harrd," Hrrula purred.

"Say, Haroola, do you folks happen to have any happy juice? Party drink? Alcoholic drink?" Kiachif pulled Hrrula cosily off to one side.

Ken glanced down to see Hrrula's tail tip describing a gentle arc. Suddenly Kiachif froze, staring at the Council table. Three Speakers remained seated, Third immobile with disapproval, the other two arguing with amiable intensity. They looked up in mild surprise at the mist closing over them before returning to their argument.

There'd be four important guests then, Ken decided, automatically checking the whereabouts of each. Hrruna, who was now accompanied by Hrriss as well as

Todd, strolled back toward the grid. No sooner had it cleared of one mist than another formed. Ken became aware now of the increased noise and activity on the Common; of groups of Hrrubans in vivid colors arriving from the woods. He could smell delicious odors and realized that he had had very little to eat since that pre-dawn stale bread and coffee. Land vehicles slowly drove up from the field, huge cylinders of fifty-gallon coffee makers lashed to their cargo beds.

The transmitter grid cleared to disclose a group of elegantly gowned Hrruban women. One good thing about rigid courtesy, Ken decided, was that females *had* to be on time. Hrruna had stepped forward with the vigor of a narrow Stripe, taking the hand of one slender lady—his mate. Hrriss doubled up in a deep bow, his tail lashing out to swat Todd promptingly on his unprotected legs. Then the group moved off toward the barn, while unobtrusive guards, three Hrruban and one Alreldep, ambled behind in a satellite course.

"Oh, Ken, did Todd behave himself?" Pat cried, rushing up to him. Her hair was damp-curly, her face flushed, her make-up and clothes fresh. "Who's he going off with? Oh, isn't that the First Speaker? Is that his wife? They say we're staying and that you'll be named Spokesman with Hrrula. Is that good? Is that what you wanted?"

"Yes, yes, yes, and yes, honey," Ken laughed, hugging her. "Todd has redeemed the family name for all time."

"Thank God!"

"Where've you been since I woke you this morning?"

Pat's face clouded and her mouth thinned with irritation.

"I had to explain to four hundred Hrrubans how to cook Terran style. Oh, for one lousy button to punch. There are times when automation had certain undeniable advantages—" She broke off with an accusing expression on her face. "Do you realize that Mrrva is a physical health Specialist—that's equivalent to having five Technical degrees on Terra. She's a full fledged doc-

tor, a biochemist and she was playing *house* on Rrala!
She was up all night planning the banquet and she admitted to me that she'd used Todd as a guinea pig to see
what Hrruban foods we can tolerate. And she and Phyllis have been going on at . . ."

"And so are you," he teased. "Hey, what's the matter?"
for Pat suddenly burst into tears and buried her face in
his chest. He pulled her around to the back of the mess
hall, away from the crowds. "Pat, darling, what's
wrong?" He tipped her head up.

"It's just—it's just too much," she gulped back her
sobs. "I'm all right, really. Nerves." But she couldn't stop
crying. "And I think I'm pregnant and I've been so
scared and all with the snakes and the mining planet
and . . ."

Ken just held her tightly to him, gently stroking her
hair. If he hadn't been so roaringly happy inside—well,
women cry because they're happy, too. It was almost a
relief to Ken to stand here, holding his wife in his arms.
It gave him a chance to catch up too. He was having a
little difficulty himself, adjusting to the fact that they
were safely ensconced on Rrala, and that the Hrrubans
were back for good.

He looked down the sweep of the greensward to the
barn. Hrrula was showing off the paces of the black
stallion to Hrruna and his lady while Hrriss and Todd
perched on the corral fence, cheering him. The guards
lounged by the water trough, the Terran offering the
Hrrubans a drink from the dipper. Beyond the barn, toward the plain, he could clearly see the black smudges
where the snakes had been lasered away by the launch
guns the day before. There was the faintest trace of
stink when the wind blew from that direction. Far, far
away he could see the dots of the *urfa* grazing. To his
right, nearer the river, stood the four vari-sized ships, sil-
ver-green in the westering sun.

Pat had quieted in his arms, comfortable against him,
warm and soft and his. As Rrala was his—and his children's.

Pat looked up at him with a tremulous smile, her lips soft and inviting. He kissed her tenderly, for her hard work today, her courage yesterday, and the promise of tomorrow. Arm in arm they returned to the Common.

L'ENVOI

THE LAST OF THE GUESTS returning to Hrruba waved good night through the transmission veil. With a deep sigh, Ken turned to check the dark Common. The barbecue pits still glowed ruddily, striking the matter grid at his feet with red fingers, flaring occasionally to light the deserted tables, the overturned benches. Above him the open sky of Rrala was star-dazzled but moonless. The last of the villagers were crossing the bridge, their way lit by yellow power beams instead of torches. Ken chuckled to himself. A race that had matter transmission carrying torches to confuse their unexpected guests!

"Rrev," purred a tired voice and Hrrula emerged from a dark splotch of shadow, Hrrestan right behind him, "we can find neither Hrriss nor Todd. Any ideas?"

"Where've you looked?"

"All over the Common, under the table, in the mess hall, at the bridge, the river," Hrrula enumerated wearily. "All the likely places."

"C'mon. We'll try the unlikely" and Ken led them toward his cabin.

They found the two boys fast asleep in Todd's bed. And chuckled at the sight. Arms around each other, heads tilted as if they had fallen asleep midsentence, it was obvious that this pair worked hard at good interracial relations. Tod wore his *mda* vest and a pair of pants, his rope tail stuffed down one pant leg. Hrriss's nether regions, too, were trouser clad, and his tail had worked down a leg, thereby equalizing the appearance of the two friends.

Hrrestan smiled at Ken over their sleeping sons. "We do not need to part such friends tonight, do we?" and the two fathers covered the boys.

"Pat must be finished at the mess hall now," Ken said and walked them back toward the bridge. They were halfway there when Kiachif's deep belly laugh broke the still night like a sonic boom. He lurched out of the shadows in front of them.

"I knew it, Reeve, I knew it," he bellowed jubilantly, swaying slightly on his feet. "Y'see this little flask? It's got spirits in it, it has," he crowed. "Every race that's got skin to cover it, hair to braid, loins to clad, if y'get what I mean, has some way to relieve the tensions of the weary weary world they live on. I knew your pussycat people were no exception, bless their velvety hides. Praise be to the everlasting stars, may they multiply forever."

The flask was tendered Ken but Hrrula stayed Kiachif's hand and sniffed delicately at the mouth of the bottle. His lips curled with distaste and he released Kiachif's hand abruptly.

"*Mlada,*" he hissed.

"*Mlada* it is, and a melodic name for a distillation of sheer delight," Kiachif replied at drive-room volume. "This planet's a joy to visit, if you get what I mean," and roaring with laughter, he reeled away toward the landing field.

"He'll not be so glad tomorrow," Hrrestan remarked drily.

The terrain dipped down from the Common to the field so they had a last look at his retreating figure outlined against the night sky, one arm holding the bottle high, like a salute.

"You don't approve of *mlada*?" Ken asked, trying to suppress his amusement over Kiachif's minor victory.

Hrrula's answering growl defied imitation but made clear his opinion of *mlada*.

"The herd drink it by the *lva*," he remarked scornfully. "Makes them sleep for hours."

"It occupies them with something," Hrrestan said.

"There is something here to keep them occupied," Hrrula replied crisply, gesturing broadly at the quiet scene. "Something new and vital and stimulating, with a whole new set of experiences and problems."

"Yes, it will not always be easy," Hrrestan said thoughtfully, catching Ken's eyes.

Quickly Ken held his hand out, felt Hrrestan's furry palm touch his; extended his left hand to meet Hrrula's.

"We will always understand each other," Ken vowed, his voice rough with feeling, "if we *listen* very hard."

"I get what you mean," Hrrula purred.

ABOUT THE AUTHOR

To be born as I was on April first imposes a challenge. In writing speculative fiction, I feel I have not failed the auspices of my natal day.

However, being 99 percent Irish indicates a certain perversity, so I tried out many other things before I settled down to write. I dabbled in the Theatre Arts, studied voice production for nine years before arriving at the horrifying conclusion that I was a better stage-director of opera than a singer. I capped off that facet with the production and stage-direction of the American premiere in Wilmington of Carl Orff's *Ludus de Nato Infante Mirificus,* which is not as far from speculative fiction as you might imagine.

I balance indifferent housekeeping with superb cooking; sew for anyone but myself, knit well, and (would you believe?) embroider; am currently raising three children, five cats, and a French poodle; swim, sail, ride horseback—western style by preference—collect Graustarkian romances, and resent being kept away from my typewriter by any one of the above-mentioned diversions.

My eyes are green, my hair is silver, and I freckle. The rest is subject to change without notice.

ANNE MCCAFFREY, 1968